REPARATION OF SIN

A SOVEREIGN SONS NOVEL

A. ZAVARELLI
NATASHA KNIGHT

Copyright © 2021 by A. Zavarelli & Natasha Knight

All rights reserved.

No part of this book may be reproduced in any form or by any electronic or mechanical means, including information storage and retrieval systems, without written permission from the author, except for the use of brief quotations in a book review.

ABOUT THIS BOOK

My husband hates me. But he's also the only man who can save me.

Taken by a stranger, Santiago is my only hope. Except that I don't know if he's dead or alive. And for as cruel as he can be, the thought he might be gone is unbearable.

But he has nine lives, my monster.

He's not finished with me yet. And soon I'm back at The Manor. Locked in my room. At his mercy.

I know I am despised.
I know I have become the face of his vengeance.

But there's something else too. Something between

us. It's a dark and gnarled thing. And it has its claws around my heart.

Reparation of Sin is the second book of The Society Trilogy. If you haven't read book one, *Requiem of the Soul*, you'll need to do that first.

You can find Requiem of the Soul by clicking here.

1

IVY

I am blind.

I reach up, my wrists bound, to touch the blindfold. Instinct.

A hand captures one arm. Strong. Cold. I smell leather and realize it's a glove.

"Keep it on," he orders.

I nod, but I'm not sure if he can make that out because I'm shaking so badly. The dampness of this place has gotten into my bones, the stone cold beneath my bare feet, dirt wet between my toes. I smell a forest. Is that possible? Where am I?

"What's happening?" I ask for the hundredth time since he brought me to this cellar-like space.

"You take it off while I'm here, and I'll bind your arms behind your back again. You don't want that."

"No," I agree although I'm not sure he was waiting for my reply. I'm sure he doesn't care.

I'm still dressed at least. Though the gown is ruined.

Has it been hours or days since he took me? Hours or days since Santiago lay dying—*dead*—on the floor of the formal dining room set for an elaborate, elegant dinner. That was ruined too. Tables and chairs turned over. The finest crystal shattered in the chaos when the lights went out.

Dead.

"Where is Santiago?" I ask, knowing he won't tell me. He has hardly spoken to me since he brought me here. "Where am I?"

I hear him move around and turn my head to follow the sound even though I can't see him. He's careful not to touch me, and when I feel him close, feel his clothes brush against me, I shudder and pull away.

But when I hear him open the heavy metal door, I rush toward it, arms outstretched even though I know there isn't anything to fall over. I'd managed to get the blindfold off before he'd come back.

"Wait!"

Powerful hands close around my shoulders, catching me. Fingers dig into bare flesh, my body forced to a jarring stop.

"Please!" I cry out, tears wet on the blindfold. "What's happening? Please just tell me what's happening!"

He makes a sound from deep in his throat. A

groan. Like I'm a nuisance. Like he doesn't have time for me.

Then he shouldn't have kidnapped me.

"Santiago," I start, clearing my throat when I choke on his name. "My husband." Another pause. "He's...is he...?" I can't say it.

"Eat. If you don't eat the food, the rats will come to have it."

"Rats?" I panic.

"You don't want that, either."

He walks me backward, skeletons of small dead animals crunching under his shoes, cutting the skin on the bottom of my feet. The backs of my knees hit the metal bed frame with the smelly, ancient mattress on top. He pushes me down abruptly, then releases me.

I remain seated because I know not to fight this man. I hear him walk away. To the door, I guess. To leave me alone in this darkness again. Maybe I should be grateful, though. He hasn't touched me. Not like that.

The door creaks as he pulls it closed. He's almost gone.

"Please just tell me if he's okay," I plead in a whisper. "If he's...alive."

He stops, and I can just about make out the silhouette of his giant body through the blindfold. He's big. Like Santiago. And just as strong. I wouldn't get past him if I tried.

"Would you have me believe you care?" he asks.

"I...Is he...?"

His approaching steps are rapid then, and I scramble backward, my back hitting the damp stone wall just as his gloved hand closes around my throat.

"Dead," he says, and I'm not sure if it's a question or a statement of fact.

My hands are on his forearm, but if he wanted to strangle me, if he wanted to break my neck, I'm sure it would take little effort. Like the snapping of the bones of dead mice beneath his shoes.

"Is he?" I choke out.

"You should hope for your sake not."

2

IVY

I push the blindfold up to my forehead as soon as I hear the lock turn. My heart is racing, but at least he's bound my wrists in front of me. They were at my back at first. I draw my knees up onto the disgusting mattress and hug them, the thick rope tight on my already raw wrists. I shudder when a cold breeze comes through the tiny square of a window high up on the forest floor. I'm at least partially below ground. An outdoor cellar from what I can make out with stairs that lead up to a door. But at least I have that window.

"If you don't eat the food, the rats will come to have it."

I glance up at the barred window. Is that where they'll come from? I look around the square space, the corners too dark for me to see if there are any holes. I'm sure there are, though. On the floor are the corpses of small animals. Most are rotted to the bone.

The dress Mercedes chose for me is a ruin of dirt and tears.

Looking at the tray set on the small table, I see a blanket folded beneath it, so I get to my feet and rush to it. I set the tray on the cot and unfold the blanket to wrap it around myself. It's rough, not a blanket at all. Something a mover would use to protect the furniture or maybe something a painter would lay down to protect the floors, but it will do.

A small bowl of soup with a spoon sticking out of it, a piece of bread, and a glass of water are on the tray.

I take a sip of water first, then set the glass down, figuring I should ration the water at least. I pick up the soup but realize why I didn't smell anything. It's cold. I don't bother with the spoon but bring the bowl to my lips and tilt it. I think it would be good if it were hot, but this isn't even lukewarm. I drink it anyway. I don't want to lure any rats or other animals, and I need to eat to keep up my strength.

The bowl is small, and it's only half-full, so I finish it quickly, set it down, and break off a piece of stale bread. I eat that too but leave the rest for later and get up, go up the stairs. There are half a dozen. The cellar is built into the earth. I try the door even though I know it's locked. There's no way I have the strength to break down this steel monstrosity that must be at least a century old.

I return to the small window and look up at it. The sun is fading, so it'll be pitch-black soon. This will be my first night here when I'm conscious. I wonder how long I was out.

It's too high to reach, not that I'm going out that way. I take the bucket he'd left for me—I guess to use as a toilet—and turn it over to stand on it. I climb up and still have to stand on tiptoes to just barely see out. Moss grows thick on the bars and against the walls of my cell.

My cell.

I breathe in, then close my eyes to ward off the panic and the inevitable dizziness. I hold tight to the bars, icy and damp. Once it passes, I climb back down and sit on the mattress, pulling my feet up again to curl into the blanket.

Is Santiago dead? No. My kidnapper didn't say he was dead. He said I should hope for my sake he's not. Which means he's alive.

Then what happened, and where is he?

I think back to the party. To talking with Colette. To the elegantly dressed men and women. The food. The champagne. To how Santiago looked darkly handsome even though I hated myself for thinking it.

I think back to my room at The Manor. To the tiny window made bigger. To Antonia. Her warmth.

And I drop my head into my knees because as bad as all that was, I know now it can always be worse. Because this is worse.

There, I am hated. But there's something else too. Something between us, Santiago and me. A dark thing. A gnarled thing. I feel it inside me, inside my stomach, my chest.

After wiping my cheeks on my knees, I draw the blanket up to cover my face and lie down to close my eyes. I don't think about the rats or the skeletons surrounding me, this burial ground, this mausoleum.

I think about him.

3

IVY

I'm startled awake when I register the sound of metal against metal. It's different than the sounds of the night with the insects and other animals out there. After a moment, the fog clears, and I sit up and squint in the shadowy dawn light as the lock turns and the door opens.

I gasp at what I see, but it's not that I've forgotten where I am.

My captor stands in the doorway in his dark cloak, the hood pulled up. I remember how Santiago had come into my bedroom the night before the wedding. How I'd been half asleep and thought it was the Grim Reaper.

Those cloaks scare me still. And this man in his reaper's coat is no exception.

Behind his huge frame filters the light of the rising sun seeping through a dense cropping of trees.

"What did I say?" the man asks, and I scramble to pull the blindfold down over my eyes, my hands shaking at the deep timbre of his voice. The threat and barely controlled hate obvious with every innocuous word.

It's damp, that strip of cloth. And doesn't cover the whole of one eye since I rolled it down, but I keep my eyes closed and hope he won't notice.

I don't know how long I've slept. I'm about to ask what time it is. What day. To ask where Santiago is. What's happening. But before I can, his hand closes over my arm, and I cry out and instinctively try to pull free. He's quiet for his size. He crossed the room without me hearing even blind.

"Quiet," he commands, and my arms are lifted. His hands are cool from the leather gloves as he forces them higher, forces me on tiptoes, and hooks my ropes into something overhead, then releases me.

I hadn't noticed anything overhead. I hadn't really searched for anything up there. But here I hang now, toes grazing the ground as the ropes dig into my raw wrists with my weight hanging from them.

"What's happening?" I ask, listening as he moves behind me and places his hands on the blindfold. It's gone, at least for a moment, but then he puts it back on so it's flat over my eyes. He knots it tightly, catching strands of hair in it, but he doesn't care when I protest.

He then walks to stand in front of me. I feel him. He's close but not touching, and I wonder what he's doing. It feels like he's just staring at me, and it's unnerving.

"How did you do it?" he asks.

"What?" I'm confused.

"How?"

"I don't understand. How did I do what?"

He snorts. "If it were up to me, I'd get that confession out of you at the end of my whip." He pauses, and I feel him step back away from me. "But fortunately for you, I've given my word."

"What?" My voice breaks mid-word. Is that why I'm here? Why he's strung me up? Is he going to whip me? "What's happening? Where's Santiago?" I can hear the panic rising in my own voice as he puts one finger on the middle of my chest and gives me a push. It's just enough to make me scramble for my feet to gain purchase and alleviate the strain on my wrists.

He moves around, and I hear different sounds. He's inside, then outside again. The door is still open, and I think I hear a woman whispering out there. I listen hard, and I hear it again. I swear I do. And then his clear voice, not whispering.

"I told you to stay in your room. Go back to the house. Now."

The woman's soft whisper again. I have to strain to hear because she's talking so quietly.

"There's nothing for you to see here," the man says. "Go." He doesn't raise his voice. It almost seems like he's placating her. He's using a different tone than the one he's used with me the few times he's spoken.

He's back inside, and I hear the clang of the bucket. I had to use it last night even though I didn't want to. It was either that or pee in a corner, though.

"What's happening?" I ask again. "Please tell me what's happening."

Nothing. Then he's close again. One arm wraps around my middle as he lifts me just a little, just enough to give the rope some slack so he can unhook my wrists. When he sets me down, he turns me to face him.

"Hold out your arms."

I do. He'll just make me if I don't.

A few moments later, the rope is untied, and my wrists are freed. I scramble away as soon as he releases me, but I trip over the bucket, send it toppling and rolling noisily. I turn back to face him even though I'm still blind. I rub my raw wrists.

"Is it over?" I ask, and for one moment, I believe he's going to set me free. Yet even as I think it, I realize it's stupid.

He laughs. It's a dark sort of unhappy chuckle.

"There's a change of clothes. Soap and water. Make yourself presentable."

"For what?"

"The Tribunal."

"The what? What is that?" I ask slowly as something heavy settles in my belly at his ominous tone and words.

He snorts, and I can almost see him shaking his head. I hear him walk to the stairs.

"Wait!"

He stops.

And although I remember what happened the last time I asked, I can't help but ask again.

"Is Santiago…is he…going to be okay?"

There's a long moment of silence, then his feet on the stairs before the loud clanging of the door. It makes me jump, and my already racing heart feel like it will beat right out of my chest. And then I hear his steps and the crunching of branches and leaves. I hurry to push the blindfold up only to see his boot pass by the window, the edge of the black cloak just grazing the ground before I'm alone again. Left in complete silence in this underground chamber not meant for human habitation.

4
IVY

I washed with the cold water as best as I could, rubbing the bar of soap on the bristles of the bath brush and then scrubbing myself, not even caring about the goose bumps left in its wake. I wanted to be clean or just a little cleaner. To wash away the dirt in my hair, I dumped the cold water over my head, but that was a mistake. It's now a half-damp mass of tangles, and it's left me shivering. He only provided a small square washcloth for my towel, and the change of clothes is a long white gown with billowing sleeves and a high collar with the ruffle detail duplicated on my wrists. It's almost like an old-fashioned nightgown or something you'd wear under your dress in the old days.

The strange dress coupled with what he said, with what I've prepared myself for, makes me feel uneasy.

The Tribunal.

It almost makes me think of witch trials of the past because what I'm wearing is ceremonial, and if there's one thing I'm sure of, it's that The Society stands on ceremony.

I pull my still-bare feet up onto the cot and hug the blanket to myself. No shoes. My feet are freezing. I've eaten the bread and another bowl of cold soup. This time, there was an apple too, and I devoured that. The water is gone. Now I sit here waiting for him to return. I'm anxious for it. The longer I sit here, the more time I have to make up stories of what happened. To ruminate over Santiago's collapse. I won't let myself go further, though. He's not dead. I have to believe that. But what happened?

I'm nodding off when I finally hear the sound of footsteps outside. When I sit up, I catch a fast-moving shadow pass by the window before hearing the key slip into the lock. Before he pushes the door open, I remember to pull the blindfold down. I tied it looser so I can open my eyes behind it. I can at least make out shapes then.

He walks in and stops. I wonder what time it is. It's pitch-black now. But the canopy of trees could be making it seem later. I've slept off and on and have lost all track of time.

"Up," he says.

I stand, dropping the blanket.

He looks me over, and I see his head move in a

nod. "Good. Arms out." He walks toward me as he says it and drops something on the cot.

"Tell me first about my husband. Tell me—"

"We are not bargaining," he says. "Arms, or I'll bind them behind your back."

My head is tilted up to his face. He's still wearing the cloak, but even without the hood up, it's too hard to make out any features between the dark and my blindfold.

I extend my arms, and he binds them, the same cool feel of leather from his gloves against my skin. I wonder if he wore them so he doesn't have to touch me. Once my wrists are tightly bound, he leans to pick up whatever he'd tossed onto the cot, and I realize it's a cloak when he drapes it over my shoulders. The heavy wool scratches my neck and smells musty. Old. He closes the clasp at my throat, then pulls the hood over my head.

My heart races. I'm on full alert as he takes my arm and leads me toward the door. I'm slow, though, too slow for him.

"Come."

"My feet," I start as I climb the stone steps and then walk out onto damp grass.

"A small price to pay," he replies before I can say more.

He leads me with an iron grip, and I have to trust he's not going to steer me into a wall, but soon, the grassy floor gives way to gravel. Small stones. And I hear the sound of a car engine start. A door is opened.

"In."

Climbing into the car, I smell the leather of the seats and feel the dry, comforting warmth of the heater. He gets in beside me and closes the door. A moment later, I feel the car shift as someone else climbs in—the driver, I guess—and we're off.

We're headed to IVI's headquarters. At least I'm pretty sure that's where The Tribunal sits. I know what it is. I think I knew when he first told me, too. The Society's version of a court where members who break the rules are questioned, tried, and sentenced. It wouldn't stand up in any court of law in the world, and I'm sure it's illegal, even, but those sort of things don't seem to hinder any IVI activities. The Society is a self-governing organization independent of the law, almost like a country in and of itself.

It's where Hazel will be sent if she's ever found. She'll have to stand before The Tribunal, where three probably hundred-year-old men will determine how she'll be punished. No trial for her. Just sentencing. It's how it works. Our father won't even be there to protect her, and there's not a chance Abel would help her.

Is that what's going to happen to me? But why? Why would I stand before a tribunal? What have I done?

A chill runs through me, and I turn my head to look in my captor's direction.

"What do you think I did?" I ask, my voice small. Because I am being punished. Or I will be. By keeping me in that cell, he's holding me until...I pause. Until things go one way or the other with Santiago, I guess.

Which means he's still alive. Or he was.

My heart sinks.

He turns to me. I see that much. "We found the source of the poison."

"Poison?" My mouth goes dry.

"Cleverly done. But not clever enough."

The car pulls through the gates at IVI, and he falls silent as I hug the cloak closer around my trembling shoulders.

5

IVY

He removes my blindfold the moment we are inside but then draws my hood back on. My cloak is scarlet red.

I look up at him as my eyes adjust to the dim lights, but all I see beneath his hood is the hard surface of a black mask.

He studies me for a long moment, then turns to walk ahead of me up the wide, winding staircase, his every step echoing off the stone.

Someone clears their throat, and I glance behind me to see two men standing there. He's not taking a chance that I'll run. Not that I'd know where to go or get far if I did.

I turn back to watch his form round the corner, then take a deep breath and follow.

We're not in any part of the compound that I've been in before. This place is darker. Colder. Lonelier.

From the window on the first landing, I pause to glance outside at the small courtyard below. The single platform there. The post.

Panic takes hold of me, and I fall back a step only to bump into the rock-hard chest of one of the men behind me.

"I..." I shake my head, backing away from him. He doesn't touch me, and I feel like a pariah. All of them avoid touching me. He doesn't come after me but waits as I steady myself. I glance once more through the barred window at that platform, and my mind wanders back to my history lessons. How the condemned man or woman would watch as the scaffold was built outside their window and see the place where he or she would be executed.

Obviously, they don't carry out executions here, I tell myself. Surely, that's a step too far. But there are other things. Other medieval punishments.

The man behind me clears his throat, and I continue up the stairs, not letting myself look out the window on the next three landings. When I reach the last one, my captor is waiting for me outside of two hulking doors, dark wood carved with the insignia IVI.

"Come," he says when I stop moving.

My bare feet are silent on the cold stone as I approach and stand before him. He unclasps the cloak and pushes it off my shoulders, letting it fall to the floor. I see his gaze drop to the strange garment, and I remember how vulnerable I am. How naked beneath this sheath.

They think I poisoned Santiago. Has he died? Is that why I'm here now?

The question of what they'll do to me is second to the echoing of *has he died* circling round and round in my head.

A sound like a gavel comes from inside, and my heart jumps as I face the doors when they are opened. My mouth goes dry as the large circular room comes into view. Raised high in the center is the dais upon which three men—The Councilors, my judges—sit behind a large desk made of the same wood and decorated with carvings as intricate as the doors.

On either side and set at a lower level is a large banister, stone like the walls and ground, with empty chairs behind it. And in the center, I'm walked to a wooden stand where a man opens the small gate, and I step up into it before he closes it again.

Ceremony. The Society loves it.

My stomach turns, and I try to swallow the dryness in my mouth. Just as the doors close, I hear a sound from behind and above me. I shift my gaze back and up to the gallery, where I see a single witness. Because that is what she is. A witness to my trial.

Mercedes.

And even from this distance, I see how red her

eyes are and how pale her face is. I feel a tear slide down my cheek, and I think it's true. He's gone. Santiago is gone.

The gavel strikes, and I startle, turning to face The Councilors.

6

SANTIAGO

"Take a slow sip."

The voice resonating above me is familiar, but he is little more than a blurry shape. A rhythmic, steady drone of beeping is a pattern I am intimately acquainted with, and the smell is one I'll never forget. Disinfectant. Cold metal. Dying flowers undoubtedly perched on the ledge of a sill somewhere in the distance.

I'm in a hospital room. That much, I understand.

Someone adjusts my bed, forcing me further into an upright position as I try to speak. A straw bumps against my lips, and that familiar voice offers encouragement.

"It will take some time to get your senses back. For now, you can relax and try to take a drink. We've already moved you to the most secure wing of the hospital. Armed guards are stationed outside, and you've been under the care of Dr. Rousseau. You're in excellent hands, Santiago."

The name Dr. Rousseau confirms there is some truth to the dissembled thoughts running rampant inside my brain. I had thought it was all a dream. The masked gala. My wife, dressed in shades of gold and black, floating across the floor like an apparition. Her half-butterfly mask shining beneath the soft glow of the overhead lights. She looked like a seductress with that blood-red lipstick. And she took that role to heart when she kissed me. A kiss that would lead to my collapse, and then inevitably, what I was certain would be my death.

If Dr. Rosseau is my attending physician, there can be no other explanation. IVI does not call him in for garden variety cases. He is the poison specialist. A master of toxicology with laser-sharp eyes and a gift for discerning even the most subtle of biological threats. He is at the top of his field, and he would not be here to treat anything else that might ail me. His presence is confirmation I was poisoned, and it does not require a stretch of the imagination to know without a doubt it was by my own wife's hand. Or more accurately, her lips.

I reach for the hem of the blankets weighing me down, trying to fling them off. But I only manage to drag them about an inch before my arm falls limp to my side. It is difficult to comprehend the weakness I feel. It's a weakness more indicative of being hit by a train and dragged for days, slamming against every object in my path. I have felt the limitations of my body before in such excruciatingly dark times, but I can no longer stew in silence while the Moreno family continues to destroy what is left of mine.

I need to see my wife. I need her to look me in the eyes and confess her sins and beg for mercy like she has never begged before. Quiet rage fuels my resolve as I imagine her falling to her knees, my fingers wrapped around her throat as she spews her lies from those pretty, poisonous lips. It's a thirst that can't be tamed. And logic isn't part of the equation when I make another attempt to free myself from the confines of my bed.

"You need to relax," the voice beside my bed instructs me. "There will be time for vengeance later. For now, you need to work on one thing at a time. Let's start with a sip of water."

I don't want a fucking sip of water. I need to see my wife. I want blood and vengeance. Nothing can mend this cavernous fissure in my chest. Nothing but the certain horror on Ivy's face when she sees me resurrected from the dead, proof that she will never escape me. In life or death, I will haunt her to the ends of the earth. And there is no time like the present—when the wound is still fresh—to seek her out and exact the punishment she so rightly deserves.

But in the face of my determination is the hindrance of my blurred vision and limp body. I may be alive, but I don't know the extent of the damage she inflicted. Try as I might, my voice won't cooperate to allow me to speak. And my muscles are about as useful as broken bow strings with my exhaustion weighing me down. I try and fail again to move myself, the monitor echoing my growing frustration as I come to terms with one undeniable truth.

Ivy thought she could be rid of me so easily. All this time, Mercedes was right. Ivy had lured me in and made me weak. She made me see something in her that never existed. Something worth saving. Now I am left to stew in the starkness of clarity as I process her betrayal from a hospital bed.

A grunt of pain leaves my parched lips as I pat around my hand and yank the IV out. I'm determined to free myself from these confines, but within moments, two sets of hands are on me, forcing me back into bed as I try to fight my way out. I might as well be fighting Goliath.

There's nothing left in me.

And despite my fit of silent fury, they've got the IV secured in a new location within seconds, pumping a sedative into my veins.

"Welcome back." The distorted voice greets me as my eyes flutter open and focus on the ceiling.

My vision has improved, and now I can make out the details of the room around me. It's dark, cold, and apocalypse-proof, judging by the thick walls. So, I know I must be at one of the IVI locations, but I'm not certain which one. Several medical facilities are located throughout the city and hundreds more around the country. Then there are the possibilities of worldwide locations, which leaves me to conclude I could be in any of them.

I spent more than my fair share of time staring at similar walls during my recovery from every excruciating operation when they tried to piece me back together and make me whole again. I swore I would never come back to a hospital. I would never again set foot in one of these rooms. Yet here I am.

I'm not certain how much time has passed since that first day when I woke to the voice beside me, informing me I was in the care of Dr. Rosseau. Since then, I have had incremental improvements in my strength, vision, and muscle control. But it has been difficult to determine to what extent since they have kept me sedated most of the time. I know because every time I attempted to move, I couldn't, and while my thoughts were screaming loud, I could not give voice to them.

I am certain they suspect I would tear them limb from limb to get out of here, and they would be right.

Slowly, I turn my gaze to the man beside my bed. The familiar face of a friend. A man I trust implicitly.

Lawson Montgomery. Or Judge, as he is better known.

He has been here every day, to some extent. I tried several times to speak to him, but he seemed to understand what it was I needed and took it upon himself to inform me that Ivy and Mercedes are both in his care until I make a full recovery. Which means he captured my wife before she could make her great escape.

I was relieved to hear the news, but that relief swiftly turned to bitterness.

She is a traitor. There is no question in my mind. I am certain of it, and I have had little else to do but replay that moment over and over. That kiss. The kiss of death she so eagerly bestowed upon me.

Poison fucking Ivy.

For days, I have laid here, strapped to a hospital bed like a goddamned lunatic, going out of my mind with alternating rage and frustration. I asked myself how she could possibly do this to me. How I didn't see it coming. And there is only one answer.

She is a Moreno. Regardless of our marriage certificate. Regardless of my mark inked into her skin. She still carries those defective genes that will forever make her a viper. And I am more certain of it now than I have ever been.

My wife will die by my hand. As sure as the sun will rise, I will spit on her grave once I've wrung every last ounce of life from her body. She thinks she has known suffering, but she has never experienced the true depths of my depravity or what I am capable of. And there will be no peace in my soul until I taste her blood on my lips as her life slips away.

She will bear my children. And she will know nothing but misery until her last breath. That is the promise I make to myself in the quiet solitude of my thoughts. It is the only solace that gets me through each passing day, waiting for the time when I can return to her, the devil reborn.

"I know what you're thinking," Judge tells me. "It's written all over your face, Santiago. But I should tell you, we haven't yet been able to find the evidence to condemn her. We've searched the compound. Her purse. Your car. Every inch of every space she encountered that evening, including The Manor. But it's turned up nothing."

I reach out for the water on my bedside table, hand trembling as I bring it to my lips to take a drink. And for the first time in days, I try again to move my lips—to form words—and to my surprise, it actually works. My throat is dry, and it's uncomfortable, but I forge on, insisting on having my answers.

"No sedative today?"

Judge cocks his head to the side and shrugs. "Not as long as you don't get ahead of yourself again."

"Tell me everything," I rasp. "I need to know."

He studies me for a moment, trying to determine something for himself. "I will tell you as long as you give me your word that you will stay here until you are given the all clear from Dr. Rosseau. I'm getting rather tired of sedating you."

"You have my word." I meet his gaze so there can be no misunderstanding about my intent.

There is no question I want to leave this place, but he is right, and I can see that now. It would only give Ivy more pleasure to allow her to see me in such a state. To allow her for one second to think she had truly hurt me. As if she could ever possess that power.

"What is the last thing you remember?" Judge asks.

"Ivy kissed me at the gala, and then I collapsed," I answer coldly.

He nods, folding his hands across his lap as he considers where to begin. "You were very lucky Dr. Rosseau was in attendance that evening. He heard the commotion when the paramedics were wheeling you away, and he rode to the hospital with you. When he'd heard what happened, he began decontamination right away. They stripped you down, and he cleaned your skin, examining the traces of lipstick. He said it was oily, which, amongst your other symptoms, indicated something quite unexpected."

"What was it?" I ask.

"A chemical nerve agent that has been used in several high-profile assassinations."

"A nerve agent?" I ask incredulously.

It doesn't sound right. How could Ivy possibly get her hands on a nerve agent?

"It's been banned in the US for decades, and by all accounts, the military stockpile destroyed. But like most things, it can be purchased on the black market. It's capable of being delivered as a gas or, in your case, dermally. An innocent touch can be deadly to the recipient since it is rarely tested for unless it is suspected. Fortunately, Dr. Rosseau followed his instincts within moments of your arrival at the hospital, by which time you had already been resuscitated twice. He gave you an atropine injection and an anticonvulsant, and they were able to get your breathing regulated."

Judge's voice becomes uncharacteristically quiet as he dips his head. "You barely scraped through this time, Santiago. If it wasn't for his immediate presence, I have no doubt we'd be planning your funeral. In fact, I was quite certain of it."

His words sink over me like a lead weight. I hung on by the skin of my teeth, narrowly avoiding death for a second time, and I can't help but question why. Why am I still here, trapped in this patchwork frame of flesh and bone and darkness? Because right now, considering the truth I will be forced to endure when I leave, I believe death might be a vacation from this reality.

For a few minutes, neither of us says another word. He allows me to digest the information quietly, processing my questions before I can give voice to them.

"You haven't found an antidote that Ivy may have taken?"

"No." He shakes his head. "She would have had to inject it, likely more than one dose. But there has been no indication where she might have disposed of it. By the time I had her secured at my house, most of her lipstick had been wiped away, which could be intentionally done if she was trying to decontaminate."

"And she has shown no signs of illness since then?"

"No."

I can tell by his tone that he is questioning her guilt, but I cannot. "Then someone helped her dispose of it. Someone helped her access the tools she required."

"It would be the only logical explanation if it is her."

"I need to find out where she has been and who she has had contact with."

"We are already looking into it," he assures me.

"Regardless, I would still like to speak with The Tribunal. And Mercedes."

Judge shifts uncomfortably at the mention of my sister's name, prickling my awareness. "What?"

"Nothing." He scratches over the stubble on his face. "She's at my house. Safe and secure. And pissed as hell that I haven't allowed her to visit."

"You can inform her you were just doing as I instructed," I tell him. "Or I will tell her myself."

"She's been struggling, Santiago," he says carefully. "I know she looks tough, but this week, I saw her crumble. She thought she was going to lose you, and it terrified her."

I draw in a sharp breath and close my eyes. He is right about Mercedes. As tough as she likes to pretend she is, she has made no secret of her terror that she might someday lose me too. Since our parents are both gone, I am the only family she has left. And I have been so focused on Ivy as of late that I have not taken the time to ensure that my sister was okay herself. Sometimes, it is easy to forget with her since she seems so capable. But inside, she is still a scared, broken girl who has been deeply traumatized by the loss of our family.

"I will see to her," I reply gruffly. "Thank you for taking care of her in my absence."

His dark and unwavering gaze meets mine. "I will always take care of her. Never doubt that."

7

SANTIAGO

"Santi." My sister's eyes fill with tears the moment she enters the room, and there is little time to brace myself before I am enveloped in her arms.

She squeezes the life out of me, and I return her hug awkwardly, uncomfortable with the display of emotion. I am not a man who expresses his feelings well, but my sister is the only reason I understand I am capable of that emotion they call love. For her, I would kill without a second thought. I protect her at all costs, and I would rain down hellfire on anyone who ever dared to hurt her. That is the only explanation of love that makes sense to me.

When she pulls away, she is wiping black makeup from beneath her eyes, choking on silent sobs. Judge was right. She's a wreck, and it's impossible not to notice how slight her frame looks.

"Have you been eating?" I demand.

"No!" She renews her crying fit with vigor, collapsing into the chair beside the bed. "Only when Judge forces me. I've been going out of my mind, Santi. I didn't know if I would ever see you again. That asshole has kept me from you, and I hate him. I hate him so much I could stab him!"

Despite her dramatic declaration, her tone lacks the conviction to make me worry. But there is something else I can't help noticing. She isn't looking directly at me. Instead, she dips her head, trying to hide her face, and it is so unlike her I can't be certain what to make of it.

"Judge is only doing what he has been instructed to do," I say. "He's protecting you. Don't make his job any harder than it needs to be."

"Harder," she mutters. "He enjoys it when I act out. I think the sick fuck gets off on disciplining me."

My lips flatten, and I try to imagine exactly how Judge might be punishing her. He knows better than to do anything inappropriate. But I wouldn't be fulfilling my duty of protecting her if I didn't ask, regardless.

"He hasn't... he's left you untouched, right?"

Mercedes peeks up at me with a strange flush on her cheeks. "As if I would ever let that sadist touch me. God, you must really be drugged up."

"I'm perfectly clear-headed," I answer dryly. "Dr.

Rosseau is giving me the all clear to leave tomorrow, in fact."

"So we get to go home?" she asks hopefully. "Things will return to normal?"

"For now. But you are to stay away from Ivy. No exceptions, Mercedes. She is dangerous."

"Ivy?" She dips her head again, wringing her hands together in a peculiar display of nerves.

"Yes." I frown. "Have you seen her?"

I don't know why I ask, and when Mercedes goes rigid, I know it was a stupid thing to do. I expect her to be out for blood, and I'm probably due for another tongue lashing about my plans for my wife. But her ire seems to have fizzled out after her outburst about Judge.

"Judge has kept us separate at his house," she says. "But the Tribunal has asked me to be a witness at her trial."

There is something in her voice I can't make out. I don't think I've ever heard it before, but she seems unnerved by the thought.

"It's standard procedure," I tell her.

She jerks her chin in acknowledgment.

"I need you to write down every location you and Ivy visited together leading up to the event. Anywhere you've gone together since she's been in the house. Every detail, no matter how small. I want them."

"Okay," she answers quietly.

Silence lingers between us for a few long moments before she clears her throat.

"Do you believe she is guilty?"

"Undoubtedly." I turn away, jaw hard, hoping she can't see the strain in my eyes. But that doesn't stop me from hearing her next question, whispered low.

"What are you going to do with her?"

"Nothing has changed," I reply coldly. "She will pay for her sins. In blood."

8
IVY

I sit with my feet up on the cot, arms around my knees and my head resting against the cold stone. I don't know how many days it's been since I stood before The Tribunal and heard what I'd been accused of. Four or five? A week? Two? It's impossible to tell with that small window as my only source of light and the trees too dense for sunlight to filter through properly.

They think I tried to kill him.

They think I smeared poison on my lips and kissed him in order to kill him.

And I'm still in a little bit of shock.

I asked how I could have done that without succumbing myself, but they dismissed that with talk of an antidote. I don't even know the poison they named. I don't know what it is. Where I would get it. How I would use it.

But they'd have none of it, then absurdly claimed it was a fact-finding mission. A preliminary and not a proper trial.

I guess I still have that to look forward to.

But I don't think they were after facts. For someone to be poisoned, they need a poisoner, and I fit the bill. Multiple witnesses, including Mercedes, saw me kiss my husband. And besides, there was other irrefutable evidence even if witness accounts were wrong.

They lied, those "witnesses." I never kissed him. Not that night.

Not that he'd let me on any night even if I wanted to. Santiago has kissed me twice, maybe three times, but never has it been me kissing him. He must allow it. Don't they know that?

I wipe my eyes with my sleeve. At least my captor hasn't bound me since I've been back. I'm still barefoot, still wearing that white dress although it's not white anymore. Nothing can stay clean in this place.

Someone tried to kill Santiago. The thought boggles my mind.

And the fact that they think that someone is me? I can't wrap my brain around it.

But then I get to the next part. The more important part.

He's alive.

There's a part of me that feels relief. And, if I'm honest with myself, something else. Something like a spark of hope. And a small bubble of something I don't want to name that quickens every time the door opens.

I shake my head.

God, what is wrong with me?

When it comes to Santiago and my situation, there is no hope, no spark of some other nameless, ridiculous thing. I can be relieved that he's alive. But I can *only* be relieved that he's alive. That's just being human. Even if I hate him, it doesn't mean I want him dead. And the hope I feel is only for my freedom. Hope that when the door opens, it will be him. My husband will come for me.

The devil you know. That's all this is. It's not that I have feelings for him.

And besides, what would they do to me if he hadn't survived? If he'd died? The Society and their precious Sovereign Sons. I don't delude myself into thinking I could ever be precious to anyone but this? Accusing me of attempting to murder my own husband no matter how much I hate him? It's insane. Unbelievable.

But he's alive.

And my mind begins its incessant circling again.

I pull at my hair to distract myself. If I could just see him. Talk to him. Explain that I was in the chapel, and when the second gong rang out, I had been hiding in one of the bathrooms. Explain that I couldn't get out.

Coincidental. Convenient. I can hear him now.

He hates me. He already believes the worst when it comes to me, and this will not alter his feelings. Not in a way that would benefit me.

I tried to explain it to the man who is holding me. I tried to tell him what happened, but he wouldn't have it either. He threatened to gag me if I wouldn't keep quiet on the drive back to this horrible place, and when he's come in to feed me and empty the bucket, he has refused to speak to me.

But Santiago is alive. He'll come for me. I have to believe that.

I stop, though, because another thought interrupts that never-ending cycle.

What if I'm wrong? What if he doesn't come? What if he leaves me here to rot until I'm expected to appear before The Tribunal again? What if he's alive but not himself? Hurt. And what if he's alive but doesn't want me back?

At that, I let out a strange, snort-laugh. It's ugly.

Yes. He'll want me back. He'll want to be the one to punish me.

I close my eyes, confused by all this, my own thoughts, my feelings, this isolation, this darkness. I tug the blanket closer, rubbing warmth into my freezing feet. It's so cold here. My captor must realize it too because he gave me a second blanket. Same as the first one. Rough and terrible but at least it's something.

Does he think I'm guilty of what they're accusing me of?

I drift off, snatching sleep when it comes before the cold, and my dreams wake me. Tonight, though, when I startle awake, it's not either of those things that rouse me. It's the key in the lock.

I blink my eyes open, my brain in a fog from the lack of sleep, lack of sunlight, and no exercise. Lack of nutrition. A half bowl of cold soup, a wedge of stale bread, and an apple a day are not enough to sustain me.

Whoever it is is carrying a lantern and there it is. That spark of hope inside me. I sit up, but the moment I recognize the cloak, the hood, the spark is extinguished.

He walks in without a word to me. That's not unusual, though.

I fumble for my blindfold. I forgot to pull it down, but I do now. I wonder if I should ask for a new strip of cloth. This one is disgusting.

"Stand up," he says.

"What?"

"Up. On your feet."

This is different. I release the blanket, shuddering as I stand. I'm not sure I'll ever get warm again.

"Arms."

"Why? I haven't done anything."

"Arms."

I extend my arms out to him and feel the familiar rope wrap around the healing, scabbed skin. I feel the warmth of tears slide down my face again.

"Are you taking me back? To The Tribunal?"

He doesn't reply. Weaving the rope around and between my wrists, he pulls me to the center of the room, where I know the ring he has hooked me to on the ceiling is. He turns me to face away from him, my back to the door.

"No, please. It's too high. It hurts..."

But my arms are stretched above me, and I'm bound in place before I even finish, and then he's leaving. Gone. I hear him go. Hear the door close. Hear the lock turn. And then the crunching of dead leaves and branches as he passes by my small window.

What does he mean to do? He can't leave me hanging like this all night, surely. All day.

I rub the side of my face against my arm and manage to push the blindfold up enough to open my eyes. I turn to look behind me, all around me. Can I at least reach the bucket? Turn it upside down and stand on it to alleviate the pain in my shoulders? I try to extend my leg, but it's too far. I'm stuck with only the tips of my toes on the floor. I shiver as a cool wind blows outside, and the rain starts to fall, the sound pretty, musical almost on the lush floor beyond my cell. It would be pretty if I were anywhere else. Even in my room which felt like a cell at The Manor. What I'd give to be back there now.

I DRIFT in and out of sleep, jolted awake when my head lolls to my arm then drops. My shoulders ache. My stomach is rumbling. I'm hungry and thirsty. I'm exhausted. So exhausted I can't think straight.

Rain now pours outside, sliding along the wall beneath the window over the trail of moss and growth on the path it must normally take. I sneeze. I'm freezing. How long has it been? How long has he left me hanging here? And how much longer does he plan to keep me like this?

Something crunches outside. A branch breaks. I hear it even through the rain. Then a moment later comes the familiar sound of the key in the lock.

I turn to look over my shoulder to watch for him, wondering what the point was to stringing me up. The door opens, creaking heavily on its rusted hinges. He's back, and I'm relieved.

"Thank God," I mutter. My shoulders ache, and my toes have gone numb.

No lantern this time. Only blackness around him.

I rub my face on my arm but fail to get the blindfold down, so I keep my face averted, my back to the door. To him. I don't want to anger him. But I listen for him. His steps are always so quiet that only the crunching bones give him away.

I swallow as he nears me, my heartbeat accelerating even more than usual. He lifts my hair and sets it over one shoulder. He's closer than expected, and I stiffen, feeling the leather of his gloved fingers running down my arm. The warmth of his breath at my neck makes me shudder.

"I...What are...?" I start, but something tickles the back of my neck, scratches the mark there. It makes my breath catch.

I swallow, my throat dry, a croaking sound coming when I try to speak and tell him to stop.

His hand slides down my side and over my thigh.

"What are you doing?" I ask, voice small as I look down at his big hand, the black glove working, fisting the fabric of the dress. "What are you doing?" I ask again, this time more forcefully. He hasn't touched me more than he's needed to since I've been here. What's changed?

But it was only a matter of time, wasn't it?

I just keep watching as my legs are exposed, my thighs, and I tug against the rope needing my arms to fight him when the fingers of that gloved hand brush against my clit.

"Oh god. Please don't. Please."

"No?"

I freeze. Even my tears seem to come to a halt.

He draws his arm around my middle and tugs

me backward into his body with a jerk. He's hard and warm and familiar, and my heart beats wildly as a thousand butterflies take wing inside my stomach.

I turn my head just a little, but he clucks his tongue, and I stop. I lick my lips.

"Santiago?"

Something cold and heavy drops over my head then, and I gasp, looking down at the rosary, the cross dangling between my breasts and over his arm, my feet off the floor as he takes my weight.

"Who else?"

I laugh. Almost. I mean, it's the closest thing to a laugh. It sounds insane, and I feel fresh tears of relief. He's come for me. He's alive, and he's come for me!

"Santiago! I was so scared." I'm sobbing, trying to turn to him, but his arm is too tight, hurting me. I hear the tearing of fabric and feel the tugging of the dress at my neck before his other hand closes over my buttock and squeezes so hard that I cry out.

He rubs his chin against my face, his rough with scruff, mine unwashed and dirty and tearstained.

"Were you?" he asks.

I nod, my eyes wide in the darkness because this is not going as I expect. He's not taking me down. He's not wrapping me in his arms like he has before.

Of course he's not.

He thinks I poisoned him. He thinks I tried to kill him.

"I didn't—"

He lifts me a little higher, arm crushing my ribs which still feel bruised from when the other man took me. With his other hand on my butt, he pulls me open. And then I feel him, his hardness, and some part of me, some sick part of me wants this. Wants him.

He brushes his cheek against my cheek, and I can just see the shadow of his face, his dark eyes black in this night. He drags his lips along my cheekbone, then closer to my ear, not quite kissing me. This is something else.

"You didn't what?" he asks.

I swallow because what I hear in his voice is not any different than the contempt I heard in the other man's voice. In the voices of The Councilors when they spoke, condemning me before my trial even began.

Contempt.

Hate.

The only one at The Tribunal who seemed conflicted was Mercedes. It surprised me. Although conflict wasn't what The Councilors heard. They heard fact. And maybe I'm grasping at straws because Mercedes has no love for me.

"What's the matter, sweet, Poison Ivy?" he asks, then bends his head to lick my neck, to close his lips over my beating pulse and suck, his mouth wet and hot and his cock when he thrusts inside me unforgiving.

I gasp, the breath forced out of me.

"Tell me," he says low and quiet, but not quite a whisper.

"I didn't..." I grunt with his next thrust. He's released my bottom and has got my jaw in his hand now, fingers digging into soft flesh.

"Tell. Me." It's a command. Voice loud. Firm. Angry.

"I didn't mean to hurt you." I say it wrong. It comes out all wrong. It's not what I meant. I meant... but it doesn't matter. Santiago laughs. He just laughs this dark, ugly laugh and shifts his grip to my hips and draws back, lifting me, bending me to fuck me. To hurt me.

And he does.

This is a punishment fuck. The first of many punishments. I know it. I feel it. And as my legs quake and my insides go raw, I realize how stupid I've been. How naïve I'd been thinking he'd come for me, come to rescue me.

When did I forget that he was the devil?

And what will he do to me now that he thinks I tried to kill him?

His thrusts come harder, his fingers agony on the flesh of my hips, my shoulders aching with his tugs, wrists raw and bleeding.

I don't come, but that's the point. He takes me.

Takes his pleasure from me. Lays claim to me. And even as he comes, I feel his rage. I feel his hate.

And I know that now, not like before, I am finished. I know that how it was before will be a thousand times preferable to what I have coming. To what he'll do to me now.

He pulls me close with his final thrust, and I feel him throb and shudder, releasing inside me. I hear his breath, his groan, and I think about what it is between us. What it is that binds us.

Because we are bound.

And he will keep his promise. He will kill me. But not before I am begging for it, begging for mercy in death.

One gloved hand comes to my face, and I wonder if he can feel the tears he's smearing away. I think he can. And I know how much he likes my tears.

"No, sweet, Poison Ivy. You didn't hurt me," he says, voice dark and low. "But I will surely hurt you."

9

SANTIAGO

"How are you feeling?" Angelo asks, his eyes moving over the case of scotch on my desk.

My fresh paranoia would be difficult not to notice. Since my return home, my vigilance has swung to the extreme end of the spectrum. Antonia's apparent happiness to see me soon disappeared when I ordered all the food and beverages in the house be tossed. She seemed horrified by the prospect, considering her menus had already been planned for my arrival. But her frown only deepened upon my informing the staff that I was having cameras installed in every room, along with daily security checks.

The atmosphere has been noticeably gloomy since I've resumed my post in my study, refusing the food I'm served and subsisting on mostly a liquid diet. It isn't doing any favors for my temperament either, and it hasn't gone unnoticed.

"I'm fine," I reply to Angelo's question in a flat tone. "Nothing some good scotch won't cure."

He sighs and bites back what would probably be some advice about my situation, knowing better than to offer it.

"I'm sorry I couldn't visit you in the hospital," he says. "I couldn't get in without being seen. They had it locked down."

"I wouldn't have made for very good company anyway," I remark dryly.

"I don't suppose so."

I tug an unopened bottle of scotch free from the case and offer it to him, but he declines. I shrug and take another drink for myself from the one on my desk.

"Any progress on the investigation into the poisoning?" he asks, skirting around the mention of Ivy.

It's become common knowledge throughout The Society that my own wife tried to poison and kill me. I don't doubt many of the member's wives are silently in agreement with her, pitying her for being wed to the likes of myself. But they know better than to speak those thoughts aloud, and as far as they are concerned, Ivy has already been shunned from their inner circle. This is the way things work. Loyalty will always lie with the Sovereign Sons.

"No news, but I didn't expect any surprise developments on the matter. I have all the information I need."

Angelo nods, a dark expression tightening his features. "So, what will you do with her?"

"What will you do with the traitor in your own life?" I arch a brow at him in return.

He understands the question perfectly well, and it doesn't require a response. I have no desire to go into the details with him or anyone else for that matter. Everyone will be watching me now. They are all desperate to know how I will handle the situation. By all rights, I could string up my traitorous wife by the neck in the middle of the compound and leave her to die and not a single soul would dare utter a protest to save her. But my agenda has always been a long game. I need heirs to the De La Rosa name. Ivy is a means to an end, and I will never make the mistake of allowing her to think otherwise.

"I believe you had something you wanted me to look into last we spoke?" I change the subject.

He drags a hand through his hair and sighs. "I do, but only if it isn't a burden."

"Believe me, anything to distract me right now is a gift."

With my assurances, Angelo reaches down to retrieve a folder from his briefcase and slides it across the desk to me. "Any information you can get on these accounts would be helpful. I'd like to know who exactly is funneling the money, but even a breadcrumb will do."

I open the folder to examine the accounts, flipping through various pages as my lips pull together in a grim line. I suspect this has something to do with his own pursuit of vengeance and his determination to confirm who betrayed him and sent him to prison. If our past conversations are any indication, he already knows, but his situation is more complex. He needs undeniable proof before he destroys his own blood.

"I will see what I can dig up. It might take some time."

Angelo rises to his feet and checks his watch. "I'll check in with you periodically to see what your progress is. I wish I could stay and visit longer, but—"

"You don't want anyone to see you." I nod. "I get it. Go, enjoy your freedom. I'll see you another time."

He disappears down the hall just as quietly as he arrived, and I spend the next few hours poring over the folder of information he gave me. It gives me something to focus on even though I'm behind on my own work as it is. It's a distraction, but not enough to keep my thoughts from wandering to my wife.

I have not been to see her in two days. Not since I locked her up in her room and barricaded any incoming light, leaving her with the solace of only a couple of candles. Antonia has been instructed to keep her closet locked, and she is to remain naked and broken for me. But I suspect when I see her again, there will undoubtedly be defiance from her as always. And I am already thinking of new ways to punish her for those future sins.

A knock on the door startles me from my thoughts, and when I glance up, Mercedes is there. Her face is drawn, and she's usually in bed by this late hour, but it seems she is still not any less rattled by the events that transpired at the gala.

"Can I come in?" she asks.

"Since when do you require permission?" I smirk, but she does not seem to notice my sarcasm.

Something is bothering her, but I haven't been able to determine what it is. She's been quiet and closed off. We sit at the dinner table together in the evenings, me drinking, and her going through the motions of eating, but it's obvious she's not really here. Her thoughts seem to be plagued by something else, and I am not quite certain how to deal with such a situation.

She enters the room and sits in the chair that Angelo vacated earlier. Her hair is braided back, her face scrubbed clean of the usual makeup she wears. And when I see her this way, it is a stark reminder she is still young and naïve in many ways, despite what she'd like everyone else to believe.

"Tell me what's on your mind." I close the folder

on my desk and secure it in my locked drawer before returning my attention to her.

Mercedes shrugs one shoulder, wrapping her cardigan tightly around herself like a cocoon even though it's not chilly in the room. "Too much to put into words."

"Don't play coy with me," I reply. "You came here for a reason, and you've been moping around The Manor since you've been home. I can't help you if I don't know what the issue is."

She bounces one leg, a nervous habit I haven't seen since she was a child, and our father sought to break her of it. A De La Rosa can never show vulnerability. That's what he told us. We all took it to heart, but I will never punish Mercedes for showing her true self to me.

"It's just hard to stop thinking about everything that happened," she says quietly. "Do you believe The Tribunal will ever have concrete proof?"

"It doesn't matter if they have concrete proof," I tell her. "It is ultimately up to me since I am alive, and I am her husband. I could feed her to the wolves, or I can handle it myself. You already know my chosen course. We will go through the motions of the trial because Ivy deserves every ounce of fear it will instill in her. But I am her true judge, jury, and executioner."

My sister nods and swallows, dipping her head as she seems to consider something. "No mercy.

That's what Father always used to say. I suppose that is the De La Rosa motto."

A chill moves over me when it occurs to me she's comparing me to him, but I don't acknowledge it. I can't.

"So, you will... end her." Her voice wavers slightly, and she clears her throat. "When?"

Her sudden lack of enthusiasm on the subject is strange, considering how she salivated over the idea before. "Why do you care?"

She shifts in her seat, glancing at the flickering flame of the candle on the end of my desk. "I don't, of course. I was just wondering."

"You needn't worry." I meet her gaze. "I know you felt I was wavering in my regard before, but I can assure you, I hold no humanity in my heart for any Moreno. Particularly one who poisoned me. She will be dealt with accordingly."

Mercedes jerks her chin in agreement, but she doesn't appear to be placated by my assurances. It's unlike her to withhold her thoughts, and I don't know if I should be concerned about her welfare. Or perhaps Judge really did begin to tame her bratty ways.

She stands up and drifts toward the door, pausing to look over her shoulder.

"Santi?"

"Yes?"

"I..." Her voice fractures. "I just wanted you to know I love you. It's so good to have you home."

IVY STARTLES awake when I slip my hand over her mouth to cover her scream. The room is pitch black, and the only sounds between us are her labored breaths as she bolts upright in the bed.

"Santiago?" She pants my name as if it's a prayer for salvation.

"What did I say about you being naked?" I growl into her ear as I wrap my fingers around her throat.

"I am naked," she hisses. "You have all my clothes locked away. Do you expect me to sleep without any sheets?"

"I expect you to do whatever I ask," I answer, my breath fanning against her face.

I've had too much scotch and not enough food, and I don't exactly know what I'm doing here. One minute I was heading for my bedroom, and the next, I was stumbling into her room.

She trembles when I yank the sheet from her grasp and toss it onto the floor. She's already trying to curl into herself when I tangle my fingers in her hair and drag her from the bed and force her onto her knees.

"You don't deserve a bed," I spit. "You don't deserve anything."

"Santiago, please." She brings her hands up to my thighs, feeling her way up my body in the dark. "I need to talk to you about what happened. I need to make you understand."

I clamp my hand around her jaw, forcing her lips to shut. "The only time you should open your mouth is to please me."

She tries to murmur a protest as I tug down the zipper of my trousers and pull my cock free, rubbing it against her cheek. I reach for her hair again, arching her head back.

"Show me how sorry you are," I command.

I release her jaw, and she renews her protest. "Please just let me talk. We need to talk."

"You want to talk?" I tighten my grip on her to the point I can practically feel her wincing. "Let's talk. I have so much to say to you, dear wife. Let's start with a refresher course. I fucking own you, and you seem to have forgotten that."

"I haven't," she whimpers.

"I control everything in your life," I answer menacingly. "That hospital room your father is lying half dead in? I could have them pull the plug with a single phone call. The nuns at your sister's school? They can make her life sweet, or they can make it one of misery. That fate is mine to determine just like everything else. Every choice you make has a consequence, and I think you would do well to remember it doesn't just impact you. Don't think for one second that any of your family is safe. Not even your sweet Hazel who ran away and left you behind."

"No," she whispers, clinging to me with a desperation that doesn't please me as much as I thought it would. "You can't do that. You wouldn't. I know you aren't the monster you want everyone to believe you are."

"You know nothing about me," I snarl, releasing her in disgust. "I have been lenient with you when you did not deserve it. And now, I'm simply biding my time. You're nothing more than a toy to be used. A doll to be fucked. And when I am done with you, make no mistake about it, there will be nothing left to salvage from the wreckage."

"I don't believe you." The tremor in her voice irritates me. Or perhaps it is her continued defiance to believe what I tell her to be true.

My growing frustration has left my cock painfully hard, and when I stroke it in my fist, it's tempting to shove her face down into the carpet and fuck her from behind. But it isn't what I want. Despite all rational thought, I want her willing submission, even if it is coerced.

"Please me or face the consequences."

She hesitates, and I close my eyes, battling my warring desires for domination and surrender. I'm intoxicated enough to admit I want her hands on me. I want her softness, even if it is false. I can think of no punishment worse than her touching me as if it is driven by her own free will. But as I suspected, she is not caving. And I will have no choice but to follow through and show her what a monster truly looks like.

With a growl, I begin to shove my dick back into the confines of my trousers when she reaches out to stop me.

"Wait!" she begs. "Please."

"Please what?" I ask gruffly.

"I'll do it."

Her voice is barely audible, and time seems to suspend as I remain there, waiting for her to follow through. Several long moments pass before she wraps a hesitant hand around my shaft.

"Your mouth." My own voice is hoarse, and I force my eyes shut even though I can't see her, and she can't see me.

She is feeling her way around me, uncertain as she brings the head of my straining cock to her lips. My breath hisses between my teeth as her tongue darts out and touches the rigid flesh. It's too soft. Too slow. I want to grab her by the head and force it down her throat. But I can't seem to move, paralyzed by the sensation of her drawing me into her mouth.

A groan rumbles from my chest as I cup the back of her skull and inch my cock as deep as she can take me. She starts to cough, and I push deeper until she's clawing at my legs and gasping for air. A brief reprieve is all I intend to grant her as I ease away to let her catch her breath, but my wife is determined, pulling me in again, her mouth warm velvet against my hardness. Already, my balls are drawing tight against my body as the urge to release overwhelms me.

I don't realize I'm petting her hair until she leans into my touch.

It's a trick. It's all a trick. Every soft sound that spills from her lips as she takes me inside. The sweet perfume of her own arousal between her thighs. She would never admit that she enjoys the perverseness of this dynamic between us. That it makes her wet to kneel before me and follow my commands. Because that couldn't possibly be true. She's trying to lure me in again. That's the only logical explanation for this insanity.

"That's enough," I bite out, trying to pull my dick free from her lips.

"No!" She clings to me, pleading. "I'll do better. Please, just let me try."

It seems I have found a way to motivate her after all. And it fucking grates at me that she will degrade herself so willingly to save her precious family. But those thoughts drift away the moment she pulls me back in, lashing at me with her tongue as she works my shaft.

I grip her hair, pivoting my hips forward as I fight my own will to make this stop. But I can't. I can't stop thrusting into her warmth as her nails dig into my thighs.

I don't know how long it goes on for. I just know that my baser desires take over at some point, and I am splitting her jaw apart as I use her mouth like I promised. She takes it. She takes every inch of it and doesn't once protest, even when she's coughing and sputtering around me.

When my muscles begin to tremble, and the tension is at a breaking point, I yank myself free of her lips at the last second, spilling my come over her naked breasts. My chest heaves from the force of my release, and the hammering pulse in my throat leaves me stumbling back from the venomous creature beneath me before I cave in to another desire. Like kissing her. Touching her. Treating her with a gentleness she could never deserve.

"Santiago?" She calls after me as I head for the door, tucking my cock back into my trousers as I go. "You aren't going to do anything to them, are you? I did what you wanted."

Silence is my only response.

10
IVY

"It's better than the cellar," I tell myself for the hundredth time. The thousandth.

I get up, go into the bathroom. It's the only place with electricity and a light bulb. There's electricity in my room too but no bulbs in the few light fixtures. That was the case since I first came here. It's not a part of my punishment. That, I know, is because Santiago doesn't like people looking at him.

I think about what I know about my husband. Not much. Not really. Yet he and I are tied together, locked in this strange, dark place acting out this strange, dark story.

The light is dim, but it's better than the three candles I'm allotted daily. I think it's daily at least. I have no idea what day it is or how much time has passed, but it feels like weeks. I have no way to mark the time apart from the meals Antonia brings in or the visits from my husband although he isn't consistent. The light from the window that I'd been allowed for so short a time has been closed up again, so I don't even have the luxury of the small square I used to have when I first came here.

No, when I first was brought here. I never came willingly.

In the dim light of the bulb, I splash water on my face, then take in my reflection. I've lost weight. You can see it on my face. And for all the sleep I'm getting, I have dark circles under my eyes. My face is starting to look like the tattooed half of his.

I step back with a rueful smile and take in my small breasts and concave belly. I think about how weak I am. How easily broken both literally and figuratively.

Bruises have created a pattern of deep blues, purples, and decaying yellows along my arms, my stomach, my legs and hips. I don't think he's seen them. It's so dark in here even his eyes couldn't penetrate it. I wonder what he'd think if he did see. It's his fault. All of it. He may as well physically beat me himself because being locked in here without light, without exercise, and with the heightened anxiety of what he'll do to me, to my family, I'm completely out of sorts to the point it's becoming dangerous. I turn a little to touch the still painful bruise on my hip, the gash. It's from the edge of the dresser.

Taking out the first-aid kit, I pour antiseptic onto a cotton pad and wince when I touch it to the wound. I should let it get infected and put myself out of my misery. Deny him the satisfaction of torturing me to death.

But that's a fantasy. God knows what he'd do to Evangeline if I took my own life. And then there's Hazel. Could he find her? Would he?

After discarding the cotton and washing my hands, I leave the light on and walk back into the bedroom to sit down on the bed and wait. It's all I do now. I wait for Antonia to come, happy for the exchange of a few words when she does. I get the feeling she's not allowed to talk to me, but she does anyway, at least a little.

I wait for him to come. To fuck me. To degrade me. To leave.

My stomach sinks, and my eyes fill with hot tears, but I am quick to wipe them away.

"It's better than the cellar," I say again, gathering the blankets up to cover myself when I hear the key in the lock.

"Dinnertime, dear," Antonia says as she opens the door.

I am greedy to take in the light of the slightly brighter corridor behind her. She must see my face because she starts to close the door but then stops and leaves it open. But her kind nature and pitying looks only make me feel sadder. More alone. More like crying, and I don't want to cry anymore. Not for him. Not in front of any of them. So, I swallow it down.

"You need to eat, Ivy," she says after looking at the untouched lunch tray. It was the same with breakfast.

"I'm not hungry. Do you think I can call my sister?" I don't even know why I ask. I know the answer, and besides, I wouldn't want to get her into trouble.

She comes over to sit on the bed, straightening the comforter. "If you eat your dinner, I'll talk to him."

I turn away. "Never mind then."

"You're only hurting yourself if you don't eat."

"I'm tired."

"He'll come around."

I turn to her. "Do you think I did it? What they're accusing me of?"

She pushes my hair behind my ear. It's a mess. I haven't brushed it in days. Haven't showered in I don't know how long.

"Of course not. I don't think you're capable of anything like that."

I smile in gratitude. "How can he think it was me?"

"Cozy in here," comes his dark voice.

Antonia and I startle and turn at the same time,

she rushing to her feet as I push up to sit straighter, holding the blanket to me.

"Sir," Antonia says as she clears my untouched lunch tray and walks past him.

Santiago looks at it, then holds out his hand to stop her as he studies the contents. "Did she eat anything?"

Antonia looks guiltily at me. "No, sir."

He glances at me, his look hateful even in the dim light. "Breakfast?"

She clears her throat, casts her gaze down, and shakes her head, and I wonder how many days it's been since his last conjugal visit.

"Is my food not good enough for you?" he asks me after dismissing Antonia.

"How can I be sure you're not poisoning me?"

He snorts. "That's rich." He enters the room, and I grip the blanket tighter, remembering how he'd torn it away the last time he was here. He closes the door. "If you don't eat the entire tray of food there, I will tie you to your bed and force it down your throat. Am I clear?"

"I'm not hungry."

"That's too bad." He pulls the chair out at the small table. "Come here."

I look away from him, rubbing my face with one hand. "I didn't do it. I swear, Santiago."

"But you lie. Come here. Now."

"Will you listen to me if I do?"

"Did I give you the impression we were negotiating?"

"No, I know you don't negotiate."

"You're smarter than I thought, then." He lifts the chair and slams it down. "Don't make me come get you."

I push the blanket back and get up, taking a moment to steady myself when a dizzy spell comes.

"Don't bother with the acting. It won't win any points from me."

"I'm not acting, you jerk!" I tell him once the spell passes, and I walk over and take the seat, being careful not to touch him. I don't even care that I'm naked. He's seen all of me. And in this light, I'm sure I'm not much more than a shadow anyway. A ghost already.

"Now pick up your knife and fork and start. I have more important things to do than babysit my wife."

"Why do you care if I eat if you hate me so much?" I ask as I pick up the fork and poke at the meat. It's underdone. Bloody. I'm sure just like he likes it.

"Oh, I don't," he says so casually I have to look up at him. He meets my eyes, the flickering candles casting shadows on his skull face tattoo. "I care that the babies you carry won't be malnourished."

"Babies again." I stab a piece of broccoli.

He leans down close to my ear, pushing my hair

over my shoulder. "Why do you think I haven't killed you yet?" he asks in a whisper, sliding his hand down, pushing the rosary out of the way and cupping my breast.

I shudder.

He straightens, dragging his fingernails along my breast before releasing it. I wonder if he realizes all that does is serve to arouse me. Because somehow, even now, I'm still aroused by him.

"Eat," he says, taking my jaw in his hand and turning my face to his. "Unless you want me to force-feed you."

I tug my face away and start to eat, knowing there's no way I'll be able to finish the entire meal. I'm already having a hard time getting just the first few bites past my throat.

He takes my hair in his hands, feels the texture. The knots. He brings it to his nose.

"When was the last time you washed your hair?"

I shrug a shoulder.

He twists my hair around his fist and tugs my head painfully backward. "Words."

"I don't remember. I don't know what day it is. I don't even know if it's night or day. I don't know how long you've had me locked up in here."

"Do you prefer Judge's cellar?"

"Judge?"

"I can take you back there. With the rats."

"You're hurting me."

"Do you want me to take you back there?"

I give a slight shake of my head.

"Use your words, Ivy."

"No," I spit.

"Then watch your mouth and do as you're told. When I come in here, you should drop to your knees eager to please me, yet what do I get? A petulant, defiant little wife who can't even be bothered to wash herself."

Tears are forming at the corners of my eyes, and the food in my mouth is turning sour, but he finally releases me roughly like he's disgusted by me, and I chew and chew as my stomach turns and idiotic tears run down my cheeks. I feel so hated, so unwanted. And it hurts so much more than I ever thought him hating me could.

He leans against the wall, arms folded across his chest, death glare on me as I finish every morsel. I'm so full that I'm sure the meal will make a reappearance. When I'm finished, I turn to him.

"Did your brother give it to you?"

"What?"

"When he was here for that impromptu visit conveniently on the day of the gala."

The poison again. I exhale, shaking my head. "Why do you ask me? You don't believe anything I say anyway."

I push my chair back and walk up to him, closer than he expects because he straightens to his full height, and I have to crane my neck to look up at him. This close, I see his gaze roam my face, slip to my breasts, then back up to my mouth. Looking at me arouses him. He's just as attracted to me as I am to him despite everything.

So, I steel my spine and stand a little taller.

"I don't know why you're hell-bent on finding me guilty when I am not. You have an enemy so hateful he is willing to poison you. To murder you. That enemy is not me. But let me ask you something, Santiago. Have you ever stood back and thought about why? Thought about how someone can inspire such emotion in another human being that they would go as far as murder? You are hated, Santiago. You. Are. Hated. How does it feel?"

Fury sparks in his eyes, darkening them, and it takes all I have not to back away.

"I'd think you'd have some sense of how that feels by now, Ivy."

His hand closes around my throat hard, making me cry out in pain as he spins me so my back is to the wall. I'm trapped between it and him. He keeps me pinned, and I listen to the sound of the belt unbuckling, the zipper of his trousers going down, and a moment later, he bends his knees to lift me, grabbing my thighs and forcing them wide.

My legs wrap around him naturally as he impales me, his face so close I can feel his breath on me. Using the wall to balance me, he puts his hands on either side of my face and brings his mouth to mine. I lick my lips, but he doesn't kiss me. Instead, he takes my lower lip between his teeth and bites just hard enough to break skin and draw blood. And I wonder if the taste of it arouses him even more because he feels thicker, fucks me harder, more frantically as my arms come to his shoulders, my breathing uneven as he draws more blood and I close my eyes because I'm going to come. I'm going to come so hard as he hate fucks me, and when I do, I cry out, digging my fingernails into his shoulders, hoping I'm drawing blood even through his shirt.

When I open my eyes again, he's watching me intently, and with one hand, he grips my jaw and forces my head against the wall.

"You stole that one," he says.

He thrusts once more, burying himself inside me as he wraps his other arm around me to carry me to the bed, to pull out before throwing me down and spinning me so I'm facedown. He grips a handful of hair and twists, forcing me to look back at him as he slides his thick cock into me and closes one finger over my back hole. He's been doing that, and I know that's coming too, and I wonder how much it will hurt.

"Do you think you'll come when I fuck this tight little hole? Because I don't think so, sweet, poison Ivy." He jerks my head back so painfully I swear I hear something pop.

"You're... hurting me."

With a snort, he lets go of my hair and grips my hips, splaying me wide as he drives into me. He's close. I can hear it. I know the sounds he makes now like he knows the sounds I make. And I want to come again just to piss him off, so I slip a hand between my legs and finger myself. He slaps my ass hard and drives deep inside me and stills, cock throbbing, emptying, the sensations calling one more orgasm from me before he's finished, before he pulls out and stumbles backward like a drunk man.

I slip to my knees onto the floor, turning so my back rests against the bed. I draw my knees up, feeling his seed spill out of me.

He tucks himself back into his pants, murderous eyes on me. That fuck did nothing to dispel his hate. He comes to crouch down in front of me and takes my jaw in his death grip.

"You steal what I don't give, and you will be made to pay."

I try to jerk out of his grasp, but he just tightens his hold on me. I wonder how much more pressure before my jaw breaks.

"Do you know what the difference is between me and you, Ivy?"

"What?" I spit.

"I know I am hated. I don't care. I use it as a strength. You? You care. Hate steals your strength.

My hate of you weakens you. Makes a pathetic victim out of you."

I swallow, shuddering in this arctic chill of his hate as I stare up at him.

"You think you will ever win against me?" he asks.

"No, Santiago, I don't." That must surprise him because I swear there's a momentary flash of confusion in his eyes. I don't think he expected that answer or any answer. "I have no doubt you will beat me. No doubt you will bury me." As I say the words, I know they're true, and they feel like a weight in the pit of my stomach.

We stay like that for a long moment just looking at each other. And then, without a word, he releases me and gets up. He turns to the door.

"I won't beg you for mercy," I call out when he opens it.

He stops and turns around.

"And I will never stop fighting you," I add.

He grins, walking back inside, and the look on his face is that of a victor as if he's already won. He comes close, so close the tips of his shoes press against my bare toes. It makes me think of the bones of the dead mice in that cellar. How they crunched underfoot.

He leans down and brushes his knuckles over my cheekbone so gently that it takes all I have not to lean into his touch. Not to close my eyes and take comfort in him.

He chuckles. He must see it. And he straightens to his full height, looming over me like the shadow he is.

"I hope you won't ever stop fighting because I will enjoy breaking you bit by bit."

11

SANTIAGO

"Antonia said you wanted to see me as soon as I got home."

I blink up at my sister in the doorway of my study, eyes bleary. I'm not even sure what time it is, but it seems late.

"Where have you been?" I demand.

She crosses her arms and shrugs. "Shopping."

I suspect she's not telling me the full truth, and it's something I'll have to follow up on with her driver and guard later. But for now, I have other things to worry about.

"I need you to make sure Ivy bathes tonight. By force, if need be. Take two of the maids and Marco with you. He will remain in the bedroom if you need assistance."

Mercedes stares at me with a vacant expression. I was expecting a fight, but her protest is minimal.

"Why can't Antonia do it?"

"Because Antonia is getting too close with her. She feels sorry for her, and I will not tolerate anyone's sympathy toward her right now. This is why it is the perfect job for you."

"I see." She offers a stiff nod. "Call in the emotionless robot when you need her."

"You've always been so proud of it." I arch a brow at her. "Why change your tune now?"

"There is no changing anything," she answers somberly. "I am who I am, Santi."

She turns to leave, and I stand and walk around my desk, calling her back.

"Should I be worried about you?"

"No." Her response is flat. Toneless. And before I can say anything else, she is gone.

I spend the next hour going over the file for Angelo while I wait for my meeting with Judge. He arrives on time, punctual as always.

"Don't you ever get sick of sitting in this office?" He takes a seat across from me and notes the disarray of the space. I haven't allowed Antonia in here to clean in days.

"I have a lot of work to catch up on."

"That must be the reason for the exhaustion on your face," he muses.

I lean back in my chair, eyeing the bottle of scotch I've been sipping from all day. It is unlike me to be so indulgent, but it seems to be the only thing keeping my mind from going to the darkest spaces.

"The final meeting with the Tribunal is this week," I tell him.

He nods in understanding. "And they will want to know your recommended sentence for your wife's crime. Or else they will impose one themselves."

I twist the cap off the bottle and take a long pull as Judge studies me.

"You're not in an easy position," he says. "Have you decided what you will tell them?"

"What is there to say?" I close my eyes and savor the burn in my throat. "She is guilty. I have nothing to offer in the way of her defense."

"That may be. But her guilt isn't the issue. The issue is what her punishment will be, and if it will be enough to satisfy them."

I tilt my head back, staring up at the shadows dancing across the ceiling. "You're the Judge. You tell me. What would you do if you were in my position?"

"She will already bear the shame of her crime every time she enters the public," he observes. "She will be shunned, whispered about, and despised. But the question is what punishment could be equal to the shame she has cast on you?"

I meet his gaze and take another long pull from the bottle. He doesn't need to explain what he means. Ivy didn't just poison me. She drove a goddamned stake through my reputation. As a

Sovereign Son, there is an expectation that my wife will have unwavering loyalty and respect for me. I knew going into this marriage the best I could expect was to have her fear and submission. She would never love me, and I could never love her. There is no loyalty or respect between us. But for her to so blatantly broadcast it to The Society is a slight that cannot be tolerated. The upper echelon must know I have this situation under control. That I am capable of doling out the harsh punishment that will satisfy them and restore the natural hierarchy of order.

"Short of killing her now, I see only one solution." My fingertips move over the scars on my face, covered in ink. A permanent reminder of the damage the Moreno family has inflicted upon the De La Rosa dynasty. Ivy too, will require something permanent. Something horrific. Something that will maim her for life and serve as a reminder of what she has done and who she really is.

"It seems to me you have already decided," Judge remarks. "But if there is one piece of advice I can give you, Santiago, it's this. If you go down this path, there is no coming back from it. When you dole out this type of justice, there must be no question of guilt because you can't take it back once it's done. As you are well aware, those scars do not fade away in time."

He rises to his feet and sets a tote bag onto my

desk. Something he must have carried in with him, but I didn't notice it until now.

"What is that?" I ask.

"Her things from the cellar. I thought perhaps you might want them back."

Fire licks across my flesh, smoke burning my eyes as I crawl through the rubble, dragging my half limp body deeper into the burning remnants. Searing pain is the only solace I have as the screams of men burning alive around me fade into the roar of the inferno.

"Leandro," I try again to call out for him, but my voice is too weak, choked by the suffocating blackness.

He was right beside me. My father and my brother were both right there. My body collapses onto the floor as I gasp for breath, stretching out my mangled arm. In the flicker of flames and shadows, I see a shiny black shoe. Italian leather. Laces perfectly knotted. A rose emblem on the sole. It could only be my father or Leandro.

Using the last of my strength, I drag myself forward again, grabbing onto the leather to pull me closer. But instead of leverage in the weight of his body, I find nothing but give. It takes me a few sputtering breaths to realize I'm holding his severed leg in my hand.

His blood drips down my arm, mixing with my own before it splatters onto the concrete. At last, darkness takes me.

"Santiago."

Something shatters around me, and I hurl myself back, crashing into what feels like a brick wall. I'm swinging without a thought, punching the air, fighting off invisible demons when Mercedes's voice drags me from my delirium.

"Jesus, Santi! Wake up! Open your eyes."

I freeze, forcing my eyes open, blinking several times as my chest heaves with ragged breaths, and I take in my surroundings. I'm slumped back into my office chair, paint dust from the wall behind me covering my shirt. There's a bottle of scotch broken on the floor, and my knuckles are bloodied from hitting something. The wall. The bottle. I can't even be sure at this point.

Mercedes is standing in the doorway, surveying the scene with undisguised frustration. "What the hell is wrong with you?" she snaps.

Her lip is trembling, emotion choking her voice, and for one terrible moment, I find myself questioning if I actually hurt her.

"You didn't come near me," I say hoarsely.

"Of course, I didn't," she hisses. "I'm not an idiot. I know what you're like. But this is getting out of hand, Santi. You haven't had nightmares this bad in months."

I scrub a hand over my face, trying to shake off the memories. "I haven't been sleeping enough. That's all."

"No, you haven't," she barks. "Because you're a goddamned mess. You're drinking night and day. Slumped over this desk every waking moment. Storming around The Manor like a zombie. You need to snap out of it."

"Watch how you speak to me," I warn her.

"No." She crosses her arms defiantly. "I'm not going to pacify this behavior because I love you too much to let you backslide. I know things suck right now. Okay, they really fucking suck. But you have to get it together. For all of us. I can't go through this again with you, Santi. I can't. I won't survive it."

Tears stream down her face, and it paralyzes me. I've never seen my sister so emotional or so fragile. And I'm horrified because I don't know how to fix this. I don't know how to comfort her. I've never learned. Neither of us has ever known comfort. We've known rules, and order, and expectations. Emotions don't have a place in a De La Rosa heart. My father ensured it when he beat them out of us at every opportunity. But Mercedes is shattering before me, and I don't know how to fix it.

"I..." Words fail me as I stand and look over the mess that is my office. "Don't cry. Please."

She blinks up at me, wiping away her tears when she hears the uncharacteristic strain in my voice.

"Santi." She hurls herself at me, her entire body quaking as she wraps her arms around my stiff frame and hugs me tightly. "Please don't do this anymore. I can't stand to watch you break."

"I'll never break," I assure her, patting her back awkwardly in an effort at consolation.

"Stop drinking so much," she pleads. "This isn't like you, and it scares me to see you going back to that darkness."

"I won't go back."

"Do you promise?" She glances up at me, and I force a nod even though I'm not in the habit of complying with terrorists. Right now, my sister is an emotional terrorist, deploying the one weapon she knows I'm unequipped for. Her tears.

She squeezes me tighter and pulls herself together while I stand there, arms dangling at my sides. After a few more uncomfortable moments, she releases me, schooling her features and drawing in a deep breath. I feel another speech coming, and I'm not wrong.

"I need to speak with you about Ivy," she says.

I walk around my desk and kneel to pick up the shattered bottle, disposing of the pieces in the trash. "What about her?"

"She's got bruises all over her," she whispers.

I pause to look up at her, puzzled by the torment in her tone. I haven't seen Ivy's most recent bruises, but I am not surprised by this revelation, considering her condition.

"Is that from Judge?" she chokes out. "Or you?"

"Why do you care?" I ask.

She doesn't answer right away. She's chewing her lip, considering her words carefully. "I just... I was just wondering."

"She has a vestibular disorder," I tell her, though I'm not sure why. It's not her business. "She does most of it to herself."

I'm not excusing myself as a monster. If I were truly responsible, I would take the credit, but my sister doesn't look either relieved or gratified by this revelation.

"Don't you think you should do something about it?" she asks.

I slice my thumb on a piece of glass and blood drips onto the floor as I cock my head, studying her.

"Again, I have to ask why you care."

"I don't," she clips out. "Just... this whole thing is stupid, and I'm tired of it. Either kill her and be done with it, or just admit that you aren't going to. There's no point in torturing her and dragging it out."

"You really must not be feeling well." I toss the remainder of the glass away and stand. "That's the only justifiable explanation I can think of for this sudden change of heart."

"I haven't had a change of heart," she declares. "God, you can be so infuriating."

"Tell me something I don't know."

"I'm going to bed," she says.

"Wait."

I grab the tote bag from my desk. I already examined the contents inside after Judge left. There's nothing much of interest in there. A pair of shoes, the remnants of her dress. A purse. The lipstick was already taken for testing, which came back clean. But that does not surprise me. The Tribunal suspects she applied the poison directly to the coat of lipstick she was wearing and disposed of any evidence, and I am inclined to agree.

"Give these to Antonia so she can return them to Ivy's closet." I hand the tote to Mercedes, and she glances inside. A strange expression comes over her face as she examines the contents.

"Are these from that night?" she asks, her voice strained.

"Yes. Why?"

She shakes her head. "Nothing. It just... it gives me bad memories. That's all."

"Get some rest," I tell her. "You'll be more like yourself in the morning."

She nods, turning away. "Good night, brother."

12

SANTIAGO

I find my wife tangled up in her bedsheets, trapped in the grips of a fitful sleep. She mutters something unintelligible as I cast the soft glow of the candle in my hand over her body. I didn't want to come back here tonight. Every night, I tell myself I won't. There has to be some resistance to this madness. But after Mercedes took it upon herself to inform me of the bruises, I had to see them for myself.

She curls into herself as I peel back the top half of the sheet, exposing her torso. A sharp intake of breath leaves my lips as I see the damage for myself. If anyone were to see her this way, they would undoubtedly think she had been beaten in places. And something is so horrific about those blemishes on the perfect canvas of her skin. It bothers me more than I had anticipated, and I can only wonder how I will feel once I see the permanent destruction I intend to inflict upon her.

I replace the sheet and turn away, chest heaving as my fist curls at my sides. Why did she have to do this? Why did she have to betray me and force my hand? And why does the prospect of what's to come bring me more torment than pleasure?

"Santiago?" Her sleepy voice whispers from behind me.

I close my eyes, tempted to leave without a word. But I can't seem to move. I can't look at her. And I can't be away from her. She truly is the slowest, deadliest form of poison.

The silence stretches between us, until finally, she asks the question on her mind.

"Have you come to take your fill of me again?"

"No," I bite out.

Against my better judgment, I turn to face her, placing the candle on her nightstand. She's peeking up at me with tired eyes, hair strewed across her pillow like strands of silk. I reach out and smooth them away from her face, my dark mood casting a shadow as I study her.

"It's a shame what you've done."

"What do you mean?" she asks.

"Just remember when you look upon yourself next week, loathing your own reflection in the mirror, you only have yourself to blame."

She flinches, yanking away from my touch as she

curls into herself protectively. "What are you talking about?"

"I told you there would be punishment for your sins," I answer. "And it will be equal to your crime."

She chokes back a quiet sob and shakes her head, reaching out for my hand again. "Please don't be cruel. You don't have to do this. It doesn't have to be this way."

"But it does." I pull my fingers from her grasp, feeling the loss of her warmth immediately. "You determined this course the day you decided to betray me."

I head for the door as she calls after me, desperation coloring her voice. "Please, just look at me. I know you want to. I know you are capable of listening, if you could just let go of this hatred for one minute—"

"Go to sleep," I command. "Your physical therapy begins tomorrow."

"Physical therapy?" she echoes in confusion.

I offer her one last fleeting glance.

"To ensure the safety of my child," I answer coldly.

13

IVY

I don't sleep after he leaves. It's been four weeks since the poisoning. I only know because I start my period again. I don't know how long I was in that cellar, but I guess I've been locked in here for at least two of those weeks.

I'm just glad I don't have to ask for tampons. I'd hidden some in a tissue box the last time.

This morning when Antonia comes, she unlocks the closet door and chooses clothes for me, a pair of jeans and an oversized lilac sweater that feels luxuriously soft against my skin, especially after spending so much time naked. So much time feeling cold and alone, both in the cellar and in this room.

I eat my breakfast because she tells me the therapist Santiago hired is already here, but I'll only be allowed to see him if I eat. I will add blackmail to Santiago's crimes against me. I wonder if it was

Mercedes who did it. Who got him to call someone. The look on her face when she got me into the bathroom and saw the bruises was one of shock. She asked me if her brother had done it. Her voice had sounded strange. I didn't answer her. I let her have a good look instead and come up with her own answers. He's a monster. But so is she. A moment of softness won't dispel what I know. She is an ice queen.

"I'm ready," I say to Antonia when I finish the last bite of toast. I wipe my mouth with the napkin, anxious to get out of my prison.

She smiles, pleased at the empty plate. "I'll send someone in to clean this up. Let's go see Dr. Hendrickson."

I nod and follow her out, almost bouncing on my heels. I'm so excited to be free. I never want to enter that room again.

My balance is off, and I have to be more careful than usual on the stairs, so I don't let go of the banister. Antonia leads me to a room I've not been in before. It's large and sparsely furnished and, most importantly, it's bright. Sunlight pours in from the clear-glass windows.

"Oh," I start, my spirits lifting already at the brightness. I don't even see the man sitting on the couch until he clears his throat, and I hear the sound of a cup placed on its saucer.

I turn to him, that smile fading. I don't know this

man, and the last IVI doctor I dealt with, Dr. Chambers, left me with a bad taste in my mouth.

"Good morning," he says, smiling warmly and coming toward me. He's middle-aged and dressed impeccably in an expensive suit. He's wearing a gold wedding band, and I can see a Rolex watch peeking out from beneath his sleeve when he extends his arm once he's a few feet from me. "I'm Dr. Hendrickson. You must be Ivy."

I look at his hand in surprise. He's offering it to shake mine like we're equals.

"Ivy," Antonia urges when an awkward moment passes.

"Oh. Sorry. Yes. I'm Ivy," I say, shaking his hand. What have those weeks in my prison done to me? Have I already forgotten how to be normal?

The doctor momentarily focuses on my right eye but then smiles at me. "It's very nice to meet you."

"Can I bring you more coffee, Doctor?"

"Oh, no thank you, Antonia," he says, eyes still on me. "I'd like to get started."

"All right. Ivy, can I bring you something?"

I turn to Antonia. "Um. No, I'm fine. Thanks."

"I'll leave you to it, then." With that, Antonia is gone, and I'm left alone with the doctor.

"Are you with IVI?" I ask first thing.

"IVI?" He raises his eyebrows.

"The Society."

He pauses. "No, I'm not with any society," he

says, looking rather confused. He reaches into his pocket to take out a business card and hands it to me. "Your husband actually flew me in from California. I have my own practice there. I'm an otolaryngologist."

I study the card, then look back up at him.

He must see my confusion now because he smiles. "Ear, nose, and throat and I specialize in vestibular disorders. Your husband called my office and explained things. He's a bit worried about you."

At that, I feel my eyebrows go up. "Santiago?"

"Yes."

"Is worried about *me*?"

He nods, again looking confused.

"Hm." I remember his words to me last night. How cold they were. He's not doing this for me. He's doing it to ensure the safety of his children should I ever become pregnant with any.

"Shall we get started?"

"Okay."

He gestures for me to sit on the sofa and resumes the seat he'd just vacated. From inside his briefcase, he pulls out a folder and opens it, and I get a glimpse of my name on the first sheet of paper.

"What are those?" I ask.

"Some of your medical records. Mr. De La Rosa was kind enough to send them along. I haven't had a chance to read them completely yet as this was rather short notice, but from what I've read, it doesn't look like you've had any treatment for the disorder?"

I shift my gaze from the papers to him. I guess I'm not surprised Santiago has my medical records.

"Just a diagnosis when I was young." My mother had decided treatment wasn't necessary. I just had to "get over it." Her exact words. Because treatment would make the condition public, and she couldn't have that. I was flawed enough. My dad argued about it with her but ultimately gave in.

"I see," he says, looking through more of the papers in that folder before taking out an electronic pad and asking me a long list of questions.

I'm not sure what to expect, but I spend the whole morning with Dr. Hendrickson. After a physical exam where he hid his shock well at all the bruises because even for me, this is extensive, we spent time on simple exercises, some of which I've found online but never really committed to doing. I didn't mind so much about those, and I thought about a bargaining chip with Santiago. I didn't tell the doctor that I'd been kept in a locked, blacked-out room for weeks. I'm not sure what Santiago had told him, but there would be no point. Even if he was horrified, what could he do? Call the police? They are in Santiago's pocket. IVI would never allow a Sovereign Son to get into trouble with the police. It would be too inelegant.

Instead, I asked him about swimming, told him

how it used to help. And I didn't have to mention going outside. He brought that up himself and said he'd add that to his discussion with Santiago.

Once he left, Antonia let me have lunch in the kitchen with her, but she had to take me back up to my room after that. I know she felt awful about it. That's the only reason I didn't fight it. I've gotten her into enough trouble.

So instead, I went back upstairs to my dark room, stripped off my clothes and handed them to her to lock away, and resumed my place on the bed to wait.

I DON'T KNOW how many hours pass before Santiago enters my room again. I've already had dinner, and I'm wide-awake, waiting for him. I don't know if it's the grin on my face that makes him pause just as he enters the room, but for exactly one millisecond, I feel like I have the upper hand. The element of surprise. I'm almost gleeful, and it's strange. Almost like a madwoman. I've rehearsed all day how I'll tell him that his seed isn't up to the task. That all this fucking and still no heir to the devil's throne. Some more crude things too. Anything to unman him. I know he'll punish me for it, but it will be well worth it.

"Wife," he greets, looking around the room at the additional candles.

"Husband," I match his tone and narrow my gaze, letting a smirk play at the corner of my mouth.

He grins too and walks over to me.

I don't move, keeping my relaxed posture of half lying down, half sitting up.

He pushes the hair back from my face, cups it to turn it slightly so he's looking at my right eye, studying it for some reason. His strange words from last night come back to me.

"Just remember when you look upon yourself next week, loathing your own reflection in the mirror, you only have yourself to blame."

I pull out of his grasp, the glee of moments ago faded. Turned uglier.

"What do you want?" I ask.

"You on your knees to start."

My belly flutters as my gaze dips from his face to his crotch and back. Fine. He wants me to suck him off? I can do that. I may bite tonight, though. So I push off the blanket that's barely covering me and drop to my knees before him. Before he can order me to, I reach to undo his belt.

He closes his hand over mine to stop me.

"No."

"What is it? Don't tell me you came in here to talk."

His gaze is on the bed at my back. I turn to it. See what he sees. That tell-tale smear of blood.

I look back at him grinning wide, the feeling inside me ugly, not me. Not at all.

Santiago's jaw tightens.

"What's the matter, dear husband? Another month gone and after how much you've tried, I dare say done your best, there's nothing to show for it? Have you considered having your sperm checked? Maybe the fire that deformed—"

He has me by the throat in an instant pushing me backward against the bed, my back bending painfully, his hand cutting off my air so I'm left sputtering. He looks like he has a hundred things to say to me. A thousand curses to hurl my way. But instead, all he does is haul me up onto the bed, sets his knee beside me, and eyes locked on mine, he closes his other hand over my sex.

He loosens his grip on my throat a little as I claw at his forearm. He must see I can't breathe, but he doesn't let go entirely.

Holding my gaze, he pulls the little string of the tampon, and I feel it slide out, slick with blood, then he pushes his fingers inside me, and I force myself to grin as he brings them up between us, looking at the bloodied digits.

He growls a curse, wipes the blood off across my face, then shifts his grip to my arm and hauls me roughly to my feet.

"Deformed?" he starts, controlled, voice low, rage just there, just beneath.

"Let go of me." I try to pull at his hand as he marches me to the door, ignoring my protests as he walks me to the stairs and down, picking me up and throwing me over his shoulder when I slip. I'm sure his grip is adding more bruises.

"Did you enjoy that?" he asks as he walks into his office and slams the door. "Had you been waiting to play your little trick all day? Practiced what you'd say. What insults you'd hurl?"

He plants me roughly into a chair in front of the desk.

I immediately move to stand, but he pushes me down. "Stay."

"You need a dog, not a wife."

"A dog would be more loyal than my wife, that is certain." He takes the sheet of paper on the desk, turns it so it's facing me, and slams it back down.

I look at it, and I gasp. I lift off my seat a little to peer closer as Santiago leans back to let me.

"Wh...what is this?" My mouth has gone dry, the blood draining from my head, a sudden cold leaving me shuddering.

"Pretty, don't you think?" He picks up the sheet.

I look up at him, mouth open, not believing my eyes.

"Just remember when you look upon yourself next week, loathing your own reflection in the mirror, you only have yourself to blame."

"What is it?" I demand although I know. My

voice rises with panic. I wrap my hands around the seat of the chair, or I'll bolt, and I don't know what he'll do if I try to run.

"It's you. Don't you recognize yourself?" he asks with a false laugh, an ugly, unhinged sort of sound.

"Santiago—" My voice breaks, cracking on his name, my throat too dry to speak as my gaze is drawn to that thing. That hideous drawing.

Because what it is is unimaginable. A tattoo. Like his. Just like his.

He wasn't looking at my eye earlier. He wasn't studying the strange pupil. That's nothing next to what he's got planned for me. He was looking at the canvas of his next work. A skull to match his.

He must know that I understand. I wonder if this is how he'd planned to tell me or if I'd instigated it. Taunted him. Poked the devil. Either way, when I stand, he doesn't stop me. And when I topple the chair behind me and stumble, he simply watches grinning that grin, that wicked, evil grin.

"This will be your punishment, Ivy," he says, more sober when he speaks.

"For the poison," I manage, my voice sounding so frail next to his.

He nods once.

"You're a monster!" I explode at him, clawing at the drawing wanting to tear it from him, wanting to rip it to shreds as if that would stop it from happening.

He laughs, catching me easily. Lifting me off my feet, he carries me the few steps back to his desk. With a sweep of his arm, he clears it, sending papers fluttering to the carpet as he lays me on it. Pushing me backward, he forces my legs apart and takes his place between them. As he undoes his belt, his trousers, that ink on his face makes him appear to be grinning as he leans over me even though he's not. Not at all. His eyes are dark, almost black, and I see sorrow and resignation along with betrayal and pain, especially pain, inside them. When he pushes into me, all I can do is grunt, reach up to hold his shoulders, and take his thrusts as tears stream down the sides of my face.

"Look at it," he says, forcing me to turn my head.

"No!" I fight him, reach up to claw his face.

He captures my wrists, and I pull against him, hauling myself up with his cock still inside me.

"Please, Santiago," I start as I hear his breath grow more ragged and see the sheen of sweat on his forehead. He releases my wrists and cups my ass to pull me to the edge of the desk. I push his hair back from his face. Our eyes are locked, and I study him as I take him and, cupping the back of his head, I draw him to me and kiss him. I kiss his face, kiss the skull side, feel the scars beneath the ink. I kiss the corner of his mouth, remembering how he bit my lip the last time, how he'd drawn blood, but I only kiss him. Kiss him full on the mouth as he leans us both back down not pulling away from my kiss, not biting.

"Ivy," he mutters against my lips, then kisses me back, thrusting harder, faster.

"Make me come," I say, my hands on his face to make him look at me. See me. "Make me come."

He shifts one hand between us, and the touch of his fingers to my clit makes me come as he watches me. I arch my back and push against him, then pull his face to mine again, making him kiss me again, taking his final thrusts, swallowing his moan as his release comes, body rigid, every muscle tight, cock throbbing.

When his eyes come back into focus, and he eases his grip, a drop of sweat falls from his forehead to my cheek.

He looks at me. We're so close. Closer than ever.

"Why?" he asks, voice broken, desperate. "Why, Ivy?"

I brush back sweat-slicked hair. "I swear to you, I swear on my life, I didn't. I did not do what you're accusing me of."

"Your life is no longer yours to swear upon." He draws back, almost sobering as he does. He exhales a short puff of air and pulls out of me, and we both look at the bloody mess on him, on me. Not bothering to wipe it off, he tucks himself back into his briefs, his pants.

I sit up. "I swear, Santiago. Please don't do this to

me. Please don't tattoo me." My god. Saying the words out loud makes it sound even more terrifying.

"Don't make you look like me, you mean? Deformed," he emphasizes the word, and my face heats as I regret the word I'd used. I hadn't meant to. I swear I hadn't meant to. I knew that would wound him.

"That's not...I shouldn't have said that."

"How repentant you are now when there is something for you to lose." He touches my cheek with the knuckles of his hand. "Your beauty."

I shake my head.

"Did you think you'd seduce me? You think me that weak? One kiss and I'd give in to you?"

"No. No, I wanted to kiss you. I needed to."

He grows rigid, ice cold. "You're a liar, Ivy," he says slowly. "A cold, manipulative liar."

My stomach turns. "No, Santiago, it's not like that. It wasn't—"

"Get out," he says, turning away.

"I didn't do it. I couldn't. I was locked in that bathroom. I couldn't get the door open. I—"

"No? You couldn't get the door open?" he asks, moving swiftly behind his desk to pull out a keyboard and push a couple of buttons. As soon as he does, the monitors all light up. I watch the blurred lines come into focus, and I hear the sounds I remember from that night. Loud talking. Glasses clinking in toasts. Jazz music. The gong. I see Colette laughing with someone, a man. Her husband, I guess. And then I see him. Santiago. And I watch as from the corner of the screen a woman enters.

And my throat goes dry. "What is this?"

He doesn't have to answer, though. I can see. Anyone with eyes can see. It's me in my black and gold dress and my butterfly mask. Except it's not. And I—she—walks straight up to my husband, and he seems momentarily surprised when I—she wraps her arms around his neck, but he takes her in his arms too, and when she kisses him, he kisses her back, and then the scene blacks out.

I blink once, twice. When I turn, I find him watching me.

"I..." I croak, touching my throat, then pointing at the empty screen, my hand trembling.

Irrefutable evidence, they had said at The Tribunal.

They must have seen this too.

"What's that, Ivy?" he asks, all false sweetness.

"That's not possible." I take a step backward, shuddering. I hug my arms around myself. "That's not me."

"No?"

I shake my head. Back up another step only to stumble over the chair I'd knocked over earlier but catching myself before I fall.

"No," I say, not even convincing myself as he replays it, and I'm forced to watch it again.

"But I have eyes in my head. The evidence is right here in front of us," he says finally.

We watch in silence, and when it's over, he switches the monitors off and turns to me.

"I will mark you so you will never forget what you did. What you tried but failed to do. So that when anyone looks upon your face, they will know your shame, and they will turn their backs on you. You are a traitor. A liar. A Moreno." My name is like a slap. I flinch. "You make me sick, Ivy."

"I—"

"And my ink to mark your face, to deform you, is the sentence I decree upon you."

14

SANTIAGO

"How are you feeling?" Councilor Hildebrand peers up at me from beneath his spectacles.

"I live to see another day," I answer flatly.

He nods and then glances at the file before him. The three councilors of The Tribunal are seated behind the ornate desk on the dais in the courtroom reserved only for meetings such as these.

Since the explosion, I have come here once a month to meet with The Councilors, elders, and other remaining family members who lost someone that day. It was undoubtedly one of the worst attacks on a single IVI sector. We lost ten Sovereign Sons that day and twice as many elders.

Unlike a civilian case, a Society case never goes cold. We have all been assigned our own duties to further the investigation, and regardless of the slow progress, we reconvene here to discuss the findings on the same day every month. A process that will continue until The Tribunal deems the perpetrators have been found and punished accordingly.

Duty would dictate that I tell them I already know exactly who the perpetrator is, and he's lying in a hospital bed, too cowardly to face his crimes. But I decided long ago not to bring my suspicions forward unfounded. I didn't require The Tribunal's approval to punish those who I know in my bones bear the guilt of the blood that was shed that day.

I may never know how many Moreno family members partook in the scheme, but the only fair sentence is that which Eli has given me. An eye for an eye. And perhaps it is selfish, but I am not willing to relinquish control of their destruction, which is exactly what will happen if I were to bring their names forward.

First, there would be a long waiting period while The Tribunal considers the evidence. And then there would be a meeting between the surviving family members and a vote of what should occur. They would all want a piece of Eli and his family. And I am not willing to settle for a piece. Not when I am the only man who left that building, clinging to life as everyone around me burned.

It will be my face Eli sees should he ever wake. My eyes will haunt him in the afterlife when I erase his existence from this earth. I can settle for nothing else.

The Councilors bring the meeting to attention, offering each family a turn to speak. Progress reports always pass by quickly, with little intel at all. Yet each man who speaks on behalf of the dead offers up the tiniest of crumbs, all meaningless, in an effort to prove that they too have not forgotten.

When it is my turn to speak, I tell them the same thing I do every month. I have leads I'm following up on, but nothing concrete. I can feel the eyes of the others on me. I may as well be a ghost in this room. They are all wondering why I survived, and their beloved family members did not. I never look their way. I never speak to them directly. I volunteer what is requested of me, and then I take my leave.

Only today, when the meeting adjourns, Councilor Hildebrand requests me to stay behind, as I suspected he would. I have not been summoned before today because they prefer to hold court at the same time, and their schedules do not bend to accommodate anyone.

Once the room is vacated of the other members, Hildebrand looks down upon me, speaking on behalf of his fellow Councilors.

"We would like to discuss the matter of sentencing for your wife, who is due back in court shortly."

"Yes," I reply. "I'm aware."

"My fellow Councilors and I have prepared

several recommendations for her sentence, which we will lay forth now."

I wait in silence as he opens Ivy's folder. My throat burns, and heat crawls up the base of my neck. I know what they will recommend. I am not unfamiliar with the expected sentence for the attempted murder of a Sovereign Son.

"There are three recommendations," Hildebrand reads from the document. "Death by a poison of the Tribunal's choice. Death by hanging. And the last alternative is the loyalty test."

I swallow the acid in my throat as I consider their options. They are as harsh as I expected, with the only option that has even a potential of survival being the loyalty test. An excruciating dance of torture Ivy would have to endure as I look on without uttering a word. It is The Society's way of reaffirming loyalty. Should I break and ask them to stop that which my wife is sentenced to endure, they would kill her. Should I watch on in silence, she may survive if she is strong enough. None of these options would please me, and I make it known.

"I have an alternate suggestion."

"You have prepared a recommended sentence for your wife?"

I force a nod. "I have."

They look at each other, then back at me. "And?"

"I propose that I will execute her punishment myself, as is my duty and responsibility as her husband. It is me who was slighted, and therefore I request that I am the one to dole out a penalty of my choosing."

Hildebrand dips his head, his face a mask of emptiness that makes it hard to discern his feelings. "Let's hear what you have in mind."

"I propose that I will disgrace my wife as she has disgraced me. I will leave her with a permanent disfiguration for all to see."

"What sort of disfiguration?" He arches a brow at me.

"A tattoo on one side of her face to match my own."

There is a long stretch of silence as he studies me, considering. "You would not have your wife put to death for the attempt on your life?"

"No." The muscles in my shoulders go rigid as I consider that they are prepared to fight me on this.

"Explain," he commands. "Explain what deems her worthy of saving. How would you ever trust her again? Why should IVI trust her?"

"I take it upon myself to guarantee her unwavering loyalty to The Society," I assure them. "And if there were to be any sign of falsehood in that regard, I give you my word that I would end her life myself."

"The sentence is too light to satisfy the requirements of this court—"

"She is pregnant with my heir," I clip the words

through gritted teeth. "And for that reason, she is still of value."

Hildebrand frowns. "We need a moment to consider. Leave the room and we will summon you back once we have made a decision."

I reluctantly leave the room, jaw clenched and irritation stirring up a fury inside me that will be difficult to hide. Ivy has put me in this position. Lying to The Tribunal to save her life, and for what? So she can continue in her self-righteous hatred and disgust every time I am near her.

I don't know what the fuck I'm doing. But I know what I'm risking by covering for her. By offering this one thing I know they will not deny me. The Tribunal is aware of the importance and expectations for Sovereign families to bear heirs, and particularly mine, considering it will be my sole responsibility now that my father and brother are dead.

I pace the length of the corridor while I wait, using my phone to search the directory of Society doctors. Then it occurs to me that I cannot use a Society doctor to examine her at risk of the truth being revealed. I need her fucking pregnant, and I need it now.

Christ.

I swipe a trembling hand through my hair and consider my options. I'll have to bring someone else in. That's the only way.

I'm scrolling through names of specialists from other states when the door to the courtroom opens again, and a guard summons me back inside. The Councilors are waiting for me in silence, their faces empty. I want to believe I know what they will say, but nothing in life is ever certain.

"You are to bring your wife to her assigned court date with visible proof that you have fulfilled the punishment as laid out. We will see it in person," Hildebrand says.

"As you wish."

"We are only granting this request on one condition," he adds.

"Yes?" I reply hoarsely.

"We want the name of the accomplice who acquired the poison for her. Either you get it out of her by the time of her court date, or we will imprison her until she produces a viable name."

"She will have a name for you," I assure them.

"Then this session is adjourned for now. We will reconvene next week. You are dismissed."

I'M WALKING through the courtyard of the compound with only one intent in mind. I need to get home. Before Ivy's court date, some things must be in order, and I can no longer put them off.

Fury is a living, breathing animal inside me. I

lied to The Tribunal to save her, and in doing so, I put my family at risk. It isn't just me I have to think about. If this goes badly, Mercedes will bear the brunt of the impact too.

Fucking poison.

That's what my wife is. She's poisoning my thoughts. My every waking moment. My hunger for her. This need that is turning me into someone I don't even recognize anymore. It has to stop. I have to fix this.

"Sir!" someone calls out as I breeze past them, but I ignore the voice, continuing to my car where Marco is waiting.

"Mr. De La Rosa, please!" The breathless voice follows me out of the courtyard, lingering behind me as Marco opens the door for me.

I turn to see a girl I recognize as Jackson Van der Smit's wife. She's a face I know well, considering how much Mercedes dislikes her. Young, innocent, and heavily pregnant. It leaves a bitter taste in my mouth as my eyes settle on her belly. They haven't even been married that long. It looks as though Jackson doesn't waste any time. I can't help but wonder when I will see my own wife heavy with my child. A thought that only serves to irritate me further.

"What do you need?" I demand.

She flinches at my tone, shrinking into herself and then squares her shoulders, seeming to rebound quickly with her primary motivation in mind.

"I was hoping I might speak to you a moment to request a visit with your wife. If you don't mind."

"My wife?" I growl.

I narrow my gaze at this girl who can't be much younger than Ivy, but she looks much younger somehow. I don't know what she could possibly want to speak to her about.

"How do you know my wife?"

She hesitates to answer, and it only encourages my suspicions. Surely, she couldn't be the one who gave Ivy the poison. She is far too innocent for that. But I have been fooled by innocence before. Eli's innocent request for my family and me to attend that meeting in place of his changed my life irrevocably. If I have learned anything since then, it is that anyone can be a traitor.

"We spoke at the gala," the girl finally confesses. "I'm Colette. Jackson's wife."

"I know who you are," I answer coldly. "Why do you want to speak to my wife?"

"She said she'd like for us to visit sometime, and I just thought... I was hoping I could come visit her, considering the circumstances."

"No."

I slide into the back seat of the car, and Marco leans forward to shut the door when Colette offers me one last parting thought.

"She didn't do it. I know she couldn't have—"

The rest of her declaration is cut short when the car door shuts, sealing me in with my own turbulent thoughts. Colette is still standing on the sidewalk, hoping I'll reconsider as Marco drives us away.

15

SANTIAGO

Ivy screams when I slam open the door to her room and startle her. The sound of the heavy wood crashing into the wall reverberates down the corridor as I stalk toward the chair where she's sitting, a horrified expression on her face.

"Santiago?"

When I don't respond, she rises up, trembling from the force of her fear. She knows what's coming. She can sense the predator in me. There is no more room for softness. There can't be. Never again.

"It's time."

My words echo between us, dark and menacing. When I reach for her arm, she bolts. Pure instinct drives her from the room and down the hall, completely naked. I prowl after her, and panic makes her eyes wide when she glances over her shoulder to see me closing in.

She pauses for a split second when she reaches the landing, trying to decide the best route for her escape, but she should know there are none. When she turns toward the stairs, I growl behind her, reaching out and narrowly missing her as she picks up speed.

I can see it happening as if it's in slow motion. She tilts to the right, stumbling as she grapples for balance. And then her hip bumps against the banister, and it jars her entire body as she rebounds and begins to topple forward.

"Fuck," I snarl, reaching out and grabbing her by the hair just in time, yanking her back against my body. "Are you trying to kill yourself?"

She screams the most horrific scream I've ever heard, wild like an animal as I haul her back and begin to drag her away.

"Help me!" she pleads. "Somebody please, help me!"

Mercedes appears at the top of the landing, a strained expression on her face as she takes in the scene before her. Ivy is kicking and clawing, attempting to fight her way out of my arms. When she throws her head back into my face, it collides with my lips and teeth, piercing my flesh as blood starts to drip down my chin.

"Fucking stop!" I roar, grabbing her chin so forcefully my knuckles turn white.

"Santiago," Mercedes calls out. "What is going on?"

"Go back to your room. This doesn't concern you."

"Please!" Ivy begs her. "Please don't let him do this."

"Santi—" Mercedes's voice breaks as I drag Ivy back up the stairs and turn us in the direction of my bedroom. She doesn't follow.

Ivy begins crying in earnest as I haul her down the corridor. She renews her fight, trying like hell to get away. Her heels collide with my shins. Her head with my shoulder. Nails down my forearms. When I hiss another warning at her, she only fights harder.

Finally, I come to a stop, forcing her facedown onto the cold marble as I dig my knee into her back and wrangle her arms behind her. When I've got them in place, I hold her down with my weight as I unbutton my dress shirt and use it as a makeshift bind, knotting her wrists together with one sleeve and her ankles with the other. She's hogtied and thoroughly exhausted when I hoist her up again, carrying her down the hall like an animal headed for the slaughterhouse.

"You don't have to do this," she sobs.

"Stop. Fucking. Crying."

She doesn't listen. The entire way, I have to hear those pitiful sobs. That panicked wheeze that sounds like a death rattle as she struggles to regulate her breathing. It's doing something strange to me, and I don't like it.

"Stop!" I demand. "Stop fucking crying."

She keeps at it, and when I finally reach my room and toss her body onto the bed, her sorrow only seems to amplify.

She's struggling against the ties, trying to break free when I head for my closet and grab what I need. When I return, she's halfway across the mattress. I grab her by the ankle and yank her back, wrapping my belt around her face and forcing it between her teeth before I secure it behind her head.

She mumbles around it, a fresh wave of tears falling down her cheeks. But for now, at least the sound is muffled. Once that is done, I remove the knots of my shirt only to replace them with a length of rope, which I use to tie her to the bedposts, one at a time. When I am finished, she is stretched wide, arms and legs pulling in the direction of each corner. She's a panting, sobbing mess, and I can't seem to look at her for more than a second as I force myself to follow through the preparations.

Perhaps I should have thought to drug her first. Knock her out cold. It would be so much easier. I reach for the case where I keep my gun and begin my preparations while Ivy continues to squirm.

"Hold still," I tell her. "Or it will hurt more than you could ever imagine."

She closes her eyes, tears clinging to the edges as

I loosen the grip of the belt, sliding it down beneath her chin.

"Don't talk, and don't move," I warn.

I go through the motions of cleaning her face roughly and forcing her head down into the mattress with my palm as I apply the stencil from my case. She's staring up at me. I can feel her eyes on me, burning a hole in my flesh.

Another solitary tear falls down her cheek, and I close my eyes, dragging in a ragged breath before I prepare the ink. When I am finished, the fight appears to have gone out of her. She is so still I have to force myself to look into her eyes to make sure she's even conscious.

When our gazes clash, something tightens in my throat and chest. A vise, squeezing me like the smoke in that godforsaken fire.

"You did this," I snarl at her. "This is your fault."

She shudders, a silent sob the last sound I hear before I turn on the gun and hover above the stencil. Her entire body tightens, her chest falling into stillness, jaw clenching.

The needle hovers for long seconds that turn into a full minute. I'm breathing hard. Trying to force my hand to cooperate. This needs to happen. There can be no alternative. She will be the other half of my dead soul, chained to me for eternity. My skeletal queen.

But when I lower the needle into her flesh,

piercing her with the first dot of ink, I make the mistake of glancing at her eyes and am rattled by the emotion I see there. I flinch back without thinking, grunting out a frustrated curse as I power off the gun and toss it aside.

"Fuck!" I yank the candelabra from my nightstand and throw it against the wall. The crash does nothing to satisfy my rage. This frustration has no cure.

I can't deny she's made me weak. She's seen it for herself now. She's seen what her fucking tears do to me.

I turn back to face her and crawl onto her body, mounting her with mine as I wrap my hand around her throat and begin to squeeze. She tries to shake her head, and I tighten my grasp.

I'm choking the air from her lungs as I lower my bloody lips to hers, smearing the evidence of her hatred across her mouth. My tongue breaches her lips, and she cries out when I relax my grip on her throat. I swallow that sound, and she drags the breath from my lungs into hers. Greedy. Desperate. Poisonous.

"Santiago," she sputters against me.

She's yanking against the restraints, and I want to see what she will do, so I release one of her wrists before I focus my attention on her throat, biting and sucking my way down the flesh. Her free hand comes to my hair, yanking and gripping and pulling me closer as she continues to repeat my name like a prayer.

"Thank you," she pants. "Thank you."

I close my eyes and shudder when her fingers caress the back of my neck, feeling the scars there. She doesn't flinch away. She's stroking them like she wants to heal them somehow.

"Tell me how much they disgust you," I whisper in her ear.

"No." Her voice trembles.

"You can't pretend otherwise." I pull back to stare down at her, and she uses her free hand to drag me back, forcing my lips against hers.

I don't know how it happens. One moment, she is bound beneath me. And the next, I have her untied, naked in my lap as I piston her body up and down the length of my cock. We're facing each other, eyes locked, breath against breath. I reach up to choke her again because it's too much, but instead, I find myself touching her softly. Reverently.

"Goddamn you," I growl. "You fucking liar."

I roll my hips up into her at the same time I slam hers down onto me, fucking her hard and rough.

"Traitor."

Thrust.

"Poisonous fucking—"

She screams as she shatters around me, her body milking mine and forcing my release before I can stop it. I'm coming inside her. Fingers digging into her hips. Teeth scraping along her collarbone. We're sweaty and sticky and hot against each other, and when I glance down, I realize it's because my shirt is off. We're skin against skin in a way we've never been before. Her perfect silk to my gnarled, inked flesh.

She follows my gaze, half breathless as her eyes roam over the designs on my chest. When her palms come up to touch them, I move to stop her, but she shoves my hands out of the way and does it anyway. Her fingers flatten against my skin, warmth sinking into a space I haven't allowed anyone to touch, and my eyes shutter closed as I consider what a goddamned mess this has turned out to be.

"I need you pregnant," I bite out.

When I open my eyes again, she's staring at me with a strained expression on her face.

"It's a matter of life or death for you." I brush her hair back over her shoulders and sigh. "No more excuses, Ivy. You'll see a doctor tomorrow. And you better pray that come next month, that test is positive."

16
IVY

"What?" I ask.

Santiago's eyes are locked on mine but my gaze shifts between his eyes and the inked, broken canvas of his body.

His expression is hard again, shut down. For a moment, for moments even, he wasn't closed off to me. He let me look at him. Touch him. And I understand so much more clearly why he lives in shadows.

I knew the damage wasn't only to his face. But the scars on his body, and the ink with which he has attempted to camouflage them, they tell a story I don't think he wants told.

"I didn't mean what I said," I start, not waiting for his answer. I need to tell him this. It's been on my mind since the night in his office. Since our blowup.

Since he told me I made him sick.

My stomach twists a little at that.

"What?" he asks flatly with the same tone he used when telling me my life depended on whether or not I become pregnant with his child. It's strange how unfeeling he can sound when physically, when he touches me, he does so with so much passion. So much rage. So much of himself, even if it is the darkest part.

I force my gaze from a deep groove on his shoulder back to his eyes. When he's not angry, raging, they lean more toward green.

"You're not deformed. I never thought that. I just wanted to hurt you."

He remains studying me that crease still between his eyebrows visible beneath the ink. "My appearance isn't something I think about. You didn't hurt me."

The first part of that may be true, but I'm pretty sure the last part isn't. I know it in fact. The tattoo on his face, the ink covering his torso, his arms, the giant skull on his back, the candles and dim lights, the constant shadow he—we—live in, it's all to hide the scars at least to some degree. And I think the saddest part is that he does it to hide them from himself not anyone else.

He shifts me off his lap and stands to cross the room into the bathroom.

"Come," he calls once he's inside.

I get up, follow him, hearing the shower switch on. I stop at the door and take it in, the dark walls, the sconces that light the space but barely. He stands naked outside the shower stall, gesturing for me to step in. I take in the wide stone counter, two sinks, the free-standing stone bathtub in the middle of the room.

There's just one thing missing. A mirror.

He watches me, maybe waiting for my reaction. For me to ask why. I don't need to ask. I know.

I step into the shower, and he follows. I turn to him, and he brings his hand to my face. He cups my jaw, and I look up at him as he smears the stencil. I grab his wrist.

"Don't."

He stops, eyes narrowing in confusion.

"I want to see it."

"No, you do not." He smears again.

"I do, Santiago."

He doesn't reply right away as if gauging the reason behind my request. But then he nods once and leans closer, forearm against the wall, hand over the top of my head, eyes on my eyes, then my lips and I think he'll kiss me again, another blood-smeared kiss. But he doesn't. And I'm strangely disappointed.

"Suit yourself."

He picks up the soap and begins to lather it, then to wash me. Moments like this, he is so gentle that he's almost tender. It's so opposite to how he usually is with me that it's confusing.

"What did you mean? That it's a matter of life or death for me that I get pregnant?"

He grits his jaw, his gaze focused on the task of cleaning me.

"It means The Tribunal is sparing your life because they believe you are pregnant with my child."

"What?"

He finishes washing me before washing himself. I smell like him now. Like he did on the night of our wedding in the confessional. Like he has every night he's come to me. It's the scent that clings to his pillow and sheets. Subtle, dark, and deeply masculine.

Once he's finished washing himself, he opens the shower door and reaches for a towel, also black. He wraps it around my shoulders, and I take it from him, drying myself off before securing it. He takes another for himself and ties it low around his hips.

I watch the muscles of his back work beneath the ink of yet another skull as he walks ahead of me not hiding himself from me anymore.

"Why skulls?" I ask. It's as if he's tattooed death on every inch of himself.

He raises his eyebrows as he opens a dresser drawer to retrieve a pair of briefs and trousers and gets dressed.

"On your body. Your face," I say.

"Our family crest."

"That's not it."

"And you know this how?" He pulls on a sweater, cashmere stretching tight over muscular shoulders and arms.

"I see you, Santiago. I think I've always seen you."

He grins, walks toward me to take the towel and tug it tighter around me, jerking me toward him. "Have you?"

"Yes."

"Then tell me what you see."

I bite my lip, glance away, my gaze catching on the tattoo gun he threw to the floor. That gives me courage. A little at least. I shift my gaze up to his.

"You can't stand to look at yourself. I don't think it's because you think you're ugly. I don't think you care about ugly or beautiful. That's too simple for you. I think you see it as a weakness. I think you're afraid when people see the scars, see what you've done to hide them, they'll know you're human. Breakable. Like the rest of us."

His Adam's apple bobs as he swallows and a muscle ticks in his jaw. "I didn't realize you were studying the human psyche at school." He secures the towel at my chest and turns away to pick up the slacks he'd been wearing. He feels through his pockets and takes out his phone.

"That's not all."

"No?" he asks, using his thumb to unlock it.

"No." I take a step toward him feeling braver. I

put my hand on his arm and push the phone away so he looks at me.

"I'm all ears," he says with an expression that says he's humoring me, but I know he's not. I'm right and he knows it and he doesn't like it.

"I think you don't have a mirror in your bathroom or anywhere that I've seen in the house outside of maybe the bedrooms you don't use because when you see yourself, you see that weakness and you can't stand it."

He smiles tightly. "You're clever but not as clever as you think," he says, tucking wet hair behind my ear, turning my head a little to study the stencil side.

I wonder if it's washed away at least a little. I am curious to see it for some strange reason I can't quite explain.

He meets my eyes. "I did this so I would remember."

I remain silent waiting for more.

"I did it so I would never forget all the lives that were lost, half of my own family wiped out in a matter of moments. I did it so I would always remember that when I walked away, I became indebted to them. I did it so I never forget that I owe them. That vengeance is due them." His fingers tighten. "And mine will be the hand that deals that vengeance."

I swallow, feel my shoulders cave a little at that because what I felt just moments ago, what we had when he made love to me—and it was love making—it's gone. And I'm the one who reminded him of his hate.

"Go to your room, Ivy."

The phone in his hand buzzes. He shifts his gaze to it but doesn't pick up.

"You lied for me," I say, realizing that the only way The Tribunal would think I was pregnant would be if he told them I was. "Why?"

His cheeks hollow out as he draws in a deep breath. "What you did is a crime punishable by death in the eyes of The Society."

My knees waver, goose bumps rising along my flesh.

"There is the law and there is our law."

"The Society's law."

He nods. "I was offered three choices for your sentence."

My heartbeat accelerates.

"Death by poison. Fitting."

"Santia—"

"Death by hanging."

He catches my arms when my knees give out and walks me backward to sit me in the chair he'd sat in the night I'd slept in his bed.

"And a loyalty test which I'm not sure you would survive."

"What is that?"

"The Tribunal has fairly archaic methods when

it comes to punishing those who betray us. You probably know this."

I shake my head but remember that scaffold in the small courtyard hidden by the towering walls of The Tribunal's building.

"Torture. Something medieval. While I bear witness."

"But...You can't let them—" the words are barely audible, my palms sweaty, fingernails digging into the leather of the chair I cling to in order to control the trembling.

"The benefit of this final method is threefold when you think about it. It will ensure you provide the name of the person or persons who supplied you with the poison as well as confirm your loyalty—"

"By torturing me."

"And it will test me as well. My loyalty to The Society as I stand by and watch my wife punished."

"But..."

"Not that they'd forego the methods necessary to draw a name from your lips if I were to choose either of the other options."

My face must go very pale. I feel the blood drain and watch him watch me.

"But, as you know, I have standing within The Society." He gives a dark smile and brushes his knuckles over the stenciled side of my face. "Since your crime was against me, as your husband, I offered an alternative."

"The tattoo."

He nods. His phone buzzes again and he silences it. "Considering the fact that you are carrying my heir—"

"But I'm not..."

"I know that."

"You lied to save my life."

His eyes narrow again. He takes a moment to answer. "For selfish reasons, Ivy. Do not be fooled."

"What if I can't get pregnant?"

"Can't?" He cocks his head to the side. "Is there something I should know?"

I shake my head quickly. Too quickly. And as I rise to my feet, for the first time in my life, I am grateful for the vertigo, for the dizziness, because when I stumble into his arms, he catches me and I hear the curse he mutters as he easily lifts me off my feet.

For a moment, just one moment, I close my eyes and lean against him and just let him hold me, cradle me, give in to this illusion of safety. I can give myself that, can't I? I can have just this little stitch in time.

He lays me down on his bed, on the bed in which we just made love. It still smells like us.

"Let me clarify then, if there's nothing you have to tell me. If there is no baby, their sentence will stand. They will not accept mine."

"What happens to you if they find out you lied?"

He's quiet for a moment. "There will be a reckoning, I'm certain, but *I* will live."

"And I won't." I can't think about that part. "And you'll be punished because of me. If I can't get pregnant, I mean."

He doesn't reply but I don't need him to.

"And the tattoo...my face, it still happens. You're still going to do it." It's not a question. The pregnancy, this non-existent, impossible pregnancy, it doesn't get me or him out of this. Me to take the punishment. Him to deal it.

"Why did you do it?" he asks, looking wretched, sounding even more so.

I can't control the emotion, the tears that come. I don't even try. Because I'm doomed. We both are.

17

IVY

Back in my room I study my face by the dim light in the bathroom mirror. The stencil is smeared but not completely gone. It matches his but is somehow more feminine.

In a grotesque way, it's beautiful. Like his.

Like him.

I turn away, fingers tightening around the counter. I can't think that. I am his enemy even if he was never mine. He hates me.

But he also lied to The Tribunal to save me no matter his simple excuse of selfishness. It's not for the reason of having me birth his babies or torturing me himself. I just don't believe that's true. Because just as ugly and beautiful are both too simple concepts for him, so is this. We are bound to one another. There is something here. And he's human no matter how much he tries to prove himself a demon.

I turn my gaze back up to the mirror, brush the hair back from the stenciled side of my face and touch the single dot of black ink high on my cheekbone. I won't be able to wash that off. And I'm glad.

But there are other, more pressing matters to consider now. I don't have the luxury of time to ruminate. To romanticize. Maybe that's a gift. A smack to the back of my head to remind me where I am. Who I am dealing with. And I don't only mean my husband.

I scrub my face and return to my bedroom, to the window. The boards have been removed. Doctor's orders. I need sunlight. I push the curtain back and look out into the distance, to the still dark night. I don't have much time.

My bedroom door isn't locked but I've been waiting until I'm sure Antonia and the others have gone to bed.

Mercedes is gone. I overheard Antonia telling Santiago that Mercedes would be spending the night with a friend. Santiago seemed less than pleased when he found out which friend even though Antonia made a point of the fact that it's a female friend. I guess the same rules apply to Mercedes even considering her rank. She needs to remain a virgin until marriage.

Santiago has been gone since walking me back to

my room hours ago. Whatever called him away seemed somewhat urgent or at least important enough to distract him. I wonder if it has to do with the calls he kept dismissing when we were talking in his bedroom.

But now that I'm sure I'm alone, I walk out into the hallway and down the stairs. I need to find a phone. I need to call Abel. Because when that doctor examines me tomorrow—today—if he were to take a blood test or look for any abnormality in my hormone levels, he will figure out why I'm not getting pregnant.

I can't think about what Santiago will do then.

Could I tell him the truth? He wouldn't be angry with me then. He couldn't be. Well, he could. I knew even if it was after the fact. But what would he do to Abel?

I'm barefoot and dressed in a bikini with a plush robe on top. My closet has been unlocked. If anyone happens to come upon me, I will let them know I am going to use the pool. Again, doctor's orders.

The first place I go to search is the kitchen hoping one of the housekeepers left their cell phone there. I've seen them use their phones around the house, both the ones who live on-site and the others.

The lamp over the stove is on and between that and the filtered light coming in through the large window from the garden I go through each of the drawers, check every possible place but find nothing.

I go into the living room. Check there. I never searched for one before, so it's possible there's a landline I just haven't come across. I look in the armoire, the drawers of the antique side tables, pause to take in the ornate gilded piano that I've never heard anyone play.

I leave that room behind, my gaze moving toward the corridor that leads to the library, to his study. I hadn't seen a phone there and if he catches me in there again, he'll kill me. I search the other downstairs rooms and the dining room, the smaller sitting room and the large one I had been in with the doctor but find nothing.

I walk back into the center of the large hall and turn a circle to see if there is any place I've missed. The bedrooms upstairs are locked and if any are open, they're not in use. I went through every unlocked room when I first had permission to roam.

I walk into the dining room and remember the night we ate in here. I stand at the window in exactly the place he'd stood, where he'd looked so solemn, so lost in thought staring out into the garden. I wonder now if it was his own reflection he had been studying in the glass and not the garden at all.

Walking to the liquor cabinet, I open the doors and move bottles around, not even sure what I'm hoping to find anymore. When I see his brand of scotch, I open it, sniff the contents. This scent lingers in his office, too.

I put it back then bend to open the drawer.

"What are you doing?"

I jump hitting my head on the shelf above before straightening and spinning to face Santiago. How did I not hear him?

"I...nothing." I close the drawer then the doors of the cabinet before hiding my hands behind my back as if to hide my guilt. I struggle to hold his gaze.

Tell him the truth. Tell him now.

His gaze moves to the cabinet. I notice the drops of rain on his hair, his shoulders. He must have just gotten home.

"Come with me, Ivy," he says and, without waiting for me, he turns to walk toward the corridor that I know will lead to his study. He doesn't look back to make sure I'm following. He knows I'll come.

Using a key, he unlocks the door and opens it for me to enter. He follows me in, closes the door.

"Sit," he commands, touching the back of the chair I'd sat on the last time I was here as he proceeds behind his desk to push some buttons on that keyboard.

Is he going to make me watch that footage again? The woman who looks like me but isn't? I open my mouth to tell him I don't want to see it when a stack of letters beneath a paperweight near the edge of the desk catches my eye. I lean closer because I recognize that handwriting.

"Don't touch," he says without even looking up from his work and I pull my arm back.

"Are they for me?" I ask, seeing Evangeline's name in the top left corner. "They're from my sister."

We look up at each other at the same time.

"You opened them? How many are there? How long—"

"Did you have anything to do with poisoning your father?"

The rest of my sentence gets caught in my throat. "Did I...what?"

He studies me for a very long minute then shakes his head and returns his attention to the keyboard and a moment later, those same screens on which I watched Santiago kiss a woman who looked a lot like me come to life.

It's not until then that I consciously realize that I was set up. Used as a weapon in an attempt on my husband's life. The woman was dressed exactly like me. I knew it on some level before, but it's like the reality hits home now, and I shudder. Because who else knew what I'd be wearing?

We watch the screens together and it's not that night at all. What I see are various rooms of the house. The kitchen. Living room. Dining room. My bedroom.

And me in those rooms. Well, all except my bedroom. That one's empty and it's just as incriminating as the others where I'm looking through every drawer, every cabinet, every nook right up until I smash my head into the cupboard when Santiago surprised me in the dining room.

He switches the monitors off and faces me.

"Do you want to tell me what you're looking for exactly?"

I stare up at him. God. What must he think of me? A thief in the night? A poisoner. Am I surprised he's kept my sister's letters from me? He thinks I tried to kill him. He truly believes it and can I blame him?

The weight of that hits me.

I shake my head and I study his face as intently as he did mine just a little while ago. And what I see isn't pure hate like before. There's a resignation there. An even deeper sadness.

He believes I tried to kill him yet he lied to save my life.

Can he save my life? What happens when they find out I'm not pregnant at all? Do they hang me?

God. I'm going to be sick.

Then there's what happens to him because of me. What if he's wrong about his standing? What about that reckoning he knows is coming?

"I have to tell you something, Santiago."

He remains silent, arms folded, a hulking shadow in this room, this house. He's ready for the worst. I wonder if he always expects the worst. After what happened to his family, to him, maybe it's the only way he can be.

"I won't be pregnant next month. Or possibly the month after, but I don't know."

His jaw tightens. "What the hell are you talking about?"

"The day Abel took me to that doctor, they gave me a shot. He said it was vitamins," I start as he sets his arms by his sides, hands fisting, knuckles going white. "But even if I knew, I don't think I could have stopped it."

I hear him swallow.

"He told me when he came to the house the day of the gala that it was a birth control shot."

I grip the edges of my chair waiting for him, for his reaction, my heart racing inside my chest.

"A birth control shot," he repeats robotically like he's processing the meaning.

I swallow, nod. I leave out the part about not wanting to have *that monster's* baby because I'm starting to wonder who the true monsters are in our world.

"I'm sorry."

His expression doesn't change, the line of his mouth stretched tight, jaw tense. His hands balled into tight, angry fists.

He's not quite looking at me. Not at first anyway because when his eyes do finally zero in on me, the look inside them sends ice down my spine.

"It's not you who will be sorry for this one." He checks his watch. "Go to your room and do not come out until I tell you that you can come out."

"Okay." I get to my feet, relieved. "Can I have the letters? Please?"

He nods once and I reach out to take them but as I'm setting the paperweight aside, he puts his hand over mine to stop me from pulling away.

I look up at him.

He gestures to my robe. "You're not to swim alone."

"Why not? The doctor said—"

"You're not to swim *alone*. Only when Mercedes or I can be with you."

"Why?"

"I don't want you having one of your episodes in the pool."

I bite the inside of my lip as I study him. Days ago, I would have made the comment that it wouldn't serve him to find me drowned. It would take his fun away. But somehow it doesn't fit anymore.

"And no guards either. I don't want them looking at you. Just me or Mercedes. Do you understand?"

"Yes," I say as I think back to my dress at the gala. To Mercedes.

He releases me and I take the stack of letters. "Santiago—"

"Go to your room, Ivy." He is dialing a number on his cell phone.

"What are you going to do to Abel?"

He glances at me, cocks his head to the side and stands.

I step backward because even with the desk between us, right now, he looks terrifying.

He grins. "You have other things to worry about, don't you? Like saving your neck. You're not off the hook with me or with The Tribunal. You still owe us a name. For starters."

"I just—"

"Go to your room." He sounds almost calm but I know that tone. There's a current underneath it. A rage. "Now."

I drop my gaze, nod and hurry away.

18

SANTIAGO

"Open the fucking door, Chambers!" My fist rattles against the heavy wood, shaking the frame with the force of my rage. "You can't hide all night."

It's well after four o'clock in the morning, but I know that fucker is lurking in there somewhere.

"Would you like me to open it, sir?" Marco asks, shrugging to indicate he's ready to use his body as a battering ram the moment I give him approval.

I prefer to do things less messily. Already, dogs are barking. A light in the neighboring house has flipped on. Curtains have moved. There is at least one possibility of spying eyes aware of our presence, and considering that I don't intend to leave here tonight without Chambers' blood on my hands, that could be a problem.

I give it another moment, waiting for some indication of life inside, but when that doesn't happen, I gesture for Marco. We walk around to the side of the house and locate a window that will be large enough to accommodate each of us.

I'm ready to throw my elbow through the glass when Marco shrugs out of his jacket and ushers me back.

"I've got this, boss."

He wraps his arm in the jacket and thrusts it through the window, shattering the glass like a missile just blew through it. Then he heaves his giant body inside and clears the way for me to follow.

The room we happen to invade is the home office. I've never been in here before, but I notice something is off about the space almost immediately. It's too clean. Too... empty. Sure enough, when I bend to open his filing cabinet, it's vacant. A quick investigation reveals the same to be true about his desk. There isn't a single trace of paperwork. Not even so much as a bill in his name.

"Fuck." I slam the drawers shut and glance around.

This situation isn't inspiring a quick resolution like I was hoping for. Marco opens the door and clears the hallway, veering toward the foyer while I head for the sitting area. The house is freezing, the air conditioner seemingly maxed out, and there's no way anyone could be dwelling in these temperatures comfortably.

"Call if you need me, boss," Marco whisper-shouts as he disappears upstairs.

My polished leather shoe crunches over broken glass as I turn the corner, and I pause, eyes scanning the fragments of a vase. It's the first sign of Chambers' haste to leave. Someone must have tipped him off that I'd be coming for him soon. He knows there would be no forgiveness for his interference into my duties to produce heirs. That's the only logical explanation I have. At least until I catch a glimpse of a shadow beneath the settee.

I move quietly, the weight of my pistol heavy in my shoulder holster as I flip on the lamp and wait for movement. But after a few breaths, it becomes apparent the body hiding beneath isn't going anywhere. A scan of the uniform and the rigidity of her muscles provides an explanation for the chilly temperatures. Whoever stuffed Chambers' maid beneath that sofa was trying to eliminate the smell of decomposition.

"Christ," Marco grunts when he appears beside me and examines her.

Using my shoe, I nudge the sofa back, and Marco rolls the body over. There's no blood, but it's evident by the bruising on her neck she was strangled. A fact that immediately leaves me to doubt it was Chambers himself who did it. Strangulation is not a quick, easy death. It takes power, strength, and endurance. Someone who is physically fit and capable of squeezing their subject's throat for up to five minutes while they fight for their life. The only endurance Chambers would be capable of for that length of time is deep-throating hamburgers.

"Any sign of him in the house?" I ask Marco.

"No," he says. "Upstairs is clear. All his clothes are still here. Personal toiletry items are untouched. If he did flee on his own, he must have left everything behind."

I drag a hand through my hair and sigh. Already, I know Chamber's didn't leave of his own accord. He's too fond of his materialistic comforts in life to abandon them. Something about this situation reeks of betrayal, and I won't rest easy until I know who's behind it.

"Call the secretary of the Tribunal," I tell him. "Inform them we need a body removal at this address. I want you to do one final sweep of the place and then burn it down when she's gone."

"On it, boss." He nods.

"Call me when it's handled."

"Dominus et Deuce." Abel bows as he opens the door to the Moreno family home, his voice pleasant but features tight. "To what do I owe the pleasure of your visit, Santiago?"

"Cut the shit." I grab him by the collar and slam him back against the banister, my switchblade grazing his throat as his eyes bulge. "I know what you did."

"Please do inform me of what crime has brought you here this evening," he says. "I am not aware of it myself."

"Two words," I spit. "Birth control."

"Fucking Ivy," he growls. "Whatever she told you is a lie."

"Don't toy with me, you piece of shit." The blade nicks his skin, crimson dripping down over my fingers. "I just came from Chambers' house. I know he's gone. Someone is trying to cover their ass."

"Chambers?" Abel repeats dumbly. "I don't know anything about that."

My eyes narrow as I dig the blade deeper, biting into his skin. Abel hisses, trying to jerk out of my grasp, but he knows he can't. There's nowhere to run. Not from me.

"And what about Holton? Will he be missing too?"

"Fuck if I know," he bites out. "What does Holton have to do with anything?"

"This is a dangerous game you've been playing," I tell him. "It leaves me to question if you value your life at all. Not to mention the lives of your siblings. Your mother. Your father. Your sister, who I should remind you lives under my roof."

His jaw flexes, but his resolve remains unwavering.

"Tell me what purpose it served to inject my wife with birth control," I demand. "What benefit could there be to risk her life in such a way?"

"Whatever agreement she made with Chambers was hatched between the two of them," he answers bitterly. "That fucking girl never does as she is told. I had no idea about any birth control, so perhaps the person you really need to speak with is your own wife. Of course, I imagine that's why you find yourself here in the middle of the night, is it not? A little difficult to trust someone who lies constantly. Someone who tried to kill you not that long ago, if memory serves correct."

His biting words do nothing to temper my rage, but I can't deny he has a point. Was it Ivy? Was she the one who made the agreement with Chambers about the birth control? And is he the one who helped her secure the poison as well?

Abel sees me wavering. The tilt of his lips and amusement in his eyes burns the still-fresh wound of his sister's betrayal, and he knows it.

"Give me one good reason I shouldn't slit you from ear to ear right now." My blade digs deeper still, slicing through layers of flesh as Abel stares up at me, unblinking. He's emotionless, and I thought for certain he'd be pleading for his life. But instead, he seems to be aware of something I am not.

"You won't kill me." He reaches up and wraps his fingers around the blade, cutting himself as he yanks it away from his throat and forces his way out of my grasp. "And you won't kill Ivy. I can see it in your eyes. She tried to murder you, yet she still breathes. There is only one plausible explanation for that. She's inside your head. She's getting to you."

A caustic laugh rumbles from his chest as he shakes his head. "Human emotion is such a weakness, isn't it, Santiago? I did not think you capable, but it appears even machines can be taught how to love."

"Love has nothing to do with it." I clip the words through gritted teeth.

"Then why did you allow her to send you on a fool's mission?" he challenges. "Chasing your answers all over the city when you already have them at home. You just don't want to accept that it was your wife's scheme. That she couldn't bear the idea of having your children. A monster's baby, I believe that was the phrase she used. Perhaps you should ask her about that."

"Ivy isn't lying about this."

I'm not sure I even believe my assertion. Abel might be a fucking flea, but he has a valid observation, and it's an obvious one. I did exactly as he says. I believed what she told me and came here for the truth, when I should be forcing it from her lips instead. Why didn't I challenge her on this? Why would I assume that, after recent events, I could chance anything she says to be truthful?

"It seems to me you have yet to weed out all the traitors in your own home," Abel says somberly.

My eyes snap back to his. "What traitors?"

He sighs as if the information he's about to relay pains him deeply. "I have it on good authority that someone very close to you provided my sister with the lipstick she wore that night at the gala. I'm sure I don't even need to mention her name. You already know who it is."

The blood in my veins reaches to a boiling point, searing me from the inside out. I should murder him for even hinting at the idea, but a dark seedling of a thought begins to take shape. Mercedes was the one who dressed Ivy that night. She helped her prepare. She purchased the clothes and did her makeup. How could Abel possibly know that? He wasn't there.

As I study him, fingers locked around the switchblade, I'm still considering the consequences of stabbing him between the eyes when he offers one last nail in the coffin.

"She's been trying to cover her tracks. Ask her yourself if you don't believe me. I'm only telling you what nobody else has the courage to say to your face. The thing they all whisper about when your back is turned. I think it's only fair someone finally tells you the truth."

19

SANTIAGO

"Where is Mercedes?"

Antonia startles, nearly dropping the tray in her hands as I intercept her in the kitchen. She's staring at me like she's seeing a ghost, and I'm consciously aware of the fact that it's morning, and I'm in one of the few well-lit areas of The Manor. But vanity doesn't have a space in my thoughts right now.

"She hasn't come home yet," she answers quietly. "Would you like me to call for you when she arrives?"

"Yes."

She hesitates as if there is something else she wants to say but isn't quite sure how.

"What is it, Antonia?"

"Will you be awake?"

There's a kindness in her tone that makes me falter, and I can't comprehend it. How can this old woman stare down the vulgar beast in front of her and find even an ounce of softness in her heart?

"I don't have intentions on resting anytime soon," I inform her. "But should I fall asleep, bring Marco with you to wake me. Just to be safe."

She nods, offering a small smile. "Can I get you something to eat?"

"Not right now, thank you." I shift uncomfortably. "Has Mrs. De La Rosa... has Ivy eaten her breakfast already?"

"Yes, sir."

"Thank you, Antonia. That is all."

I turn and take my leave, stalking down the corridor and up the stairs to Ivy's bedroom. When I open the door, a small gasp flies from her lips, and she wears the same startled expression to find me lurking about at this hour.

"Santiago?" Her voice is tinged with concern as she tries to uncover the meaning behind the stormy expression on my face.

"I need to know now." I shut the door behind me, securing me inside the room with her.

Her eyes dart to the walled-off escape and then over my body. She looks as if she's trying to determine her options but accepts there are none left.

"What do you need to know?" she asks carefully.

"I need the name of your accomplice," I growl, stepping toward her. "Who gave you the poison, Ivy?"

She sucks in a sharp breath and shakes her head.

"I can't give you a name because I wasn't the woman who poisoned you."

The wording of her declaration confuses and infuriates me.

"This isn't a game." I seize her by the arms and drag her up, pinching her face in my grasp. "You will tell me, or they will kill you. It's that simple, Ivy. Surely, even a fucking Moreno can comprehend that much."

"Don't talk to me like I'm stupid." She presses her palms against my chest, trying to shove me off. "You're the one so blinded by your hatred for my family you can't comprehend the only logical conclusion, which is that I'm telling you the truth."

"The truth?" I echo her words darkly. "What truth should I find in the constant stream of lies you have spewed since you walked into this house?"

"It wasn't me!" she yells, shoving with all her might.

I grab her arms and pin them behind her back, walking her backward until she hits the wall. The breath leaves her lungs in a grunt as we collide, and despite the fury surging through my body, I am so hard for her I just want to fuck the confession out of her.

"Tell me." I wrap my icy fingers around her throat and squeeze. "Who gave you the poison?"

"Nobody," she snaps. "Because it wasn't me!"

"Goddammit." My lips hover over hers, breath

fanning against her skin. "They will kill you if we don't give them a name. What part of that don't you understand? There is no alternative. You give up the traitor to save yourself. That's the only way this will play out."

"I can't." She wheezes, straining against my grasp. "So, torture me all you want, but I can't give you what I don't know."

"Was it Chambers?" I demand.

"Chambers?" she repeats, eyes narrowing. "Do you really think I would be in on something with that sick fuck? You know what he did to me."

"Colette then."

This she laughs at.

"God, sometimes you really can be incredibly paranoid. Do you even realize that?"

The last accusation leaves my lips on a choked whisper. "Mercedes?"

Her face sombers, and my fingers fall from her throat as she peers up at me with a sadness I don't understand.

"It must be so lonely," she answers softly. "To hold such little faith in the people around you. To see everyone as an enemy. Even your own blood."

"Tell me." My voice fractures as I press against her.

Ivy manages to pull one hand free from behind her. Instead of using it to claw or fight, she reaches up to stroke my face. The scars I have no doubt she can see clearly beneath the ink.

"Don't," I warn her, but I'm not stopping her, even as I say it.

My eyes fall shut, and I let her touch me, telling myself I will end it. One more second, and I will end it. But I don't. She studies me with her fingers, smoothing over the rough, taut skin, tracing the lines of the skull.

"You aren't as much of a monster as you think," she whispers.

My eyes open, cold and hard as I grab her hand and force it away. "I know what you're doing."

"You always do." She smiles up at me sadly. "You always know what everyone is doing, though. They are all full of evil intent. Lies and shady motives. Isn't that right, Santiago? Nobody can be trusted. Not even your own sister apparently."

"Did she give you the lipstick or not?" I demand.

"Of course she did." Ivy sighs. "But it doesn't matter that she gave it to me because that woman in the footage was someone else. Someone dressed just like me. Someone who wanted to look like me that night."

"Convenient," I mutter. "But not even remotely believable."

"God, you are such an—"

I cut her off with a violent kiss, arching her head back to devour her mouth. Ivy freezes momentarily but then surprises me when she starts to devour me too. We are two rabid creatures, clawing at each other with staged hatred but desperate for more of this toxic attraction between us.

I nip at her lip and draw blood, and she digs her nails into my arms, moaning softly as I savor the copper crimson on my tongue. I'm hoisting her into my arms, and she's wrapping her legs around me as I carry her to the bed. I can't get her naked fast enough. Buttons are scattering, cloth ripping as I work to free her of the barrier to the sweetness of her flesh.

Her tongue is in my mouth, tasting me as I spread her over the mattress and mount her. She's struggling with the zipper on my trousers, and I pause briefly just to watch as she grunts in frustration, desperate for my cock. I've never been so hard in my life as I am when she finally gets it free and strokes me in her palm.

"Take me because you like it," she pleads, her eyes meeting mine. "Not because you need a baby. Not for any other reason. Just because you like it."

I indulge her, the notion of babies a distant thought in my mind as I resume control and settle my body against hers, thrusting between her legs. She arches into me, fingers slipping under the hem of my shirt to press against the skin on my back. I let her have it. Just this once. The same thing every addict tells themselves.

Tongues and teeth and hips collide as we come together. I fuck her into the mattress, and she hangs on as if her life depends on it, groaning out my name when she shatters around me. A muttered curse leaves my lips, and it's my undoing. I'm coming inside her. Spilling all of my frustrations in the pulsing throb of my cock, emptying within her for the sole purpose of exactly what she said.

Because I like it.

My head dips against hers as I collapse onto my forearms, catching my breath. I'm trying to think of a way to destroy this sickness between us when a knock sounds at the door.

Ivy blinks up at me, eyes heavy and face glowing. So fucking beautiful. Why does she have to look this way? Such a beautiful little liar.

The knock comes again, and I growl.

"What is it?"

"I'm sorry to bother you, sir," Marco answers. "But there are guests waiting for you downstairs. Jackson and Colette Van der Smit. He asked to speak with both of you."

A gust of air leaves Ivy's lips as she looks up at me pleadingly. "Can we talk to them? Please?"

I pull out of her, watching my come leak down her thighs with satisfaction. For now, I suppose the interrogation will have to wait.

"Get dressed."

20

IVY

Santiago has one hand wrapped around my arm as we descend the stairs.

I glance at him. The way he's holding me is almost his brand of affection, I think. The only way he knows to be. This is as close as he'll come to actually holding my hand. I almost have to smile, but he looks too wretched, so I stop and turn to him. Before he can ask what I'm doing, I pull free and link my hand with his.

He appears almost startled, but he's quick to school his features, and I wonder what is going on inside his head as he looks at the knots of our fingers. When he shifts his gaze to me, I want to ask him what happened. Because I'm sure he's been to see my brother. Did he hurt Abel? Or did Abel spin some story, make up some lie to cover his ass? Is that the cause of this strange look on his face? This uncertainty. Because Santiago is always certain even when he's wrong.

A cough comes from the foot of the stairs, and Santiago blinks, banishing any emotion. We both turn to find Antonia standing there.

"They're in the sitting room, sir."

"Why not the formal living room?" he asks as we get to the bottom of the stairs, and he unwinds his fingers from mine.

I clasp my own hands, disappointed.

"Mr. Van Der Smit wanted to be assured you'd have complete privacy."

Santiago sighs. "Fine." He takes my arm again and leads me toward the sitting room. When he opens the door, we find Jackson standing at the window that overlooks the eastern side of the garden. Colette is sitting on the couch with a shopping bag at her feet. She looks anxious.

"Ivy!" She jumps to her feet, her rounded belly looking even bigger than before. I do the math. She's due any day now.

"Colette." I slip from Santiago's grasp and go to hug my new friend. This woman I've only known for minutes but who has a warmth I'm not sure I've felt from anyone except my own sisters. "I'm so happy to see you," I tell her.

One of the men clears his throat, and we draw apart. Santiago and Jackson are both watching us, and I realize Jackson must be around Santiago's age, the difference in years between him and Colette about what it is between us. With blond hair and stark blue eyes, his expression is stern or at least appears so, and I remember the high heels he'd made Colette wear, knowing they were uncomfortable especially considering the pregnancy.

"Ivy," Santiago says, and I realize my face reveals exactly what I'm thinking. He turns to Jackson. "Jackson," he says by way of greeting. "What brings you here?"

Jackson nods to Santiago. "Your wife, actually."

"My wife?" His eyebrows rise. "Well, sit down," he says as the door opens, and Antonia enters with a tray of refreshments that she sets on the coffee table before leaving.

I sit on one side of Colette as Jackson takes the other. She smiles up at him warmly and slips one hand onto his thigh as he tucks his around the nape of her neck. She seems to lean into it, and it takes me back because the way he's holding her isn't what I expect. It's not possessive like some animal needing to mark his territory. Well, it is, but it's something else too. Tender. I expect Jackson to be a brute, a cold and insensitive man when it comes to his young, pregnant wife, but that's not what I see. Not yet at least.

"Her shoes, actually," Colette says and reaches for the bag beside her. "Ivy had lent them to me before dinner the night of the gala."

"Thank you for that," Jackson leans over to say to me. "Colette thinks I have expectations of her that I do not." He and Colette exchange a private look.

"Well, isn't that wonderful?" Santiago stands and checks his watch. I don't know why he's being so rude.

Jackson doesn't miss the rudeness either. "It will be when you hear the rest of what I have to say."

"Go on then. Don't keep me in suspense," Santiago deadpans, sitting down again and leaning back in his chair. He crosses his ankle over the opposite knee.

"As you know, I'm one of the advisors to The Tribunal."

My heart drops to my stomach, and Colette closes her hand around mine like she feels this shift in me.

"And?" Santiago prods, unimpressed by his status, which I guess he already knew.

"Colette has been convinced your wife wouldn't have done what she's accused of and I've come to trust her intuition."

"Intuition is all well and good, but facts are facts," Santiago says. "And I'm not sure your visit is appropriate, considering those facts."

"Hear me out, Santiago."

I'm trying to follow the dynamic between the two men. They're not friends, obviously, but not quite enemies either. Or is everyone an enemy to my husband at least in his own mind?

"You've seen the footage," Jackson says.

Santiago's lips move into a tight line, and I want to scream at him that it wasn't me. That I didn't try to kill him. He can't believe I would, can he?

"Her sandals," Jackson says. "My wife was wearing the same pair the woman in the security footage was wearing, but those aren't the shoes she left home with. They're your wife's sandals."

"Oh my god!" I clasp my hand over my mouth, understanding what this means, tears of relief ready to spring from my eyes.

Santiago is as still as stone for a moment before he uncrosses his legs, hands on his knees and leans forward.

"Her sandals?" he asks.

"Mine, actually," Colette says. "Ivy was wearing them. We'd exchanged shoes before the dinner. It's not possible Ivy was wearing the sandals the woman in the video was wearing because I had those on."

I can almost see Santiago's mind working as he processes. Then without a word, he stands and walks to the door then out of the room.

"Um," I start, standing too as Colette and Jackson get to their feet. "I'll see where he's going."

They follow me as we head toward the corridor that leads to Santiago's office. I turn the corner to see him disappear inside. He leaves the door open, and we all follow. No one takes a seat as he moves around his desk to push a few buttons on his keyboard, and a moment later, those screens come alive with a scene I wish I could forget. But today, this morning, I move closer, peering intently at the monitors.

"There," Jackson says just as Santiago pauses the video. It's just a corner of the screen. Easily missed. The flat sandals Mercedes had been irritated by. She'd wanted me in heels but obeyed Santiago's order. And there's the woman in those same flat sandals. In the distance is Colette in a matching pair standing beside her husband.

Santiago plays the rest of the video, but it's only in that one shot that her feet are visible.

"Play it again," I ask, but he's already doing that. He slows the video, and we see it again.

"I had Colette's sandals on by then. And I was locked in the bathroom," I say. He's never let me tell my side of the story. He's never wanted to hear it.

He turns to me, and I guess I expect to find relief on his face. Maybe joy even, but even I know that's a stretch. What I see, though, is at least a sliver of the former. It should hearten me, shouldn't it? But there's something else in his eyes.

"Thank you, Jackson," he says stonily.

Jackson nods. "I'll take this to The Councilors today. You'll still need to bring your wife in on her appointed date, but I believe this will be enough to clear her name."

It's over.

A sob escapes me, and I catch the edge of the desk to steady myself. It's over. This one part at least.

Santiago nods tightly. "I need to talk to my wife," he says, voice hoarse.

"Of course," Jackson says and turns to Colette. He gestures to the door. That's when I see it. The ring on his finger. The insignia with the two hammers on the hand of the man talking to Holton on the night of the gala. The name my brother wanted.

"Ivy," Jackson says, and I shift my gaze up to his. "I hope the next time you and my wife see one another, it will be in happier circumstances."

I nod nervously. "Thank you. Thank you both of you."

Colette takes my hands and squeezes. "Your wedding veil is in the bag too," she whispers when she hugs me. "See you soon."

"Thank you so much, Colette. Really, thank you."

"We'll see ourselves out," Jackson says.

I watch them go then turn to my husband to find him watching me with a strange expression on his face.

"Tell me about that night."

"You're going to listen?"

"Tell me."

"After your friend came to talk to you, I walked around for a little bit, then went into the chapel. I wasn't going to hang around your sister or mingle. That's where I met Colette and offered to swap shoes with her. She'd taken hers off and had been walking around barefoot. They must have been so uncomfortable, especially considering the pregnancy. Anyway, we stayed there talking until the first gong went off. She had to rush back, but I didn't want to, so I found a bathroom and hid there for a while. I knew I couldn't hide out forever, though, especially after the second gong, but when I tried the door, it was locked. I mean, it locks on the inside, so it wasn't so much locked as barricaded I guess. I don't know. I called out, but no one heard me, and then someone screamed. I think it was Mercedes. I'm sure, in fact. And then I could open the door, and well, you were lying on the ground." I feel myself waver, remembering that moment. Remembering him like that. "And then the man—"

"Judge."

I don't repeat it. I don't care about his name. I never want to see him again. "He knocked me out, and when I woke up, I was in that awful place."

"Bring me the shoes you were wearing."

"What?"

"Colette's shoes. Go get them."

"I don't have them. I guess they got lost somewhere between the gala and the cellar. I—"

"Mercedes had them sent to your room."

I pause. "No, she didn't. I don't have them."

His face becomes stone-like, and I swear I can see him thinking, trying to make sense of things. His jaw is tight, body tense. Before I can ask why it matters, he storms out of the office and down the corridor. I rush after him as he hurries up the stairs to my bedroom. By the time I get in there, he's in the closet, and when I get to it, I see him inside, pulling clothes off hangers, opening drawers, and shoving things aside wildly.

"Santiago?"

With a roar, he knocks a whole shelf of shoes clear off, and I jump backward. He turns to me, and the rage I see in his eyes is nothing like I've seen yet.

"Where are they?" he demands.

"Not here. I told you!" I back away into the wall. "You're being crazy!"

"Where the fuck are they?" He slams his fist into the wall, and I jump, letting out a scream.

He shakes his head and storms out of my room to barrel down the hall to Mercedes's bedroom.

"Mercedes!" He bangs his fist against her door, and when he finds it locked, he rams his shoulder into it so hard I hear wood splinter. It takes only two times for the door to crash open.

"Santiago, stop!" I rush in after him and am glad for his sister that the room is empty.

But then he begins to tear her closet apart, and

when he doesn't find what he needs there, he destroys her bed, then her desk, pulling out the drawers, dumping their contents, and smashing a beautiful antique lamp against the wall.

"Santiago, what are you doing?" I scream as I try to pull him away, try to make him stop, but he just shakes me off. "Santiago, stop!" I grab his arm and cling tight, but it's a mistake. He's out of control, and when he next shoves, I go flying backward and crash against the large, heavy armoire, slamming the back of my head so hard that for a moment, time stands still.

"Fuck! Ivy!"

I blink, sway on my feet as the room spins. When my knees give out and I reach for something, anything, he catches me, big arms wrapping around me, sweeping me up just as consciousness slips away.

21
IVY

His smell is all around me. I breathe it in, but when I turn my head, pain makes me hiss.

"Shh. Just relax," Santiago says, fingers gentle on my face.

"She'll be all right. Probably have a headache, though," says a vaguely familiar voice.

I open my eyes to find Santiago and Dr. Hendrickson standing over me.

"There she is," the kind doctor says, smiling as he tucks something into his bag.

I look from him to my husband, who looks absolutely tortured, and I remember what happened. Colette and Jackson coming over, the shoes in the security footage that will exonerate me. The brief relief followed by Santiago's madness.

Does he think Mercedes has somehow betrayed him? No. I can't believe that. If there's one thing I know, it's that Mercedes loves him. She'd do anything for him. He must know that.

The moment I try to sit up, Santiago's arms are around me, hands lifting me, pushing a pillow behind my back.

"You'll need to take it easy today, but it's just a bump. Santiago will keep a close eye on you to be sure there's no concussion, but I don't think so."

"Our session," I say, vaguely remembering an appointment.

"It's actually why I happened to be here at the right time. I don't think we'll have our session today, Ivy, but I'll be back next week."

"Thank you, Doctor. I'll see you out," Santiago says.

"No need. You stay with your wife. I think Antonia is nearby anyway."

"Let her know Ivy's fine. She's probably worried."

"Will do."

They shake hands, and I watch the doctor leave. The moment he does, Santiago turns to me. He sits on the edge of the bed and pushes hair behind my ear. He studies my face in a way he hasn't before and touches the spot where the tattoo gun left a tiny dot of ink.

"Christ," he says, wrapping his big hand around the back of my head, gentle with the bump as he weaves his fingers into my hair and draws me against his chest. He holds me like that for the longest moment.

I breathe him in and can't help the tears of relief as I wrap my arms around his middle, feeling his strength and the power of his protection.

"What I almost did to you," he says, the words barely audible as if they weren't meant to be spoken at all as he brings his lips to the top of my head.

I draw back, and he cups my face, his hands on either side, thumbs wiping away old or new tears. I can't tell anymore. The look in his eyes, though, is pure torture.

"I'm sorry," he says. "I am exactly the monster you prayed I wouldn't be the night of the wedding."

I shake my head, touch his cheek, and lean up to kiss his mouth. It's a chaste kiss, salty with tears. He doesn't kiss me back, but he lets me kiss him.

"No. You're not a monster. Not even close."

He draws in a deep breath close to my head as if he'll draw my scent into his lungs, inside himself.

"The foundation of my own home is cracked," he says, and I try to understand what he's thinking. The dress and the sandals, Mercedes was supposed to bring them to my room? She never did. I didn't realize he'd somehow gotten hold of them after my days in that cellar. But that alone has led to this? It seems a bit far.

"No, Santiago. It's not right. I know it. She—"

"Enemies inside my own home. Inside my own heart."

"Mercedes wouldn't..." He starts to pull away, but I grab his face with both hands, getting up on my knees so we're at eye level. "She loves you fiercely."

"She sent you knowingly to The Tribunal. She would have you bear the consequences. She would see you executed—" His voice cracks on that last word. "And you would defend her?"

I swallow hard.

He stands and turns away, running one hand through his hair while the other rests on his waist.

"I don't know your sister at all, apart from the fact she's a bitch. But I know one thing. She would kill for you, Santiago."

He turns to me, face hard, that mask firmly in place. "Then where the fuck is she?"

I just watch him, see the threads he's tying in his head, putting things together, putting things in place. Maybe in the wrong places.

"There's an explanation. I'm sure. You can't think based on just the clothes missing that she's somehow responsible."

"I have cause," he says vaguely.

Just then, I hear the clicking of heels in the hallway. Santiago hears it too and turns to the door where Mercedes, her face red, steps inside.

"What the hell did you do to my room?"

I hurry out of the bed, ignoring my aching head

when Santiago moves toward her, and Mercedes, seeing his face, jumps back.

"Stop, Santiago! Think!" I yell.

He pauses, drawing in a deep breath. "Ivy. I don't want to hurt you again. Get away from me."

"No. I won't."

Mercedes looks from me to Santiago. I realize her makeup is faded, eyeliner smeared. She looks like she's had a very long night. "What's going on?" she asks.

"Where are the clothes I asked you to put in Ivy's room? The clothes from the night of the gala."

There's a shift in her stance. It's a tiny change, a stiffening, and I wonder if Santiago catches it.

"I threw them away," she says.

Santiago's eyebrows rise high on his forehead. "You threw them away? When I told you to put them in Ivy's room?"

"I didn't want a reminder of that night. Is that what this is about? Is that why you tore apart my bedroom? What the fuck, Santi?"

I don't know if it's the nickname that has him softening or the fact that what she's saying makes sense.

"You almost died," she says, her voice passionate as tears spring to her eyes. "Can you blame me for wanting to erase that night?"

Santiago turns away, wraps his hand around the

back of his neck, takes two steps, and then faces her again.

"Get cleaned up. I want you in my office in twenty minutes," he tells her, then walks out.

"What about my room?" she calls after him.

"We have about two dozen others. Pick one." He doesn't bother to turn around, and I wonder what is going on in his head. What I don't know. Because there's something.

Mercedes turns to give me a nasty look. I want to tell her I just defended her, but I keep my mouth shut.

"Don't look so smug," she tells me.

She doesn't even give me time for a comeback before she spins on her heel and disappears in the direction of her bedroom.

22

SANTIAGO

"Santi?" Mercedes lingers in the doorway, watching me carefully with her hands clasped together in front of her.

She is the picture of contrition, confirmation enough that she was involved in this somehow. The problem is, I'm not certain I want to know the extent.

"Come sit down," I tell her.

She enters the office on wooden legs, forcing herself into the chair opposite my desk. Although she has done as I instructed and cleaned herself up, there is still something chaotic about her appearance. Her normally polished, smooth black hair is wild, falling around her face almost as a shield when she dips her head. The shadows beneath her eyes are evidence she did not sleep much last night either, and I can only speculate on the reasons.

"I'm offering you one chance." My sharp tone

slices through the heavy silence between us. "To clear your conscience and come clean. It will be the only chance you have, Mercedes. If you don't take this opportunity now, I will never forgive you for whatever it is you've done."

She peers up at me, eyes glassy, her lip trembling as she tries to hold it together. "Don't freeze me out, Santi. I can't bear it. Please."

"Tell me." I glower. "Tell me what your involvement in this scheme is. The poison. The lipstick. Why did you do it?"

Horror washes over her features as she shakes her head fiercely. "I didn't poison you, brother. I would never do that!"

When I don't respond, she flings herself forward, reaching for my palms flattened against the desk. She grabs them desperately, clinging to me as the tears she's been trying to hold back splash against her cheeks.

"Please believe me. I would never hurt you that way. You must know that. I'm your family. We are all each other has left right now."

I pull my hands from her clutches and stare at her, empty. "How did Abel know you gave Ivy that lipstick?"

She pales, her brows pinching together as she considers how to answer. "Abel?"

"How did he know?" I lean forward, biting the words so forcefully Mercedes flinches back.

"I... I don't know. That doesn't make any sense. I haven't spoken to him, and Ivy hasn't spoken with him since before. There's no way he could have—"

She pauses abruptly, an odd expression taking over her face.

"What?" I ask.

"I can't." She stumbles to her feet, swaying slightly. "I don't have the answers you need right now, Santi. But I will. I can promise you that I will. All I'm asking is for you to give me some time. Trust me, please. Know that I would never hurt you."

"Mercedes." I stagger to my feet, but she only offers me one last glance over her shoulder before she runs from the office, her heels clapping down the corridor as she goes.

"Fuck."

I stare at the empty doorway, considering my options. Considering that there is very possibly a traitor in my own home, and she's my own blood. I could go after her now. There are ways of getting the answers I want from her. I know them intimately and can still recall the sting of my father's methods for situations such as these. But I don't have the stomach to torture her myself, and I can't bring this to anyone else within The Society without raising alarm and confirming her guilt. There is one alternative. Someone I trust, who could execute a harsh but fair punishment and draw the answers from her efficiently. Judge would do that for me. But before I go that far, I have to consider my sister's desperation to prove whatever it is that occurred to her when she was speaking with me. And the fastest way to do that is also the easiest.

"Marco." I press the intercom button, summoning him, and he appears within a few moments.

"Yes, boss?"

"I want you to follow Mercedes when she leaves this house. Wherever she goes, I want updates on her location. Don't let her know you're there. Stay hidden, but don't lose her."

"Of course, sir."

He takes his leave, and I call some of my other men, instructing them to scour the city for Chambers. Once that is arranged, I stir my computer back to life and resume the video from the night of the gala, playing it from the beginning, trying to catch any other glimpse of the woman who attended that night. The woman who kissed me.

I think of my wife in her room. How many times she must have tried to tell me, and I would not hear it. How close she could have come to facing execution if it weren't for this revelation.

I am not familiar with these churning emotions deep in my gut. They are feelings I don't recognize, but I think perhaps it is guilt.

It appears that nothing is as simple as it seems, and if I was so wrong about this, it leaves me to question my resolve on other matters. The matter of Ivy's family. Her father was poisoned, but by who? At some point, I will need to go to the hospital.

He's been asking to see me since he awoke. A fact not even Ivy or Abel is aware of. The moment the doctor informed me, I had him placed on restricted lockdown while he recovers. The only visitor he is allowed right now is me, and so far, it hasn't proven to be an issue, considering his own family hasn't been to see him in some time. As far as they know, he is still in the same unyielding condition. They are all oblivious to his progress, and he is painfully aware that they are not at his bedside while he fights to regain his strength.

I am still determined to take his life and exact my revenge. It's the only logical conclusion to this scenario. The only way I can ever know peace. But there is no pleasure in snuffing out a sick, weak man. I need him at his best, whatever capacity that may be when he's fully recovered. I need him to feel the immense deal of pain he will face and remember every agonizing detail.

Except, I can't help considering how that might sour Ivy against me. Right now, she is... different. Instead of running away, she is leaning into me. Stealing opportunities to touch me. In place of her hatred, there is something... more. Something sweeter. Softer.

I feel it. And I don't want to admit that I will be at

a loss without it when she realizes what my plans are for her father. Once I carry them out.

But what about her? Can I follow through on my threats to her?

My eyes are bleary as I watch her on the screen. A goddess in black and gold silk. A butterfly with only one wing. How fitting it is.

With painstaking clarity, a realization hits me without warning.

I can't kill her.

Because I don't want to.

My eyes shutter closed, under the weight of exhaustion and delirium, and that's the last peaceful thought I have.

No, I won't kill her.

I will keep her instead.

"SANTIAGO."

A strangled groan rumbles from my chest as her fingers stroke my hair back from my face.

"Hmm?"

My eyes are so heavy, it is difficult to open them. But I can feel her weight in my lap. Her scent surrounding me. The warmth of her body pressing against mine.

"You need to sleep," she says softly.

I half nod. Sleep sounds good.

I'm not thinking clearly when I scoop her up into my arms and stagger to my feet. Ivy lets out a soft little laugh, and I freeze, opening my eyes to look at her.

"You're delirious," she says, amused. "Put me down."

"I've never heard you laugh." The words are strained when they leave my lips.

Her face sombers, and she gives me a gentle nod. "I know."

I force my rigid body forward, carrying her down the corridor and upstairs despite her protests. I'm not thinking clearly, but it only becomes evident when I enter my own bedroom and spread her across my bed before I collapse beside her.

She works to free some of the bed covers, pulling them over us. I'm already falling asleep again when I reach out and grab her waist, tugging her against me like a caveman.

Ivy lets out a little sigh, burrowing deeper into my body as I bury my face in her hair and inhale her. She smells so good, and I don't want to let her go. I'm not thinking about the consequences of what I'm doing right now. Not until I start to drift off, and she touches my arm, and I jerk awake, startled.

She blinks up at me, confused.

"Did I hurt you?" I ask.

She frowns. "What?"

"This isn't a good idea," I mumble almost incoherently. "You shouldn't be in here. Not safe."

"You won't hurt me," she whispers, curling into me and kissing my jaw. "I know you won't."

There's an argument somewhere in my mind. Logic trying to alert me to its presence. But logic isn't winning when I close my eyes and breathe her in. One breath becomes two, and two becomes three, and soon I am drifting off into peaceful oblivion.

23

SANTIAGO

*F*ire.
Fire in my lungs. Fire on my skin. Thick black smoke curls around me as I crawl, dragging my useless body. Searching. Screams pierce my ears, but I can't find them. They are all around me, reverberating like a nightmare.

I call out for my brother. My father. The names of the other men who were just standing beside me only moments ago. It doesn't feel real. I can't believe it's real. But the melting, searing pain is too visceral to be false.

"Santiago."

The name echoes through my consciousness, and I roar in frustration, choking on thick plumes of smoke.

"I can't find you."
"I can't find you."
"Santiago."

Fingers dance over my jaw, dragging me back to

another time. The present time. I explode upright, violent breaths stalling in my lungs as I scan the room with wild eyes. They latch onto the first thing they see. A bedpost. A blanket. *My bedroom.*

I turn slowly and find Ivy staring back at me with concern etched into her features. We're in my bed, together, still dressed in our clothes. We must have fallen asleep like this.

"It's okay," she whispers, reaching out to stroke my arm. "It's okay."

I'm still shaking, the fit seizing every fiber of my muscles as moisture clings to my forehead. My palms are clammy, and it takes me several moments to regain a normal breathing pattern before I can choke the words from my lips.

"Did I hurt you?"

"No," she reassures me. "I promise you didn't."

I collapse back onto the pillow again, staring up at the ceiling as she curls closer, the warmth of her body pressing against mine. It calms me faster than anything else could. A strange revelation, only compounded by the fact that I don't want her to leave, even though I know she should.

"You shouldn't ever try to wake me," I tell her gruffly. "For your own safety."

"Okay." She acknowledges my declaration. "I just didn't... I didn't like to see you so lost to it. The nightmare. It was so intense, and I was worried for you."

I turn my head to the side, studying her. I want to

ask her why she cares. But it's already written on her face. Her emotions are changing. Evolving. She sees me as something she shouldn't. Not a saint, but not quite a monster anymore. I'm somewhere in the middle of the spectrum, I think. And that is a dangerous thing to believe.

For both of us.

"It must be terrible," she says softly. "To experience something like that over and over again."

I avert my gaze. It's not something I care to discuss. She seems to understand, choosing not to press the matter.

"Is everything okay with you and Mercedes?" she asks.

I swallow, and it feels like broken glass gets caught in my throat. "It will be."

I have to believe that. But the truth is, I don't know.

Ivy continues to stroke my arm. It does something to my nerves I can't quite explain, but I'm on the verge of falling asleep again when her voice stirs me.

"What will happen when the Tribunal finds out I'm not pregnant?"

There's an undercurrent of fear in the question, and for once, it doesn't bring me pleasure to hear it.

"As far as they are concerned, you are." I roll onto my side, reaching out to drag the pads of my fingers along her jaw. "That is what we will tell them if they ask. There can be no question. You must act as if it's true."

She closes her eyes, shuddering softly against me. "So, we need to get pregnant as soon as we can."

"Yes."

She's quiet for a long moment, and when she opens her eyes again, something has changed in them.

"If we bring a child into this world together, it should be out of love. Not duty."

Love?

Tension bleeds into my body as I shake my head, but Ivy is quick to stop me before I can speak.

"I know. We have to do this to save my life and protect you from the Tribunal. I understand that. But I need some reassurances from you, Santiago. I need to know if I bring a child into this world with you, that child will be loved. I would rather face my own execution than agree to any other condition. I will not allow my own child to suffer."

"The child will be cared for beyond measure," I force out. "Far beyond any other child."

Ivy studies me, lost in her own thoughts for a few long moments before she gives voice to them. "And what about me? When you get what you want from me, you will kill me?"

I don't want to look at her. I know if I do, my face will betray everything. So instead, I close my eyes, and I kiss her, conveying the truth my words can't.

She whimpers against me, curling her fingers into my shirt. I pull her closer, squeezing her so tightly it must border on the point of pain. But she doesn't protest. She leans into it, giving herself over to me. The nightmare she can't wake up from.

"A child needs a mother," I murmur against her lips.

A confession. Not quite the truth. But I am not willing to admit that perhaps I need her too. Not yet.

She pulls away, breathless, still clinging to my shirt. "A child needs a father too. Not just a disciplinarian. But someone to love and guide them."

Her statement isn't a question, but it feels like one. Can I be that for someone? Am I even capable?

My cell phone starts to vibrate in my pocket, but I ignore it, trapped by my wife's eyes. She needs an answer from me. Assurances. And I am aware I don't need to give them to her. Regardless of her feelings, she will carry my child. But perhaps she is right. Perhaps I want her to want this as much as I do.

"I will do what is necessary," I tell her. "I will provide for you and the children. I will discipline, but I will also... do what fathers do."

It's the closest I can come to saying love at this moment. Truthfully, I don't know what that bond feels like. I fear that I am lacking. I may never have the ability to love unconditionally or understand the true meaning of love at all. But I am not my father. I will not hand out only punishments and withhold the necessary softness for humanity. Though I know even when I fail, Ivy will care enough for both of us to compensate for my shortfalls. I see that in her. This desire in her to love her own children will not allow anything, even me, to stand in her way.

My phone vibrates again, and I sigh, releasing my wife to drag it from my pocket. When I see Marco's name, a cold chill moves over me.

"Yes?" I answer.

"Did you get my texts?"

Texts?

"Hold on."

I pull the phone back and click on my messages. There must be at least a dozen updates on the screen regarding my sister's whereabouts. She's been to the club at the compound. Abel's house. A long list of different hotels around the city. And then finally, there's a message alerting me that she's been driving around aimlessly, scanning the streets in areas of high prostitution. At that point, Marco asked me what I wanted him to do, but I was asleep.

"Where is she now?" I ask.

"She's still driving around. Seems to be looking for someone."

"Keep following her," I tell him. "Until further notice, that is your full-time job. Wherever Mercedes goes, you go."

24

IVY

If we bring a child into this world together, it should be out of love. Not duty.

My own words haunt me for days.

Love. What am I thinking? So much has happened between us. But none of it has anything to do with love.

I put my hand to the back of my neck to touch the place I know his mark is and I'm more confused than ever.

"Here you are, dear," Antonia says, drawing me out of my reverie. She comes around the corner carrying a beautiful cream-colored lightweight coat and helps me put it on.

"Thank you," I say, feeling the luxuriously soft fabric. I'm dressed in cream from head to toe, my hair in a pretty twist, the knee-length dress shapeless on purpose. Not that they'd expect me to show yet. I'm grateful I don't have to wear the dress I was made to wear the last time. *The sheath of the accused.* I shudder at the memory.

Santiago comes around the corner looking striking in a charcoal suit stretched tight over broad shoulders and muscular arms. His head is down, eyes locked on whatever it is he's looking at on his phone. He's been distracted since the other night. Since Mercedes. He hasn't said what's going on, but I've hardly seen her since he tore her room apart. All I know is that tensions are still high and I'm not sure brother and sister have seen each other since.

A man I don't recognize opens the front door. "Your car is ready, sir," he says.

Santiago finishes typing something out and drags his gaze up to me before replying to him. "We'll be right there," he says, walking toward me.

"Where's Marco?" I ask.

"Occupied elsewhere."

He puts a hand at my back and looks me over. I'm about to ask if he's occupied with Mercedes but he pulls me to him and kisses my mouth. It's a deep kiss, sensual and erotic and full of promise and desire.

"You're beautiful," he says, and I'm flustered. I look up at him, see him smile and I falter. His kisses affect me physically. It's the strangest thing. The attraction between us has always been powerful, raw and violent even, but it's even more so now. "Let's get this over with."

I nod, but anxiety has my stomach in knots. I don't want to go but I have no choice. The Tribunal will dismiss the charge against me but the thought of being in there again, in that awful building, seeing that scaffold out in the courtyard, it terrifies me.

"Don't be afraid," Santiago says, squeezing my hand. "I'm with you. I will not leave your side."

I look up at him, squeeze back, my hands clammy. I nod.

He pulls me to him and kisses my forehead, holding his lips there for a long moment as his fingers brush the tattoo at the nape of my neck. It's exposed today at his request. I'm his. He wants The Tribunal to know it. He wants everyone to know it.

When we step outside, I see the small sports car rather than the Rolls Royce. He opens the passenger side door, and I climb in, realizing he'll be driving. It would be fun if it was any other occasion.

Santiago slips into the driver's seat and seamlessly shifts gears to drive off the property. By the time we arrive at IVI, the sun has set, and the lights cast on the building make it look even more ominous than it must look by daylight. I know the timing is by Santiago's design. He doesn't come out in the daytime unless he absolutely must, and The

Tribunal has agreed to it. Santiago tucks the keys into his pocket and comes around to help me out of the low sports car.

We enter the building, and the men who'd escorted me up the last time greet him with reverence. They still barely acknowledge me. Santiago takes my elbow, and we climb the stairs together, the guards following us. I don't let myself glance out the window. I won't look.

Once we stand outside the large wooden doors, Santiago helps me out of my coat and hands it and his to someone standing nearby. A moment later, the doors are opened, and we enter the cavernous, cold room, our footsteps echoing. Santiago's hand is firm at my back when I draw away, guiding me to stand in the pulpit. I'm surprised and grateful when he steps in beside me, and I realize I'm shaking when he wraps a hand around the back of my neck and leans close to tell me to relax.

How did I do this that first time around? How did I stand here before these men sitting in their cloaks high above me ready to judge me? How did I do this alone?

I glance at where Mercedes was sitting that day, her eyes red, skin blotchy from crying, and see Jackson looking at us, expression unreadable.

When the gavel hits the block, I startle and turn. I listen as The Councilor formally reads the charge of poisoning against me, the way he says my name sending a shiver down my spine.

I don't hear much of what he follows up with because I'm too anxious until his final sentence. "In light of new evidence, the charge is dropped and the case against Mrs. De La Rosa dismissed." I wonder if he's disappointed by the fact. I get the feeling he is. When he's finished with the formal statement, he removes his glasses and looks down at me. "You owe Mr. Van Der Smit for that, young lady."

I nod, not sure what I'm supposed to say, too nervous to tell them off, tell them that I hadn't done anything wrong to begin with. That, at the very least, it is they who owe me an apology.

"Santiago," one of the other Councilors starts.

"Councilor," Santiago says, no note of nerves in his tone. More an irritation. Is he truly not even a little bit intimidated by this?

"It is troubling that there should be yet another attempt on your life. Have you any intelligence you can lend on the matter?"

I am confused. A *second* attempt? I turn to Santiago, but he doesn't look my way. I do, however, see that tic in his jaw he gets when he's annoyed.

"With all due respect, I don't believe this is the proper forum to discuss that other, separate matter, Councilor."

"Very well," The Councilor says, his irritation seeming to match Santiago's. "Then I adjourn this session. Mrs. De La Rosa, The Tribunal wishes you a healthy pregnancy. Let us hope you deliver a strong, healthy male heir to carry the De La Rosa line."

I nod, feeling heat flush my face.

"You are free to go."

"Thank you," I say, but it's drowned out by the sound of the gavel striking the block.

We remain where we are while the three robed men leave the room. The double doors are then opened, and Santiago leads me out, collecting our coats along the way.

I feel a physical sense of relief as we descend the stairs but find myself shuddering once more when a light coming on out in the courtyard catches my eye. I glance out the window to see the scaffold has been lit, and several people have gathered.

My throat goes dry, and I pause. "What's going to happen?" I ask, going to the window.

"Nothing you need to see," Santiago says, taking my hand and walking me the rest of the way down the stairs and back out to our car. He helps me into the passenger side, and this time, I can appreciate it.

"What is this car?" I ask when he gets in.

"It's an Aston Martin." He pulls out of IVI, and I see the gates close in the side mirror.

"Can we drive around a little? I don't want to go home yet. Just have some fun maybe."

"Fun?" he asks, almost confused by the word.

I reach over and put my hand on his thigh. "Fun. It means doing something you enjoy."

"I enjoy many things I wouldn't call fun."

I sigh, the relief still a palpable thing. "Please?"

He glances at me, then back to the road and nods slowly exactly once.

"Yay! You think I could drive?"

"Don't push your luck."

When we get home late that night, Antonia has an elaborate dinner prepared for us. We sit down to eat, the candles feeling more romantic tonight than before. But as I sip on my half-glass of wine, which he allowed since we know I'm not pregnant, and after The Tribunal, well, I earned it, my mind wanders to our lie. To a few nights ago. To the baby and the reasons for having one.

If it came down to it, we could say I had a miscarriage as far as IVI is concerned. I'm sure Santiago could pull that off. But there's so much more going on that I don't know.

"Santiago?" I ask when we're at dessert.

"Yes?"

"What did The Councilor mean when he said this was the second attempt on your life?"

"My, what big ears you have," he says lightly, but his mood darkens palpably.

"Tell me."

"It's not a matter for you." He puts his fork down after only having a bite of the chocolate cake and wipes his mouth.

"Does it have to do with my family?"

He sits silent, watching me.

"The other attempt on your life, does it have to do with us? Is it why you hate anyone with the last name Moreno?"

"Stop, Ivy."

"Is it why you chose me?"

His phone buzzes, and he glances at it. It's been beside him on the table, but he's ignored it mostly. He pushes his chair back. "This doesn't have anything to do with you," he says, emphasis on the word you.

"But my family, though?" I remember how he's accused me of being a Moreno as if it is a horrible thing.

"Enough." He stands. "I need to take care of some things, and you need to get to bed. It's late."

"I'm not finished."

He glances at the single bite of cake still on my plate. "All right. Finish."

I break the piece in half and put one part into my mouth. "Why didn't you tell me Evangeline had come to see me?" She mentioned it in one of her letters. She'd taken the bus to get here, an hour of travel time, and she'd been turned away at the door.

He sits back down. "Do I need to remind you of the circumstances?"

I grit my jaw and cut the other already bite-size piece into an even smaller one. "Can I see her? And my dad?"

"Not your father."

"Why not? What harm could it do? You know now it wasn't me who tried to kill you. You know someone set me up too. Doesn't that put us on the same side for once?"

"That's enough." He stands again and pulls out my chair. "Go to bed."

"He loved you. Did you know that?"

There's that tic again. And a flicker of emotion. "Go to bed, Ivy. Now."

"You were like a son to him. His favorite son, in fact. It's why Abel hates you. I used to be jealous of you, too. Did you know that?"

He draws in a sharp breath. "Your father did not love me," he says tightly with an emotion he's trying to hide. "If you hate him, that's for different reasons."

"Hate him? I don't hate him. I'm sick with worry for him, and you won't let me see him, and I don't understand why." Now, I stand. "Especially now. After the other night."

"The other night? What does the other night have to do with anything?"

"We talked about a baby."

"An heir."

"A baby. A life! And you said he'd be loved."

"I said I would do what is necessary. I never used the word love. That was you, Ivy."

I falter. Did I misread things? The emotion I thought I saw? The connection we'd made?

His phone vibrates with yet another message, and his expression turns ugly as he replies to it. "Go to your room." He takes a step to leave.

"*My* room. Not yours?"

He stops, then turns back to me. "I sleep alone. It's better—"

"It's not better. I'm your wife!" I push the chair in, but it catches on the carpet, and I have to pick it up to do it.

"Ivy, you're picking a fight. Tonight is not the night. What I meant is—"

"I can't live like this. I'm going crazy. My head is spinning. One minute you hold me, make love to me, talk to me about babies. The next, you dismiss me, sending me to my room, not yours. Not *ours*. You don't tell me anything even when I'm the one who would have paid the steepest price for what happened to you. You still don't tell me anything when I know you know much more than you're letting on, and I have a right to know."

"A right?"

"Yes. A fucking right!"

"That's more than enough." He takes my arm

and starts to walk me out of the room. "I'm going to blame the alcohol."

"Get off me! I'll go on my own. I know when I'm not wanted."

Without a word and without missing a step, he marches me up the stairs, hand tight around my arm but not bruising. And some part of me knows he's taking care with me. But it's not enough.

When we get to my door, he opens it and releases me only when we're inside.

I take two steps away. "Are you going to lock me in? Don't worry, I won't try to sneak into your bed!"

He comes toward me, takes my arms, rubs them as he walks me backward. "Ivy, Ivy, Ivy. Don't you think I want you in my bed?"

"No, I don't." I shove his hands away, but he traps me between the wall and himself. "You've given me every indication that you do not. Except when you want a fuck."

"Shh." He brushes a loose strand of hair back, then dips his forehead to mine. "Are you going to listen?"

"No."

He sighs, drawing back. His phone goes off again, and I can see he wants to look at it.

"Just go. I don't want to keep you." I fold my arms across my chest and look away from him.

He reads the message on his screen, and I try to

catch it, but I only see one word, *Mercedes*, before he tucks it into his pocket. He looks back up at me.

"You're not unwanted," he says.

I feel myself soften and my eyes warm with tears.

"What I meant about my bed is that I have violent dreams. And sometimes, I lash out in my sleep. I don't want to hurt you any more than I already have." His thumb comes to the dot of ink from his tattoo gun. I know he feels guilty about that. The tiny but constant reminder of what he almost did to me.

I want to say something. I want to have some reason to lash out at him, but his sad smile and gentle touch disarm me, and what he's saying makes sense. He'd been worried about the other night too. Even warned me never to wake him.

"You won't hurt me," I tell him.

"I won't take a chance."

I exhale, dropping my head.

He takes my face in his hands and turns it up to his. "All right?"

I shrug a shoulder, very aware I'm pouting. "Fine."

"I'll arrange for you to visit Colette tomorrow. Would you like that?"

"Why Colette and not my sister or my father?"

"Don't push. Not now. This is what I am offering."

"I just don't understand. We had fun tonight."

His phone goes off again. "I need to go. Would you like to visit Colette?"

"Yes."

"All right." He leans in to kiss me, but I turn my head away. He clears his throat. "Good night, Ivy."

25

IVY

I toss and turn for what feels like hours. Guilt gnaws at me. He was trying. For Santiago. We did have fun tonight, so I shouldn't have pushed. And he did give me something. He has nightmares. I saw that myself. I want to know what the dreams are. What the cause is. The fire?

That takes me back to the comment The Councilor had made. A *second* attempt. That fire was caused by a gas leak. Or at least that's what the public was told. Is that not the case? Did someone try to kill him and succeed in killing so many others? All Sovereign families. All males. I think it was more than a dozen dead, and I remember my father's reaction to it. I'd just thought he'd been relieved he wasn't there but also guilt-ridden that he'd sent Santiago in his place when he'd been too sick to go.

Is that what this is about? Does he blame my father? Is he punishing me to punish him?

No. That makes no sense.

I push the blankets off and get up. I want to go to him. I want to sleep in the same bed as him and feel his arms around me.

I want to tell him I'm sorry I acted like a brat.

The house is quiet as I pad down the hallway to his room. Mercedes's door is hanging at an odd angle. I don't know which one she moved to, but no one has cleaned this one yet. I bypass hers and get to his. I knock lightly so if he's asleep I won't wake him up. I'll just slip into bed beside him.

I turn the handle, grateful it's not locked. But from the dim light in the hallway, I can see he's not here. His bed is still made. He hasn't slept in it. The clock by the bed tells me it's past three in the morning. Is he still up?

I turn and head down the stairs to his office. It's the only other place I can think he'd be. And I'm right. I know it before I even reach his door not only from the light coming from beneath it but from the melody streaming out. Something dark I recognize. Mozart's Requiem. My father loved Mozart, and I remember this piece especially well. The haunting tune, the escalating soprano.

Without thinking, I let my feet carry me to his door, and this time, I don't knock. I push it open, and Santiago's gaze snaps up from what he's doing. The volume is so high I can't hear myself think, but from the candles on his desk, I can see how red his eyes are. It makes me wonder how much of the bottle of scotch that sits half-empty he consumed after dinner tonight. I don't know all that he's carrying, but it's heavy. I see it. And I feel doubly guilty about pushing him earlier.

I walk inside and close the door behind me. I don't say a word as I go to him. He drops the pencil into the notebook and lets it close as he pushes his seat back when I come around the desk. I pull my nightgown off. I'm not wearing anything underneath but the rosary, and I stand before him and let him look at me with his sanguine eyes and his sad skull face.

Something about the look in it breaks my heart a little. What was so terrible that he's gone from the man driving the sports car too fast through dark, winding streets to this one? This broken man.

I drop to my knees between his legs, and he leans back when I reach to undo his belt, then his trousers. I take him out and look up at his sorrowful face.

He puts his hand on my head as if giving me his blessing, and when I lean forward and close my mouth around him, I hear a choked sound come from deep inside his chest. His hand soon turns to a fist in my hair as he takes over, moving fast, pushing deeper, both hands on me now as I taste the first salty drops before he pulls me off, the pop strangely loud as the suction of my mouth is broken. He lifts me, laying me on his desk, and the leatherbound book digs into my shoulder before he shoves it to the floor.

He spreads me open and looks at me like a starved man before a feast, and when he dips his head between my legs, I arch my back and close my eyes, fisting handfuls of his hair as he licks hungrily. He brings me just to the edge of orgasm before straightening. Tugging me closer, he locks eyes on mine when he thrusts into me, leaning closer to me as I claw at his shoulders. I pull at his hair, wanting him closer still, deeper because it's not enough. It's not enough. He's still too far, and I need him.

"Ivy," he grunts, these final thrusts punishing. And then he stills, and I watch him, watch his beautiful face as he comes. Something inside me flutters and twists, and it's bittersweet, this. Our lovemaking. Our violent, raw lovemaking.

And I think in time he will break me whether he wants to hurt me or not.

26

SANTIAGO

I'm still inside my wife, touching her and breathing her in. I can't seem to stop. My head dips to her neck, lips trailing over the tender flesh. How did she know I needed her tonight? Why does she come to me like she needs this too?

Already, I can feel myself hardening inside her again. Perhaps it is just her and this cloyingly sweet intoxication I seem to find myself indulging in far too often. Or perhaps it is because I know this could be the night I finally claim her in the most primal of ways.

"You've been here for three months now," I murmur against her skin. "Did you know that?"

She stills beneath me, her palms flattening against my back.

"I have?"

"I did some digging in Chambers' practice," I tell

her. "Scoured through his drug inventory. On the day of your visit with him, there was only one injectable used. That shot you had was a progesterone shot. It was only effective for eight weeks."

When I pause to look down at her, Ivy curls her fingers against me, her expression soft, eyes wild.

I brush the hair away from her face, staring into her eyes so deeply it feels as though we are tethered together by some unbreakable cord.

"You could be pregnant right now." My hand comes to rest possessively on her belly. "Any day now, you could have my child inside you."

She sucks in a sharp breath, and I swallow her exhale when my lips crash against hers. Logically, I'm aware that fucking her all night won't increase our chances, but it doesn't change the fact that I want to try regardless.

My phone rings as I grope her breast in my palm, and she arches into my touch with a moan. I swallow that sound, desperate for more, only to be interrupted by the phone again.

A feral growl leaves my lips as I yank back, glancing at the ID, torn between answering it and testing how long Ivy can withstand my obsession tonight before she collapses from exhaustion.

"Santiago," she pleads beneath me, reaching up to cup my face. "Please don't stop."

I grunt and pivot my hips inside her, just enough to let her feel what she does to me. The glazed softness in her eyes has me leaning in her favor. Fucking wins out over every other priority. But when I pull back to thrust into her once more, the phone rings again.

I know it's Marco, and as pleased as I am to be inside my wife, I can't quell the quiet dread creeping up my spine.

Reaching across the desk, I grab the phone and bring it to my ear, rolling my hips against Ivy as she stifles a groan.

"Yes?"

"Boss?" Marco replies, half breathless like he's been running.

"What is it?"

"I think Mercedes found who she was looking for," he tells me. "She's been on the trail of some woman who left Abel's house tonight. Followed her to a shitty apartment building in the 7th Ward and forced her way inside. I've been trying to let you know."

"Is she still inside?" I swallow, pausing as Ivy looks up at me.

"She's been in there for twenty minutes and hasn't come out. I thought I heard a scream. I asked you if you wanted me to break in."

"Fuck." I pull my cock out of my wife and tuck it back into my pants as she leans up on her elbows.

"What do you want me to do, boss?" Marco asks, his voice tinged with the same uneasiness I feel.

"Go in after her," I say. "Make sure she's safe, and don't let either of them leave. Send me the location. I'm on my way."

"Will do."

The phone disconnects, and I reach out to stroke Ivy's face one last time. "We'll have to continue this another time. I need to leave now."

"Is everything okay?" She sits up, squeezing her thighs together.

"It will be. Get yourself cleaned up and go to sleep. I'll check in on you when I get home."

I pull away, prepared to leave, but Ivy reaches for my hand and tugs me back. When I glance down at her in question, she leans up and gives me one last gentle kiss to take with me.

"Be safe, Santi."

Be safe.

Her words echo through my mind as I navigate the dark streets to the 7th Ward. Wondering what Ivy meant by that request is the only thing keeping my thoughts from drifting to darker territory.

During the drive, Marco called to update me that he's inside the apartment, and Mercedes is safe. But he requested that I get there right away, and something in his voice alarmed me. It was an urgency I seldom hear from him.

It takes me thirty minutes to reach this part of the city. The part that isn't safe for anyone really, let alone girls like Mercedes. These apartments are a high crime area, and almost everyone will turn a blind eye for a bit of cash. There's a level of paranoia in this district that separates the residents from the outsiders. Anyone who isn't local is a threat, and it isn't uncommon for lost tourists to wander into these areas only to get stabbed or mugged.

If the mystery woman Mercedes is following lives here, it's because the apartments are cheap, and she can pay cash. The neighbors won't talk, and it's a good place to hide. Without even seeing her yet, I can take a stab that she is the same woman from the gala. The question is, why is Mercedes chasing after her?

I still don't want to accept the correlation. Not until I see it for myself. But the evidence is stacking up against her. She's been avoiding my calls and hasn't returned to the house. The updates I've received from Marco indicate that she's been staking out the Moreno house, which means this has something to do with Abel.

I can't believe Mercedes would ever lower herself to the level of Abel Moreno as a companion or even a participant in her schemes. But the connection can't be denied.

I pull up onto the street in one of my guard's cars, something inconspicuous with a fake plate.

The second I shift the car into park, my phone chimes with another message from Marco with instructions on where to enter.

I follow his directions to the back of the building, where he's waiting for me at an exit door that's riddled with bullet holes and large dents from previous break-ins. So far, the gloomy state of this place isn't inspiring any faith that I'm going to like what I find inside.

Marco gestures for me to follow him silently, opening the door and leading me down the hall. When we reach the apartment door, he glances over his shoulders, checking for prying eyes before we enter.

His large frame blocks my view at first, but almost immediately, my shoes are stepping over the debris of broken furniture and glass. And then Marco steps aside, unveiling a scene from a horror movie. That's the only way to describe it.

Lying in a gory heap on the floor is a woman I don't recognize, but even if I knew her, I doubt I could recognize her. Her hair is matted with blood, clothing torn, and pieces of what I think are a lamp shattered around her.

"Is she—"

"She's dead," Marco answers quietly. "I already checked."

Glass crunches under the weight of someone's shoes in the hall, and a second later, Mercedes appears. Her hair is a tangled mess, blood spattered across her face, a large gash down her cheek. She's visibly shaking, wobbling in her heels as if she's on the verge of collapse, and when her eyes collide with mine, a mournful sob bursts from her lips.

"I didn't mean to, Santi." Tears splash against her cheeks as she shakes her head violently. "I was going to bring her to you so you could do it."

Fragments of sentences eject between her ragged breaths. "She wouldn't listen to me! She just kept fighting me. I had no choice. She was going to kill me. She tried to kill you."

On this last sentence, she breaks down entirely, dropping to her knees and hiding beneath her hair as she dips her head. "Oh God, what have I done? What have I done?"

For a few long moments, I can't even speak. I can't bring myself to move or think. I'm paralyzed by her confession. This is the woman who tried to kill me. Somehow, Mercedes knows that, and right now, I don't know if I want to strangle her or comfort her.

"We need to handle this, boss." Marco gives me a gentle nudge in the right direction. "Perhaps you should take your sister home, and I can call for a body removal."

"Yes." My voice cracks as I nod. "We should probably do that."

27

SANTIAGO

It's late morning when Mercedes emerges from the bathroom in one of the lodging rooms at the IVI compound. She's wearing a pair of cheap sweats from the only store that was open on our way here. Her hair is clean, face completely free of makeup, and the gash on her cheek is starting to scab over as a bruise forms around it.

She looks like someone I don't recognize anymore.

"Santi?" She lingers there hesitantly. "Why are we here?"

I can't bring myself to answer that question. But I don't need to. Mercedes is aware the conversation we are about to have will determine her fate, one way or the other.

"Tell me everything," I order gruffly.

She pads farther into the room and sits down

on the bed, squeezing her hands together in her lap. "I will. But I need you to promise you won't hate me. No matter what. I need to hear that from you."

"I can't promise you anything." I glower at her, angry she's put us in this position. We shouldn't even be having this conversation. None of this should have ever happened.

She chokes up again, and I give her a moment to collect herself, but only a moment.

"Now, Mercedes. If you don't tell me now, you will decide for both of us. You will never hear from me again."

She peers up at me as gut-wrenching agony twists her features. "No. You can't do that."

"You aren't in a position to argue anymore." I walk to the window and pull back the curtain just slightly, glancing down into the courtyard. The compound is mostly empty right now, apart from the few other guests utilizing similar lodgings on this level. These rooms are reserved for out-of-town members or those who imbibed too much at the club. It isn't somewhere I would have ever considered bringing my sister. But now, I can't imagine taking her home.

"It wasn't supposed to happen this way," she blurts out. "I never meant for any of this to happen. I was just so irritated with you, Santi. To see the way you looked at that Moreno girl. You were falling for her right before my eyes. I could see it, and it felt like such a betrayal."

I release the curtain and turn to look at her. There is no mistaking the misdirected anger in her features. She's envious of Ivy. A confirmation that she's too dangerous to have around my wife.

"She was going to take you away from me," she says. "I had to do something. I just wanted to make her hate you. So, I hired that courtesan who used to work for IVI to lure you away at the gala and seduce you. All that was supposed to happen was that Ivy would come out of the bathroom and see you together. That was it. Nobody was ever supposed to get hurt."

I pace a few steps across the room, and Mercedes rushes to cry out the rest of her confession.

"I know it was a stupid idea. I was naïve to think I could trust that woman. I didn't know she was one of Abel's regular conquests. He used to meet with her at the club here until she was shunned by The Society. I didn't figure that out until after the fact. He paid her for information about the members of IVI, and when he found out what I'd asked her to do, he was the one who gave her the poison and the antidote. He put her up to it and paid her three times what I did. They double-crossed me, Santi. I had no idea they would put you in harm's way. If I had, I would have stopped it. You have to believe me."

"How can I believe anything you tell me?" I turn

my back to her and shake my head. "How can I believe any of what you're telling me now is even true?"

"Because she told me so herself!" Mercedes shouts.

"When you were beating it out of her?"

A long silence follows my question and then a shaky breath. "It wasn't like that. I was fighting for my life. I didn't mean to kill her, but I had no choice. It was either her or me."

When I collapse into the chair, Mercedes starts to sniffle again.

"Would you rather it was me? Is that it? Do you wish it were me who was dead on that floor?"

"What I would have rathered was that you never lied to me at all!" I roar. "You betrayed me. You schemed. You nearly fucking killed me. My own sister. Do you understand that?"

She sucks in a sharp breath, a fresh wave of tears falling as she watches me pleadingly. "I would rather die than hurt you, brother. Please believe that. If nothing else."

My throat is tight, stomach tied up in knots when I look at the girl who used to follow me around constantly as a child. The one person in my life I thought I could always trust without question. But right now, her every word, every tear is just salt in the wound. It feels like I'm being torn in half by this decision, her betrayal. It's an agony unlike any I've ever known.

I know what I need to do for both our sakes. At this late stage, my harsh words will be of no benefit to Mercedes. I could verbally eviscerate her, and it would make no difference because this is the monster I've allowed her to become. I've watched it happen. She's been coming unglued since the deaths of our father, Leandro, and subsequently, our mother. Lost to her grief, she has turned into a shallow, manipulative, hateful shell of a woman. A reflection of myself, if I'm being honest. And while I can accept that I am who I am, I can't accept that fate for her.

I won't allow her to destroy her life or anyone else's any longer.

"Get in bed and try to get some sleep," I tell her.

"What's going to happen now?" she croaks.

"Now, you are going to sleep," I answer flatly. "And when you wake up, you will start fresh."

She looks relieved but hesitant. Regardless, her exhaustion wins out, and she does as I ask, pulling back the covers and curling up to sleep. For a long while, I remain in the chair, unmoving. Frozen by the understanding of what it is I must do. I can't have her in my house any longer. I can't have her under the same roof as my wife and my future children because it will be impossible to protect them both.

Mercedes has made her bed, and now she must lie in it.

It is the hardest decision I have ever had to make when I drag my phone from my pocket and dial a familiar number.

He answers on the third ring, greeting me by my first name.

"I'm ready," I tell him. "I need it to happen now."

Three hours later, Mercedes stirs from her sleep, gasping for air as she bolts upright, clutching the blankets to her chest. She seems to sense the danger lurking in the corner of the room, and her eyes move to the dark figure sitting opposite me in the shadows. Watching. Waiting for her.

"Santi?" she whispers, her eyes moving back to me. "What's going on?"

I rise from my seat on rigid legs, steeled by my retreat back into numbness.

"You are dangerous," I tell her. "And you have proven that I can't trust you. Not in my home. Not in my life. And now, there is only one solution that can save you."

Her eyes move to the figure again, widening with fear as she begins to shake her head. "No. You can't send me away. You can't!"

"It's done." I tear my gaze away from her, breathing fire into my lungs as I nod to Judge.

He steps forward from the shadows, and Mercedes

scrambles from the bed, prepared to fight. To flee. But for one split second, her eyes connect with his, and she pauses, almost... relieved. It doesn't last. She's bolting for me when Judge intercepts her, capturing her around the waist. Within seconds, he has her arms pinned behind her back as she screams for me, her desperation clawing at the last shred of my sanity.

"Santi, please don't do this!"

"Go," Judge tells me. "Leave, Santiago. I will handle this."

I look at him and then at my sister. Our eyes connect for one last fleeting glance. In mine, she can see the anguish I tried to avoid, and even now, after everything, she tries to exploit it.

"You won't do this to me. I know you won't."

"It's already done."

My stomach sinks, and I walk out the door.

28

IVY

I clean up in the bathroom attached to the study, then return to the now empty room and look around. I'm pretty sure that was Marco on the line, and I know I heard Mercedes's name. It must be big given the urgency with which Santiago ran out of here.

It feels strange being in here without him. Feels like I'm not supposed to be here. And I guess I'm not. He did tell me to go to bed. And I will in a few minutes.

I close the door he'd left open and turn back to the large, ornate desk and the chair he'd been sitting in when I came in here. I think about how he looked, and again, there's that feeling inside my chest. That tightness. A constriction.

I put a hand to my stomach.

Is it true that I could be pregnant? That I could

get pregnant now? I look for a calendar on his desk. I don't even know what day it is. Have I really been here for three months?

Taking a seat in his plush leather chair, I roll myself closer to the desk. I don't see a calendar, and it feels wrong to open his drawers to search for one. A few weeks ago, I wouldn't have thought anything of it, but now, it doesn't feel right.

The bottle of scotch is still somehow on top of the desk after our lovemaking. I cork it, and I notice the book we knocked off the desk. I bend to pick it up and set it on the desk, the pencil marking his place still inside.

I glance at the door and bite my lip as I consider. It's not an invasion of privacy really. Not if I let it fall open to the page he'd been looking at. The pencil is right there.

I'm not sure what I expect to find, but it's not this.

On the page is an unfinished sketch, the lead of the pencil worn down. It's his book. His sketches. I hadn't realized it when I'd seen it briefly that night so long ago that it feels like another lifetime. On the page are two lovers in profile, and although they're not close to finished, I know it's us. I know it from the skull side of the face that I see.

My face is less clear. Mostly lines and shadows and the fingers of my hand are just grazing his cheek. There's something hopeless about this image, and it matches what I saw on his face when

I first walked in here. Something sad and too broken.

And I know this is an invasion. I know I should close the book and leave his private thoughts private. But I can't.

I turn the page instead and work backward and what I see is pain. His pain. Poured into this book. Sketches of his sister. Sketches of the woman I'd seen the last time. On one page, there's a photo stuck inside, and it's Santiago, Mercedes, and another boy. They must be in their teens. Santiago wears the expression I've come to know even then on his young face. He's too young to look like that. But the other boy is smiling wide, and he has one arm around Santiago and the other around a pre-teen Mercedes. She's smiling too, and you can already see the beauty she will become.

The two of them are wearing swimsuits, but Santiago is fully dressed in a school uniform. His hair falls into his eyes, and it's strange to see him like this, without the ink that is so much a part of him. That is the only way I really know him.

He's sketched the photo, but he's changed just one thing. He's smudged out half of his face. I touch the shadow there, smear the pencil, and something catches in my throat. What must it be like for him? What must it have been to survive the fire only to find yourself not yourself? To feel you're better served to wear a skull for a face.

I take a deep breath in and force my gaze away from his. The other boy must be Leandro, his brother. I wonder if they were close. Strange that we've been married for three months, and there's still so much I don't know about my husband.

I take a breath in and close the book. It's late, and I need to get some sleep, but I want to ask him about the book, so I take it with me up to his bedroom, not mine, and I lie down in his bed and put the book on the pillow beside me. I want him to know I'm not hiding it. And when I close my eyes, I sleep.

"Ivy," a voice calls. Someone gives me a shake.

I groan, rolling away.

"Ivy, dear, Mrs. Van Der Smit will be expecting you soon. It's almost two o'clock."

I blink, rub my eyes and turn to find Antonia standing over me. "What?" I look over at the other side of the bed. It's empty. The book right where I left it.

He never came home.

"The driver will take you to Mrs. Van Der Smit's house in less than half an hour."

"Oh." I sit up and run a hand through my hair. "Where's Santiago?"

"He called earlier to ask me to arrange a driver for you."

"He didn't come home?"

"No, I'm afraid not."

"Do you know where he is?"

"I'm sorry, dear." She looks at her watch. "Why don't you go get dressed? I'll make the bed up."

"Um, okay. Do you think I could call him?"

"He said he'd be offline for the rest of the day and possibly tomorrow."

"Tomorrow?"

"I'll ask him to talk to you if he calls in again, all right?"

I nod and push the blanket off to get ready to go. At least he remembered to arrange for me to go to Colette. But where is he?

AT ANTONIA'S INSISTENCE, I eat a quick piece of toast in the kitchen once I'm dressed before a driver I don't know takes me to Colette's house. It's a beautiful, cold but sunny day, and I'm grateful to be out of the house. And visiting a friend feels like a normal thing to do.

When we pull up to the beautiful mansion in the Garden District, the front door opens, and Colette comes outside, wrapping a shawl around her shoulders and waving happily. It puts a smile on my own face to see her. To feel so welcome.

"Ivy!" she calls out when I step out of the car, and

we hug halfway up the path to her porch. "I'm so glad you came!"

"Me too. It's good to see you." She draws back, and I look down at the huge belly between us. "How is it going?"

"Still pregnant." She turns, takes my hand, and we walk back toward the house like we've known each other forever. "I'm a few days late. This little guy doesn't want to leave. I'm evicting him if he's not out by Saturday," she says, rubbing her belly affectionately.

I raise my eyebrows.

"They'll induce if I don't go into labor naturally by then."

"Oh, I'm sure it will be fine either way."

"Yes, it will. I just wish he'd come already. I'm anxious to meet him."

"Do you have a name picked out?"

She smiles. "Well, Jackson thinks we'll name him Jackson of course." She rolls her eyes.

"Of course."

"But I have my heart set on Benjamin. That's my grandpa. Or was. He's gone now, and he was always so wonderful to me," she says, her face falling a little. "It will be a remembrance."

"I'm sorry he's gone."

"It's okay. It's been five years, and he had a good long life."

"Well, I say since you do most of the work, you get to pick the name."

"That's what I've been telling Jackson," she says as we enter a casual sitting room. "I hope you don't mind if we sit in here. Jackson's got someone in his office, and I don't want to see him if I can help it."

"No, this is great. And your house is so beautiful." I go to the window and look out over the vast garden. It's a very different house than Manor De La Rosa. Much more lived in, more colorful.

"It's my favorite one."

"Favorite?"

"Jackson's family has several, but they're a little too stiff for my taste."

"His family or the houses?"

She laughs. "You caught that." The door opens then, and a woman walks in carrying a tray of tea, coffee, and cookies. "Thanks, Lindy," Colette says with a warm smile.

"You're welcome, Mrs. Van... Colette."

"See, it's not so bad," Colette teases, and the older woman smiles and leaves us alone. "Tea or coffee?"

"Coffee, please. I just woke up and haven't had a cup yet."

"Just woke up? It's the afternoon." She hands me the coffee, and I take it.

"Oh, we had a late night."

"Did you?" She waggles her eyebrows. "I bet."

I feel my cheeks flush.

"How did it go at The Tribunal? Jackson said they were dismissing the charges."

"They did, but it was still nerve-wracking."

"I can imagine. I've only been there as a witness for you, but that was scary even with Jackson beside me."

"Thank you so much for what you did. To you and Jackson."

"Of course, Ivy. I knew you couldn't have done what they accused you of. Have they found the woman?"

"I don't think so."

"Well, they will. The Society always does in the end."

I think about the comment The Councilor had made about the second attempt on Santiago's life. "Can I ask you something?"

"Sure." She takes a bite of a cookie.

"The fire a few years ago where a lot of members died, was that a gas leak?"

"That's what they say but..." She shrugs a shoulder. "Who knows. I've asked Jackson, but he's pretty tight-lipped. So many rules."

"Tell me about it. How long have you been married?"

"Just over a year."

"Oh, I didn't realize it was so recent."

"No? Hasn't Mercedes filled you in?" she asks,

saying Mercedes's name with a tone that doesn't hide how she feels.

"Mercedes and I aren't exactly friends. She hates me, in fact."

"Well, that makes two of us then! We'll have to toast on that once Benjamin has vacated the premises."

"Why doesn't she like you?"

She glances at the door, then back at me. "Are you up for a walk?"

"Absolutely."

She puts her tea down. I finish my coffee and do the same. We get our coats on and step out into the garden arm in arm. She glances toward one of the back windows and waves.

I turn to find Jackson standing there looking out. He raises his hand in a less enthusiastic wave.

"It's Holton. That man always puts Jackson in a bad mood."

"Holton?"

"Cornelius Holton," she says in a haughty accent. "I can't stand him, honestly. Gives me the creeps."

"Me too."

"You know him?"

"I wish I didn't. Tell me about Mercedes."

"You really don't know any of this?"

I shake my head.

"You had to have felt the tension when Jackson

and I came to your house the other day. Between Santiago and Jackson?"

"You'd have to be dead not to feel that. What's the story?"

"Mercedes had her eye on Jackson. They dated a long time ago even though that's not technically allowed. I think they had some make-out sessions is about the extent of it."

"Mercedes and Jackson?" I'm shocked.

"I know. She's an ice queen."

"You're being nice."

"Well, my family only moved to New Orleans less than two years ago. We're from Atlanta originally. I guess by then Mercedes and Jackson, although not engaged, were officially courting right up until the night he saw me."

"What?"

"It was my family's first event at IVI in New Orleans."

"Love at first sight?"

"It's what Jackson says." Her eyes get shiny, and I feel goose bumps rise on my arms. "For me too, though." She doesn't say it in a gloating way. I think she's just in love with her husband.

"Anyway, we met that night briefly, and by the next week, he'd broken it off with Mercedes. He told me he'd been wanting to for a while, but she wouldn't accept it. She wasn't happy about the break, obviously. And again, I don't blame her, but it's not like something like that can be helped. And she's been pretty awful since."

"Awful to you?"

Colette nods. "I don't exactly have an abundance of friends at The Society, at least not among the women."

"Well, I like you."

She smiles, shrugging a shoulder. "Mercedes has done everything she can to freeze me out, and her family ranks higher than Jackson's, so you know, the sheep go along."

"I'm sorry to hear that."

"It doesn't matter. Those women are too snooty for me anyway. Anyhow, the week we met, Jackson was at my door asking my father's permission to court me."

"Are you serious?"

"You know how things work with IVI. It's so old-fashioned. I hope you don't think—"

"What would I think? My brother told me I'd be marrying a perfect stranger days before our wedding."

"You didn't know Santiago at all?"

"Well, he worked with my father. He was close with him when I was younger so I'd seen him around. We'd barely had a conversation though. But I want to hear about you and Jackson. I have to admit, the night of the gala, I'd assumed he was some ogre for making you wear those shoes and be out late when you're so...so pregnant."

"Jackson?" She giggles. "Nah, that's his Society face." She makes a face herself at that. "He's just a big teddy bear behind closed doors."

"He sounds great, actually. You seem very happy."

"I am. I love him. I'm *in love* with him. But aren't you? With Santiago, I mean?"

"Um..." I look away as we walk, and I think about how to answer. "Our relationship is a little different. I mean, we didn't start like you and Jackson."

"No, I guess not. But you're happy, right? I mean, love is hard in these arranged marriages. At least right at first. But you care about him, right?"

I nod. It's true. I do.

She tugs me closer and smiles wide as we pick up the pace. "I think it's more than that, Ivy."

"What do you mean?"

"I have eyes in my head. I've seen how he looks at you."

"How he looks at me?"

She nods.

"Well, Santiago is...complicated."

"That he is."

"Do you know the history between my family and Santiago's?" I ask.

"What do you mean?"

"I don't know. Just..." I turn to her. "I guess I don't

know why he chose me. He can have anyone. Even with...what happened." The scars. The skull face tattoo. "I'm certainly not elevating him within The Society."

"He was close with your dad. And now that he's taken over his care, maybe he felt—"

I stop. "What did you say?"

She stops too and looks at me, forehead wrinkling.

"He took over my dad's care?" I ask.

"Didn't you know?"

I shake my head.

She glances nervously at the office window then back. "I probably wasn't supposed to say anything. I'm sorry."

"I won't tell. Just please tell me. I feel so lost. I don't know what's going on. I feel like there are moments I'm so close to him, but then, I'm so completely in the dark. I don't understand...I guess it just doesn't make sense he'd choose me without some motive, and at least in the beginning he hated me, Colette. I think he married me to torment me, and..." I shake my head and Colette pulls me in for a hug.

"It's okay, Ivy. I didn't mean to upset you. I just had overheard Jackson say something to someone the other day. I thought you knew. Please don't say anything. I don't want Jackson to know I know."

I draw back. "Of course not. Is he okay at least? My dad?"

"I think so. Nothing bad happened or anything. Haven't you been to see him?"

I shake my head, my mind elsewhere now. My chest feeling constricted. The memory of last night in his office, him inside me, the things I felt and the knowledge that it wasn't enough and that it wouldn't be enough. And that it would break me.

Santiago isn't the man I make him out to be. The man I want him to be. He's had an agenda since the first day, and he hasn't made a secret of it. If my heart breaks, it's my own fault.

29

IVY

Santiago doesn't return home that night or the next, and he doesn't call either. Or if he does, it's not to talk to me.

And all the while, all I can do is make up scenarios to try to understand why he would take over my father's care. What it means. And why he hasn't told me. I feel isolated and alone, and when I ask if I can at least call my sister, Antonia only gives me a pitying look and tells me I must ask Santiago.

It's an infuriating circle because I can't ask him if I don't have any way to talk to him.

I want to trust him. I know it will take time for us to trust each other, but what Colette told me and then this, his absence, combined with my isolation from my family, from anyone outside these walls, it makes it hard.

By the third night, I'm worked up and feeling

more angry than anything else. At least anger is better. Anger means I'll fight, not roll over and let him plow over me.

When the staff have all gone to bed, I make my way down to his office. It's locked again. I guess Antonia has a key. But I know another way in, and I go through the library to that secret entrance. I'm not even really hiding anymore. Or at least I tell myself that. I need to know what's going on with my dad. How could Abel have approved Santiago taking over his care? And why hasn't Santiago told me? Why hide it from me?

His office is dark apart from the monitors, and it's been cleaned since I was last here. I set the notebook with the sketches on his desk and sit in his chair. If I concentrate, when I inhale, I swear I can smell his aftershave.

I take a deep breath in and tell myself I have no choice but to do what I'm about to do. Even though just a few nights ago the thought of looking through his things felt so wrong, tonight feels different. But a part of me wishes he'd tell me, too. Wishes he'd just be honest with me.

I pull open the top drawer at the center of the desk, but this one has some pens in it and a few sheets of heavy paper embossed with his crest at the top center with envelopes to match. I close it and try the next one. It slides out easily, but it, too, like the first one, is neat and almost empty. Not even a paper-clip out of place. I lean down to peer at the far back, but there's nothing there.

The third drawer is locked as are all three on the other side. If there's anything here, I won't find it unless I break into them.

Standing, I go to the antique armoire against the far wall and open it. I don't expect to find files, and I don't. Instead, I see two unopened bottles of the scotch he likes to drink, some crystal tumblers, and, on the shelf beside those, a glass box that looks a lot like the one he keeps that mask in in my room. The one he hasn't made me wear since the night I passed out.

My heart races, and my brain tries to tell me that what I'm seeing can't be. Because it would be too humiliating. Too horrible.

I open the lid. It's not locked. Maybe it's my imagination, but I swear I smell the coppery scent of blood as I take out the neatly folded, unwashed sheets. The bloody sheets from our wedding night.

I try to make sense of this. Why would he have this? Why would he keep it? But then I remember. After he'd taken me and I'd had that awful mask on my head, I remember what he'd muttered that my mind hadn't quite processed, not then.

"I wonder if Eli will be pleased to see how I bled his daughter."

Is he planning on giving this to my father if or when he wakes? Still? After everything?

I drop the sheet and push my hands into my hair. God. I am a fool! I wonder if he's laughing at me now wherever he is. This fool that is his wife.

"Fuck you, Santiago!" I pull the sheet out of the glass box so violently that the box drops to the floor when a corner of the cloth catches. I'm glad for the carpet, or it would have shattered, I'm sure, but as I bend to pull the sheet free, I see a single long crack across the bottom of the box.

I don't care. I'm not hiding from him. I'll tell him I burned the damned thing. Because that is exactly what I plan to do with it.

So, I leave the glass box where it is and make my way back through the dark house. I'm fully aware as I head to the back door that he has cameras everywhere and will see what I've done, but again, I remind myself that I don't care because he obviously doesn't. Colette was wrong. What she thinks she saw in the way he looks at me isn't anything but ownership. Possession. Hate.

I slip on the pair of shoes I'd left at the door earlier when I'd gone for a walk, unlock and open the back door, pausing when I do, wincing as I wait for an alarm. But nothing comes. I'm not actually sure if the house has an alarm, but if so, it's not on.

The night is black, moonless, and cloudless, and it's cold. My sweater will have to be enough, though, and before I know it, I find myself at the doors of the small chapel. When I push one open, I see the red of the Tabernacle lamp and step inside.

The door closes behind me, and I'm alone inside the old stone church. The place has an eerie feel to it now, and it's no less cold than it was outside.

I walk to the front of the church and drop the sheet on the stone altar. I pick up the box of matches to light more of the altar candles feeling less sure of what I'm about to do now than I had just a few minutes ago.

Once more candles are lit, I see the photographs on the altar, and although Leandro is an adult in the framed photo, I can still see the child he was in that photo in Santiago's book. I shift my gaze to his father and meet his cold eyes. They stare at me from inside the frame, accusing me from beyond the grave.

It's his fault Santiago is the way he is.

And I wonder if we do have a baby together, what kind of father will Santiago be if the only role model he had was this cold, brutal man?

What kind of father could he be if he can do to the mother of his child what he plans to do with this soiled sheet?

"You are a fool," I tell myself and light one more match. I set it to the bloody sheet and watch the flame take and spread.

30

SANTIAGO

Exhaustion is settling heavily into my bones by the time I pull through the gates of The Manor. The fresh sting of my sister's betrayal has left me empty. Vacant. I need sleep and a moment of peace.

Ivy will be upstairs. Soft and warm and available as a balm to the chaos in my wretched soul. The thought of being inside her, close to her, is the only solace I can find in the current landscape of reality.

Those thoughts drive me forward, sustaining my last shred of sanity as I park the car and drag my rigid body from the metal frame. The scars on my torso are aching tonight. A pain that surges again during the most inconvenient times, threatening to incapacitate me. My limbs are weighted down like lead, causing my feet to drag as I turn toward the front steps. In my desperation to get inside my sanctuary and collapse, I almost miss the sight of Marco darting across the garden on the east side. He catches sight of me at the same time I notice him, and we both freeze.

"What's going on?" I ask.

"Mrs. De La Rosa," he answers tightly. "She's in the chapel, sir, and the groundskeeper informed me—"

Without waiting to hear the rest of his explanation, I pivot and move in that direction. Adrenaline floods my veins in response to the urgency in Marco's tone. Whatever it is can't be good.

My natural inclination is to suspect the worst. Someone has come for her. Another threat. Another scheme. Another hidden enemy I have been unaware of. My fists clench at my sides as murderous thoughts plow through my mind at lightning speed.

I will kill anyone who even thinks of touching her.

The chapel door screeches open beneath the weight of my palm, my haste pushing me forward with only one thought in mind. I have to get to Ivy. But the moment I see the flickering flames up on the altar, I stop short, my breath seizing in my lungs.

It feels like a hallucination. Another vivid nightmare. Because this can't be real. That can't be my wife up on the altar, burning what I soon realize is a length of fabric. She turns to me, the shadows dancing over her features as an orange glow reflects in her eyes.

A sharp pain lances through my chest, and I stumble forward, grasping at the end of the pews to catch my balance. Smoke suffocates the oxygen, a putrid smell that never leaves my thoughts. My eyes shutter closed as I try to focus on the present, fighting the past that keeps trying to drag me back to hell. When I open them again, I can just make out the faces of my father and brother staring back at me.

"No!" I roar.

I'm back there again. In the midst of the flames, dragging my body through the rubble trying desperately to get to them. Sharp metal scrapes against my torso, forcing an animalistic sound from my throat as I try and fail to push it away. It cuts me deep, and flames lick along my clothing, singeing my skin. The smell of burned hair and flesh nauseate me, but I have to keep going, for them.

Footsteps move past me, echoing across the floor like heavy artillery.

"Get back!" someone yells.

I try to see through the smoke. The flames. The pieces of bodies around me. But I never can. A cough explodes through the air and sweat drips down my neck as a familiar voice calls out to me.

"Take her outside."

Heat seeps into the fibrous tissue of my scars, deepening the ache. The itch. My brother and father aren't here anymore. I can't see them. And when reality yanks me back, it's Ivy standing in front of me, wide-eyed and horrified.

"Take her outside!" Marco yells, shoving her in my direction. "I'll put this out. Go!"

It takes me a moment to find my balance and re-orient. And slowly, the pieces start to fall into place as I dissect one nightmare from another. My fingers curl around Ivy's arm like an iron trap, and she cries out as I drag her from the chapel out into the fresh air.

She yanks away from me, coughing and trying to catch her breath as I blink at her, trying to understand. Chest heaving, venom filling my veins, souring any sweetness there may have been between us. My traitorous fucking wife.

"What did you do?" I growl.

She wipes her face and shakes her head, refusing to answer. Refusing to look at me. She may as well have poured accelerant on my already volatile mood.

"What. Did. You. Do?" I snarl, capturing her around the arms and shaking her.

Her mouth falls open, the picture of horror as she looks up at me like she doesn't recognize me. And I suppose she doesn't. She hasn't met this monster yet. She hasn't known a rage like she's just provoked.

"Answer me!" I roar, my breath whipping strands of hair across her face.

"Let me go!" She hurls her words back at me, shoving against me with all her might.

"Let you go?" I mock her pathetic words. "Let you go? Haven't you figured it out yet? I'm not letting you go until you're fucking dead."

"I hate you!" she screams. "I would rather die than stay here with you."

"That can be arranged," I answer darkly.

Her lip trembles as she looks up at me, eyes shining in the moonlight. "Then do it. Quit threatening me and just do it."

I grab her by the throat and drag her forward, forcing her onto her toes. "Don't tempt me."

Whatever vitriol she has left is choked down by my fingers as I tighten them around her neck. I'm a raging bull, and any softness I may have had for her has abandoned me in the face of this fresh betrayal. When I look at her right now, the only thing I can feel is disgust.

Disgust that I could ever care for a Moreno. That I would ever think she could be loyal. That she wouldn't have taken every opportunity to stab me in the back and exploit me like she's just proven she can.

"You don't deserve the De La Rosa name," I grit

out as she fights for her balance, raking her nails over my hands. "You don't deserve my mark. I should cut it out of your skin."

She whimpers and tries again to speak, but her words are suffocated under the weight of my palm. When I finally release her, she's coughing again, but there isn't an ounce of sympathy left for her.

Marco opens the door to the chapel and nods at me. "The fire is out. I'll get someone in here to clean up the mess." He pauses momentarily, his eyes darting to Ivy and narrowing slightly. "But you should know the pictures of your father and brother are ruined."

Ivy sucks in a sharp breath and flinches when I grab her by the hair, hauling her body in front of mine.

"Thank you, Marco."

He turns away, and I force Ivy forward, her knees nearly buckling as she stumbles to put one foot in front of the other.

"What are you doing?" she croaks.

"You want to burn down the memory of my family?" I ask. "It isn't enough that you've already destroyed them?"

"Me?" She tries to turn her head to look at me, and I tighten my grip on her, enforcing her stillness.

"You're a Moreno, aren't you?" I sneer. "You've just proven it. You may as well have spit on their graves."

"That wasn't what I was doing," she whispers.

"Lies," I sneer. "That's all that ever pours from your lips. Fucking lies."

When she tries to protest, I squeeze my free hand over her jaw, pinching it shut. "As far as I'm concerned, you don't have a voice anymore."

She shudders against me, tears splashing against my fingers as I march her into the house. When the door slams behind us, I pause in the foyer, squeezing my fingers between the seams of her shirt and tearing them apart. She fights me at every turn as I repeat the process on her leggings, shredding them with my bare hands while she kicks and slaps at me, screaming out a rage she wishes was equal to mine. Her lace underwear and bra are the last to go, and I discard them in a pile onto the floor and force her onto her knees.

"Crawl," I command, tangling my fist in her hair.

She grunts out in frustration as I move forward, leaving her no choice but to crawl along beside me, all the way up the stairs, bruising her knees as she howls like a wounded animal.

"I'm not doing this anymore!" she yells, coming to a dead stop at the top of the landing. "You can't make me do this."

"No?" I release her hair and cock my head to the side, studying her. "You think I can't make you do whatever I want?"

She tries to scramble to her feet, and I force her

down against the marble, mounting her body and pressing her face against the cold floor. She arches up like a cat, only to grunt in pain when I exert all of my weight against her.

"Tell me again what you won't do," I whisper in her ear.

"I hate you!" she sobs.

"So you've told me about a dozen times." I glower at her. "Do you think I care? Do you think it makes one goddamned difference to me what a Moreno thinks? Your insults are pathetic and weak, just like your bloodline."

For a split second, she tries to look at me, and I refuse to let her. Dragging myself up, I seize her by the ankle and tug her along, her naked body sliding over the marble floor as she claws at it desperately, scrambling for purchase. That fight lasts all of a minute before she's twisting and flipping onto her back, her legs splaying apart in the chaos, baring her pussy as she tries to use her other heel as a brake. When my eyes move between her legs, she flails, trying to squeeze them together as if that act could save her from her indecency.

All of her fighting is for naught, and when we reach my room, she is breathless, too spent from the struggle over something so simplistic she has little energy left for what comes next. Her body bounces against the mattress when I yank her up and toss her onto it. Using the lengths of rope from when I tied her to my bedposts to tattoo her face, I push her face down and tie her hands behind her back and stretch her legs wide, securing the ropes to each ankle and forcing her onto her knees to keep her in that position.

"Santiago," she chokes out. "Just let me go. Just send me away. Please. I can't bear this hatred from you anymore."

"You will bear it." I lean down to look into her face, annoyed by her foolish request. "Because you earned it."

I unbuckle my belt, and she starts to cry in earnest as I slide it from the loops. She pauses her simpering to glance at me over her shoulder again, and I bark at her.

"Turn around."

"No."

"Very well." I offer her a cruel smile. "Have it your way."

I tug the pillowcase from the pillow and force it over her head, obscuring her face from my view. If I can't see her, I can't succumb to her tricks. Not anymore.

I retrieve the belt, gliding the leather edge along the curve of her hip before I fold it in my palms and crack the loop against her ass. She jolts forward, a scream piercing the silence as red blooms across her skin.

I crack the belt against her again, colliding with

her thigh this time. Another scream erupts from her throat, and I savor that sound, creating a beautiful, haunting melody as a pattern emerges. The leather snaps against her skin, a trail of heat blazing over her swollen, red skin as I cover her ass, thighs, and calves with the evidence of my rage. Every time she tries to edge farther away, I yank her back, forcing her endurance.

She cries until her tears dry up and her throat is raw, and her ass is so sore she won't be able to sit for a week without being reminded of the consequences of her actions. But it isn't enough. It still isn't enough.

I can't look at her without a fresh wave of fury rolling through me. My breath is ragged as I loop the belt around the pillowcase covering her throat and latch it, leaving one end in my fist as I tug down my zipper with the other.

"You can't even look at me," she clips out. "That's why you're doing this. You can hide my face, but it won't change anything, Santiago. I can promise you that."

"Stop. Fucking. Talking."

I free my throbbing cock, jerking it in my fist as my eyes move over her pussy, and then up to her ass. I splay her apart with my palms, and she makes a strained sound in her throat as I slide my dick against her. Once. Twice. Three times before I circle her clit with the head, toying with her until she's squirming against me unconsciously in half pleasure, half pain. Her ass is tender. I can tell when it brushes against the fabric of my trousers, and she whines. It's a glowing red ember against my white knuckles when they graze her curves, and when I hoist her back up, her body begins to sag into the bed again. Exhaustion is wrapping its ugly claws around her, but I'm not even close to being done with her yet.

I slide my cock against her, smearing it with her traitorous arousal. Even when she hates me, she wants this. She's as fucked up as I am.

I wrap my fingers around the leather belt end and tug, arching her head back as I slam inside her with one deep thrust. She screams, a shrill sound that vibrates my eardrums and rattles my cock. In and out, I slide against her, soaking my rigid dick with her arousal.

Her fingers curl behind her back, shoulders squeezing as she struggles to hold herself up without the use of her arms. I release the belt and she collapses again, panting against the pillowcase covering her face. When I slide my fingers against her, she arches into my touch, unaware she's even doing it, but freezes when I circle the tight forbidden hole I have not yet sampled. I press against her with my finger, pushing past the barrier as she tries to jerk forward, out of my reach. My hand on her hip stills her, and I slide my finger in and out as she begins to breathe harder, faster.

"Santiago," she gasps when I pull my finger away and replace it with the head of my cock, nudging against her.

"You can address me as Dominus et Deuce." I squeeze her ass hard as I push past the tight barrier. "Your lord and your god."

She falls completely still, completely silent as I slowly bury my cock deep into her ass. Her knuckles are white, tears soaking through the pillowcase as she gulps in mouthfuls of air.

"Oh God." She bucks against me as I pull back and start to thrust forward again. "That's... too... I... Santiago."

Her broken fragments turn to garbled incoherence as I close my eyes and settle into a steady rhythm, rocking back and pivoting forward, stretching her body around my dick to accommodate me. She's clenching against me, desperate for stimulation where she needs it the most, all while she squeals and groans and mutters indecipherable curses.

"You don't get to come," I bite out through gritted teeth. "Don't even try it."

"I'm sorry about the pictures!" she shouts. "That wasn't my intention."

"Your words are meaningless." I thrust hard, fingers digging into her. "They always have been."

"You don't mean that."

I fuck her harder. Angrier. Pinching her skin as I use her like a fuck toy, thrusting, grunting, rolling my hips while she folds under the weight of my palms, sinking lower and lower, only for me to yank her back up.

"I can't stay up anymore," she cries out, choking on her tears.

"You will." I punctuate my words with two quick, deep thrusts, hoisting her ass up into my hands and holding half her body in the air while I fuck her into my oblivion.

Shudders move through me, muscles tightening, ears ringing, and finally, I slam into her one last time, unraveling. Filling her with my come.

She trembles when I release her, dropping her back onto the mattress, half limp. Branded by my belt and my hands and my seed leaking from her body. For a long moment, I stand there, catching my breath as I watch her. This woman I can't trust. The woman who has managed to get inside my head. The darkest spaces of my mind. The emptiest spaces of my chest cavity. The beating heart no other soul has ever dared to trespass. And at that moment, I realize two things.

I hate her.

Yet I feel something else for her too. Something inexplicable. Something dangerous.

Something I can never allow myself to feel.

With tremulous hands, I release her ties and the belt around her throat, leaving the pillowcase over her face. My tone is ice cold, almost demonic as I give her one final command.

"Get out of my sight."

31

SANTIAGO

Days pass, turning to nights, and then, inconceivably, to weeks. I spend them locked in my office, alternating between work and poring over every detail of the reports that come in on Abel. He's a loose end. Something that needs to be dealt with. A fucking Moreno who doesn't deserve to breathe the same air as the rest of humanity. I know what needs to happen. I dream about it all night and all day. Bleeding him out slowly. Torturing him until he gives me the answers I want. The confirmation of everything I know to be true. Their blood is a stain on society, a systemic disease, and the only way to cure it is to cut it out.

Every day, reports arrive on Eli's progress in the hospital. He is regaining his mobility, recovering slowly. I'm told he demands to see me. Demands answers on the whereabouts of his family. And one day, he will have them.

This has always been my plan. My intention. But even behind a locked door, stowed safely out of sight, my wife manages to poison my thoughts.

I have not seen her since the night of the incident in the chapel. I have not asked her about the broken case or her reason for burning the sheet because it doesn't matter. She lit the fire on my altar and in my soul with one intention. To wound an already wounded animal. I am too proud to admit that on some level, she succeeded.

I'm drowning myself in scotch, trying to forget her. Trying to get back to a time and a place when I didn't think about what her feelings might be when she learns the fates of her brother and father. The fates delivered by the same hands that touch her at night. The same man whose mark she will bear for eternity.

She will never want to look at me again. Slowly, I am coming to understand that. But there can be no alternative.

"You look like hell."

My eyes snap up to find Judge standing in the doorway, his concern evident on his face.

"Nothing new," I remark dryly.

He enters the room and examines the space. The scattered folders on my desk. The scotch from my breakfast and lunch. The monitors streaming a steady pattern of figures in front of me.

"You shouldn't be so hard on yourself," he says solemnly.

When I don't respond, he takes a seat across from me, studying me.

"Mercedes is fine," he assures me. "She couldn't be in better care."

"I didn't ask for a progress update."

My fingers tap the glass of amber liquid. Judge watches me with the precision he is known for. He has always had an eerie ability to get under your skin, as if he can see into your soul and read your secrets like an open book. It's what makes him so effective at his job.

"You may not have asked, but I believe it would do you well to know. She is healthy and safe. In time, I have no doubt she will blossom in my care."

I nod tightly, unwilling to admit that he's right. It does relieve me to hear it. But that relief is temporary at best because it changes nothing. Nothing will ever be the same again.

"Have you been to see Eli?" Judge asks.

"No." I bring the glass tumbler to my lips, drinking the liquid in one long swallow.

"You always knew it was going to come down to this," he says. "Why put it off any longer?"

When I look up at him, the torment must be evident on my face.

"Oh." He frowns.

"Whatever you think you see, you don't. Don't make something out of nothing."

"I didn't say a word." He scrubs his hand along his stubbled jaw.

"You never have to."

He chuckles a little, but his mood sobers after a moment. When he rises to his feet again, he glances at the open sketchbook on my desk. The image of Ivy left half-finished.

"It seems you have a lot to consider, so I won't waste any more of your time. But if I may..."

When I glance up at him, he offers me the closest thing to solace I have ever witnessed on his face.

"The choices are clear. But I think the question is, which can you live without? Your revenge... or your wife's affection?"

He doesn't wait for me to answer, and long after he's gone, I'm still staring at the door, that question hanging over my head.

32

IVY

It's been two weeks since he locked me in here again. The light blocked again. I know because I'm counting meals. Three a day.

I'm angry. I'm tired. I'm tired of being so fucking angry. So confused. Heartsick.

I keep going back and forth with what I'll do when he does finally come to see me. *If* he comes. This time is different than before. He's different.

Maybe he's heartsick too.

No. He's not heartsick. You can't be heartsick if you don't have a heart. And I need to stop being an idiot when it comes to Santiago.

I get up off the bed. At least I'm not naked. Maybe he forgot to lock the closet. Or maybe he just doesn't care as long as he doesn't have to see me.

"Get out of my sight."

I shake my head. I want to forget his words. The hate inside them. Forget his disgust of me.

What will I do when he finally comes? Will I explain what I was doing? Burning the sheet? I didn't mean to destroy the pictures of his father or his brother. I didn't care about those. Although it's just as bad that I didn't care about them, isn't it? But I'll explain how I felt when he left for days when I thought he'd be back that night.

I'll tell him I'm sorry.

But then I get angry. Why should I apologize? What have I done to him? Nothing that validates what he did to me. Using his belt like that? Marking me for days. And then how he took me.

Shame, anger, and hurt war inside me. I tell myself that he's the one who should get down on his knees and beg for my forgiveness, yet the longer he keeps me here, the more I think it's my fault. The more I think I'm the one who should kneel to him.

I am so confused. So sick of this.

And I know one thing for sure. I can't do this much longer.

I stand at the bathroom mirror. I look a mess, my hair unbrushed and a tangle of knots. I showered a few days ago, but I don't even care. I'm going crazy in here. He won't let Antonia bring my meals. It's another girl who is too scared to even look at me when she delivers the new trays and takes away the old.

I've had exactly one communication from him during these weeks. A threat. If I don't eat, he will have Marco force-feed me. The act itself is violent enough but what hurts the most is that he'd send Marco.

Why the fuck does that hurt me? God. What is wrong with me? Why can't I hate this man who hates me? Because even when I tell him I do, even when I scream the words at him, I don't. It's like there's this sick, masochistic side of me when it comes to my husband. I want him.

And I want him to want me.

"Fuck!"

I pull at my hair, trying to make sense of my thoughts, my feelings. It's all this isolation. This darkness. Solitary confinement.

I pick up the empty dish I'd set on the counter after flushing the food and go back into the bedroom. Antonia may have figured out I'm not eating, but the girl hasn't. I wonder if he's pleased with himself when he hears the report that since his warning, I've licked my plate clean. Asshole.

I'm tempted to smash the dish against the wall, but last time I did that, I cut my feet on the shards I couldn't see in the too dim bedroom. So, I set it down on the tray instead and go to the window using the dull knife to try to dislodge the board covering the glass. It's pointless, I know, but it's something.

A key slides into the lock on my door, and I turn, hating myself for that little swell of hope that maybe it'll be him. After what he did to me, how do I still feel hope? I'm not even sure what was worse, the humiliation of it, of how he took me, or the pain of the whipping that lasted for days afterward.

But when I see the girl again, it's like someone's just pricked that bubble of hope with a pin. My shoulders slump, and I hug my arms around my middle, feeling cold and alone and unwanted.

"Is he coming?" I ask her.

She's been instructed not to talk to me. Maybe not even to look at me.

A man I don't know stands at the door as she sets the new tray down.

"Is he coming?" I push, more forceful this time. More angry.

Nothing. She picks up the old tray.

"Look at me! Fucking look at me!" I scream, lunging to grab her wrist, sending the tray toppling, empty dishes scattering. "I'm here! Look at me!"

The man is on me in an instant, backing me into the wall and keeping me there as the girl drops to her knees to clean up. I hear her sniffle. She's crying.

"Just tell me if he's coming. Please. Tell him I can't stay here any longer. Tell him I'm dying. Tell him—" A choke cuts off my sentence. The girl scurries away, and the man releases me. "Please," I try. I'm not sure they hear that. It's a pathetically small sound, and even the door closing and the lock turning are louder.

I sit down where I am and lean my back against the wall, hugging my knees to my chest. The smell of the meat turns my stomach. I breathe through my mouth as the wave of nausea slowly subsides, and as soon as I can, I get to my feet and take the dish into the bathroom to flush it. The smell lingers, though.

Switching on the tap, I wash my hands and my face. My hands tremble as I pick up a towel. I open the medicine cabinet and take out the bottle of aspirin Mercedes had left the night of the gala. I twist off the lid, drop two into my palm and swallow them dry. I'm just closing the lid when I think of something and stop.

I remember when Mercedes had left the whole bottle. I'd thought I was desperate then, but I wasn't. Not like now. Because this isn't going to change. He hates me. Even knowing I didn't lie to him, knowing that whoever it is that tried to kill him was willing to let me die too, he still hates me.

Santiago will always hate me, and I don't even know why.

I empty the contents of the bottle into my palm, watching as some spill over and drop onto the floor.

How many would I need for it to cause kidney failure? For it to kill me.

Do I want to die?

No, of course I don't want to die. This is stupid.

I pour the pills back into the bottle, but I can't get the lid back on with my hands trembling like they are. I carry the bottle back into the bedroom and sit on my unmade bed. The sheets haven't been changed in two weeks. He's really leaving me to rot. I wonder why he bothers to feed me. But I know that part. If I'm pregnant, he'll want his heir. Not his baby, but his heir.

Would he cut the baby out of me and let me bleed to death once he has what he wants?

God. I'm truly losing my mind.

I lean my head back and look up at the camera pointed right at me. I stare at it, but he's not watching. I know because the little blinking light went out a few days after he put me in here. He doesn't care about me. Why do I need him to? Why do I care? I should be glad he's abandoned me.

Using the back of my hand to wipe away my tears, I reach into the bottle to fish out two more pills. I swallow them. Then another two. And another two. I cough those up, though, and have to get up to drink the water the girl brought. And I keep swallowing, digging out two at a time until the bottle is empty.

My heart races, a sick feeling in my stomach at what I've done. But what else is there to do? Slowly rot? At least this way, he can't control it. He can't decide it.

I let the empty bottle drop to the carpet and walk

backward to the bed to lie down. When I roll over, I see my sister's letters scattered beside me through the haze of tears that are so much a part of my life now. Every day. Every day too many tears. I am so tired of it. I've read the letters a hundred times. I can't think about how she'll feel when she hears what I did. I can't bear how confused she'll be. How hurt.

I think of Hazel when she left. How I felt. How there was a time I hated her. I felt betrayed and left behind. It's what I'll do to Eva, and I hate myself for it. I don't want to die, do I?

So I get up and go to the door. I try it, but I know it's locked. I call out, but no one answers, and I don't know what I want. I go to the desk, opening the drawers until I find a pen and some of that De La Rosa letterhead. I tear off their family crest, crushing that part and dropping it at my feet, then return to the bed where I lie down again and set the paper beside me.

When I start to write, the pen punctures the paper at the *Dear*. The aspirin can't be working that fast, though. This is probably exhaustion. Starvation. I feel dizzy, a different sort of dizzy than usual, so I close my eyes for a minute. But when I open them again, I know it's been longer than a minute.

I feel sweaty, disoriented, and heavy. I sit up, squinting against the double vision. I swing my legs off the bed, and a wave of nausea hits me so hard, I drop to my hands and knees and vomit before I can even think about trying to make it to the bathroom. Another wave comes, and I throw up some more. After dry heaving, I sit back, one hand on my belly, the other on my forehead, my breathing shallow and labored.

My ears are ringing, and I swear I can hear my own heart beat too fast.

A noise at the door has me turn my head, but when it opens, the room spins, the girl freezing when she sees me, her mouth falling open.

I think I reach out for her and try to say something. The man is inside, the look on his face panicked. The girl screams, and the man calls out for help, but that ringing is too loud. I can't seem to keep my eyes open, and the last thing I see is the empty bottle of aspirin rolling under the desk.

33

IVY

I'm not in my bedroom anymore. The smell is different. The sounds. The light. I lie still and listen and try to remember. Something tugs at my arm, but when I try to pull away, I can't, and the first thing I think is I'm back in that cellar.

Panic grips me.

"It's all right," a woman says. "Shh. Nothing to worry about, love." She has an English accent. "There you go. Just relax."

I try to open my eyes, but the lids are too heavy, and a moment later, I'm gone again. The light is different when I next wake to the sound of men's voices talking quietly.

"Dehydration in addition. She vomited most of it on her own from the sound of it."

"Why is she restrained?" This voice I recognize.

Santiago. He's here. He's come back to me.

I want to call out to him. Touch him.

"She tried to pull the IV out. We'll remove those as soon as we can."

IV?

"When will she wake up?"

"When she's ready. Her body is exhausted. It's working twice as hard now. Give her time, Santiago." I hear affection in the voice of this man.

"You're sure about that?" Santiago asks. He sounds worried.

"Blood tests don't lie."

I hear him exhale. "Thank you, Doctor."

Doctor.

I realize what that smell is. Why the light is different. I'm surprised I didn't recognize it before. I'm at the hospital.

A door opens and closes, and someone moves, footsteps coming closer. I smell his aftershave over the antiseptic, and despite all that's happened and all that he's done to me, it's a comfort.

Fingers brush my forehead, then my cheek.

I turn my face into his touch and feel a chill as the blanket is pulled away. But he's touching me again then, touching me gently, fingers feather-light over my arm, my belly. A hand laid flat there, big and warm.

I want to open my eyes, but I can't. I'm so tired. I try to move my hand at least, try to touch his, but something doesn't let me.

"Shh," he says. "Sleep." The blanket is tucked up around my shoulders again, warm but not as warm as when he touches me, and I feel myself drift even though I feel him move away. I want to tell him to stay with me. And when I manage to momentarily open my eyes in the dim light coming from a machine to my right, I see him sitting in the chair across from mine, one ankle crossed over the other knee, eyes dark and intent, watching me.

I WAKE up because I'm hungry. Ravenous. Someone is humming, and the light is suddenly too bright.

I groan, turn away, blink, but then it's dimmed again.

"There she is. I know it's early, but you need to wake up. You need to eat. Doctor's orders. Come now, love."

Opening my eyes, I see the needles and tube sticking out of one arm. "What...?" But it's when I try to pull at my arms that the real panic sets in.

The door opens, closes.

I look up, meet his eyes, and freeze. He freezes too.

"You can go, nurse," Santiago says, not taking his eyes off me.

"I'll just give her—"

"I said go."

My gaze shifts to the elderly nurse standing beside my bed, looking up at Santiago's face, riveted by it.

He's wearing a hat, keeping it in shadow. At least half of it. It's daytime. I see the light coming in from around the blinds. It's not like him to be out during the day.

"I should make sure she eats, sir."

"I am capable of taking care of my wife. My family."

Family? That's an odd way to say it.

The nurse nods, glancing once at me before hurrying away. I watch her go, and when the door closes, I turn slowly back to find Santiago's eyes still locked on me.

I don't speak right away. I can't. I try to pull my hands up again, but the leather restraints don't allow me to move.

"What's happening?"

He pulls up the chair and sits down, taking off his hat and setting it on the table beside my bed. My heart races, my stomach in knots as I watch him roll the tray containing my breakfast closer, something dark in his eyes, something hard in the way his hand is wrapped around the tray.

"You're going to eat. That's what's happening." He picks up the bowl and spoons up some oatmeal. He brings it to my mouth. "Open."

I do.

"Swallow," he says when he pulls the spoon out. Again, I do.

We don't speak until I've eaten the whole bowl and drank the juice out of the little straw he holds to my mouth.

"Why am I tied to the bed?"

"Where did you get the pills?"

"I...I didn't mean...I changed my mind."

He raises his eyebrows. "Did you?"

Did I?

"You changed your mind about dying? Well, lucky for you, you vomited most of the aspirin, or it may not have been up to you." He sounds angry. "Do you know what happens with aspirin poisoning?"

I turn my face to wipe it on the shoulder of the hospital gown. "Please untie me."

"Answer my question. Do you know?"

I do. Even if you change your mind, it may be too late for your kidneys. I nod.

"Where did you get the pills?"

"Mercedes left them."

The hand I can see fists and warring emotions darken his features. "I see."

"Please untie me."

He shifts his gaze down to one wrist, and without comment, he undoes the buckle. He then moves to do the same on the other bind.

I watch his dark head as I rub my wrists. "Isn't it what you want?"

He looks at me. "What?"

"Me dead." I feel sick to say it. Feel myself start to tremble with a sudden cold.

He stands, runs a hand through his hair, and shakes his head like he's having some private conversation in his head. He then looks at me again. "You're pregnant, Ivy."

"What?"

"You could have hurt the baby."

"But..." I shake my head, try to remember my last period. Days and weeks all meld together, time lost in my prison where it's always night. "I can't be."

"You are. And you'll have a guard 24/7 once you're home. You will not harm my child again."

"I didn't know. I didn't mean to—"

"You will eat, you will get fresh air, you will exercise. Your body will be a healthy host for my child."

"A host?" I shake my head, hating the hurt inside my chest. "That's all I am?"

His eyes narrow. "You've proven untrustworthy too many times to be anything else."

"How far?"

"Four weeks. Five."

"It's not possible."

He leans down to take my chin in his hand and force my head up. "It is reality. My child grows inside your belly. You will not hurt him again."

Does he think I really wanted to hurt a baby? I tug free of his grip. "Get out." My voice breaks.

"You will never be alone again. Isn't that what you've been whining about?"

"Get out." I can't look at him as my hand moves over my belly, my throat tight, vision blurry with tears. I'm pregnant. I am pregnant.

"Marco will bring you home once you're released later today."

I look at him now. "Your house is not my home. It will never be my home."

His jaw tightens, and he stares at me for a long minute before he relaxes it. "Do you think that matters to me, Ivy?" he asks, head tilted. "Do you think I care even a little bit whether or not you feel at home in my house?"

"The other night, you...What happened to us?"

"Us? What *us* are you referring to?"

"You're not human. Do you know that?"

His eyes narrow, and I watch his Adam's apple work as he swallows. "I know what I am, dear wife." He leans toward me, and I find myself leaning the back of my head into the bed. "I know perfectly well. And more importantly, I know what you are."

34

SANTIAGO

"How is your wife?" Judge greets me in the entryway.

"She's...alive." I swallow and glance over his shoulder, beyond the vast space of his foyer.

The familiar notes of Beethoven's "Moonlight Sonata" are a distant murmur in another part of the house, and it brings me back to another time and place.

"She will come home soon, I hope?" He gestures for me to follow him into the sitting room.

Home.

That word leaves a bitter taste in my mouth. Ivy said my house would never be her home, and I know she's right. Too much has happened. We are living like strangers beneath one roof. A practice that is not uncommon in arranged marriages within The Society. But ours feels wrong. Tainted. And there is no fixing it.

"I believe I made a mistake." The confession spills from my lips freely as I collapse onto the sofa and close my eyes. I'm too exhausted to keep the truth inside.

"How so?" Judge asks.

I blink up at the ceiling. The music changes to a faster, angrier tune.

"I never should have married her."

The words settle over us, dark and heavy, much like the current atmosphere of my life.

"But you did," Judge responds, unmoved by my admission. "Why regret it now?"

I drag a hand over my eyes, attempting to revive myself. But how can I? All I see is Ivy, lying lifeless on the floor. I can't erase that image from my mind. I can't deny I'm responsible for her actions. And logical or not, I can't forgive her for the constant throbbing ache in my chest.

What is this pain? This feeling of suffocation I get when I think of how desperate she was to escape me. I don't recognize it. I don't know how to navigate it or how to make it stop. I've tried, but it won't go away.

She's having my child. Everything is as it should be. But she hates me so much that she would rather kill herself than continue in this life with me. I can't say I should have ever expected anything else. There was never any possibility of changing the rules of the game halfway through.

"This plan was never going to work," I tell Judge. "It was foolish."

The housekeeper appears, asking if I'd like a drink, which I decline. Judge tells her to set dinner for an hour later, and she leaves again. Then he leans back, cocks his head to the side, and studies me.

"You're falling for her."

"Don't be ridiculous." I wave his suggestion away. "This isn't a joke."

"I'm not joking."

When I look at him, I can see that he's not. His face is as serious as ever, and it concerns me.

"You really think me that weak?"

"It's only a weakness if you believe it is." He arches a brow at me. "I think the only real conflict you're having is that you never intended to. But you are. And now you have to face the facts."

"You know I'm not capable of those emotions." I laugh grimly. "I can't believe you'd even suggest it."

"Alright." Leaning back, he crosses one leg over the other and takes a sip from the glass of whiskey in his hand. "Then let's discuss your options."

I don't think I'm going to like wherever he's going with this, but for reasons I can't quite understand, I allow him to go on.

"How do you plan to kill her?" he asks. "When all is said and done."

I shift in my seat, my eyes flicking to the clock on the wall. Anything to keep myself from thinking about what he's asking.

"I haven't decided yet."

"You want her father to suffer for his crimes," he points out. "So perhaps, slow torture. Strangulation. Mutilation. You could send her back to her family piece by piece."

Fucking Christ.

My jaw clamps shut as my eyes drift to the empty table beside me, wishing I had taken the housekeeper up on her offer of a drink.

"But first, you need to determine how many times you will breed her," he remarks. "Ideally, you should have at least two sons. There might be girls in between, so that could take time. Although she only needs to be healthy during the pregnancies, I suppose. There's still a possibility for torture in the downtime."

The music from the other part of the house seems to grow more frantic. Haunting. Punctuating the violent images of Judge's words with a soundtrack to match his casual horrific suggestions that I myself had indulged in not that long ago.

"Of course, you'll need to ensure your children hate her too," he adds. "There would be no sense in fostering an attachment for a mother who won't be around to see them grow. That will surely bring her the suffering she deserves. Effective, but if you really want to break her, death might not be the only option."

My fists curl at my sides, my pulse throbbing in my neck.

"What do you mean?"

"Perhaps when you are done with her, you could send her to work at the Cat House. Offer her up as leftovers to any man who might use her for a few minutes of pleasure. That would surely be a dagger to her father's heart."

"Enough!" I stagger to my feet, pacing toward the fire as I fight to rein in my temper. "I know what you're doing."

"I'm doing what you always said you would," he replies calmly. "You said you wanted to torture her. You wanted every Moreno to pay."

"I know that's what I said," I snarl.

"So, what is the problem?" he presses. "Make your plans and be at peace with them. Unless there is a reason you can't or won't."

I turn to glare at him, and when I do, there is a small hint of amusement on his face. He gives me a moment to come back to myself, to regulate my breathing and calm this strange new beast living within me.

"It would not bother you if you didn't care," he observes. "You can only live in denial for so long.

This was always going to be a possibility, whether you saw it yourself or not. Mercedes sees it too. There are rumblings through IVI how your wife has softened you. Changed you."

"No." I shake my head. "I don't accept that."

"At some point, you must. It's the only way to move forward. You can spend your time fighting it or implement a solution to both your problems. You're in it now. Find a way to satisfy your revenge and keep her, or you will lose it all."

"That isn't a solution," I scoff. "When I kill her father and brother, Ivy will never get over it. She isn't like me."

"So, don't tell her." Judge shrugs. "Keep it to yourself and let your wife be happy in her ignorance when she puts her grief behind her."

Doesn't he know I've already considered that? I've considered every option. But I can't. Already, I know I won't. There is no room for emotions in our marriage. We have too many secrets between us, and there is always the potential they would come out later and poison her against me. Why allow something to bloom only to have it snatched away when the truth inevitably comes to light?

"Ivy could never be satisfied without answers. She wouldn't stop until she had them."

"And you couldn't live with yourself if you kept them from her."

When I meet his gaze, I can finally see there is

some truth in that. And at least to myself, I can admit that he's right. I couldn't keep that from Ivy. But it isn't because I have the potential to care for her. My father proved time and again that I wasn't capable of such a weakness. It was the only thing he ever praised me for. My coldness. He said it would serve me well in this life, and it has. I would be a fool to think for a second that things could be different. These feelings inside me are only temporary. They are new and unfamiliar but not permanent. They will go away, and I will return to the same man I've always been. The same unfaltering, empty, soulless shell.

The music in the other part of the house stops for a few moments, and when I glance in that direction, Judge watches me closely.

"She's playing again," he says softly.

A new ache lances through my chest at his confirmation. Mercedes hasn't played since our father died. And it gives me a strange sense of hope for her. Perhaps, she will be alright after all.

"Would you like to see her?" Judge asks.

I consider it carefully, weighing my options. Truthfully, part of the reason I came here was to see her. I needed to ask her about the aspirin. But now, I am questioning it.

"She would like to see you," he adds. "I am certain."

When I don't respond, he rises to his feet and

sets his glass aside, gesturing for me to follow. "Come. I'll take you to her."

MERCEDES SITS AT THE PIANO, her body swaying as her fingers whip over the keys with a proficiency that betrays a lifetime of study. The tune is beautiful and violent. Melancholy and deep.

I had forgotten what it was like to witness her this way. In our father's absence, I have often noticed my sister molding herself to be more like me. For reasons I have never understood, she idolizes me, and she has made herself colder because of it. She would have everyone believe there is no passion in her heart, but when she plays, it is undeniable. She feels deeply. But she has become too good at hiding it.

When I glance at Judge, he's watching her with an expression I'm convinced I've never quite seen before. Equal parts awe and frustration, maybe. But something else. Something much more intense.

I glare at him, and it seems to break the spell, at least momentarily.

He clears his throat. "She's very good. But she can do better. I make her practice several hours a day."

The sound of our voices behind her alerts Mercedes to our presence, and she glances over her shoulder briefly, her fingers halting over the keys.

"Don't stop," I tell her gruffly. "Finish the song."

Relief shines in her eyes, and she offers a tiny nod, swiveling back around to resume. For the next two minutes, Judge and I watch her in silence. The performance is moving, even for me, and I find that it brings up unexpected feelings. There is a tightness in my throat and chest. A gloomy shadow settling above me as if to say this is what sadness feels like.

The song makes me think of my wife. My child inside her. And for a moment, I consider perhaps there is some truth to what Judge said before. Maybe I am broken. Because I can't deny that there are feelings in me I don't recognize. Feelings I still haven't figured out how to identify. But they are there, lurking in the depths. And the notion of extricating them now feels almost as unbearable as ending her life.

Still, there is a part of me that knows I must extinguish them. These seedlings will continue to grow if they are fed in her presence. It has to be now or never. I have to figure out how to hate my wife forever or live with the uncertainty that the decision might not be my own.

The song comes to an end, and Mercedes turns, eyes shining with sadness. She's searching my face for the hatred she is certain she'll find.

"Santi?" she whispers. "You came to see me?"

"Yes." My tone is cold, and a small part of me

wishes it wasn't when her face falls. "I came to ask you about the aspirin you left in my wife's room."

She clasps her hands together in her lap, answering softly. "Aspirin?"

"Yes," I grit out. "The aspirin you gave her. The aspirin she used to try to kill herself and my child."

"Child?" she repeats, her voice fracturing. "You... you got her pregnant?"

For a moment, her anger returns. Her eyes harden, and she shakes her head as she rises to her feet, sneering in disgust. "How could you? She's the enemy, Santiago. What part of that don't you remember?"

Judge walks to her, his shadow falling over her face as he clasps her jaw in his hand, leaning in to whisper a threat that seems to hold more power over her than I'd expect.

"Behave."

She glances up at him, her face softening a fraction before she dips her head and nods begrudgingly. Admittedly, I am surprised by this. I knew Judge to be more than capable of guiding her, but I did not expect her to be so pliable just yet. It leaves me to wonder if there is more between them than he is letting on. If I should have even left her here at all. But Judge wouldn't betray my trust by exploiting Mercedes's vulnerability. He wouldn't risk his position within The Society by ruining her for another man who actually would intend to marry her. And I feel more confident in that knowledge when he turns back to me, his expression as cool as always.

"You think I gave them to her intentionally, to kill herself," Mercedes says. "That's why you came here."

"It isn't out of the realm of possibility," I reply sharply. "I need to know what other schemes you may have left unfinished."

She casts her eyes to the floor to hide the tears she's fighting back. And after a moment, she regains her composure enough to look up at me again.

"I didn't have any other schemes, Santi. I gave her the aspirin for pain. That was my only intention. I never meant to hurt your precious wife or child."

The last of her words are colored with bitterness, and I know it's because she feels like she's losing me. The only family she has left. I knew she would not bear the news gladly, but it bothers me more than it should. I consider offering her my assurances that she will always be my family, but how can I? After what she has done, how can I ever trust her again?

"For your sake, I hope that isn't another lie," I answer.

She crosses her arms and casts her eyes to the floor, closing herself off. Clearly, we are both finished with this conversation, and I think it is best to leave any other pleasantries for a time we might actually mean them.

I turn to go, Judge by my side. But when we reach the hall, Mercedes calls after us.

"Goddammit. Wait a second. I have something to tell you."

I turn slowly, weary this might be another confession. Another trap she's set. Another threat to my wife.

"I'm not telling you for Ivy's sake," she clips out. "I'm telling you because I want to show you that you can trust me."

"What is it?" I demand.

She hesitates again, shifting her weight as she glances at Judge as if to seek his approval. He nods at her, and she returns her gaze to mine.

"It's about Chambers," she says. "That doctor."

"What about him?"

She glances briefly at Judge again, and then back to me. "After the poisoning, when you mentioned Abel, and the pieces started falling into place, I was following him. I wanted to see how he was involved. And there were a few times I followed him to a storage unit. I figured there must be something in it. A reason he'd keep going back there. So, I broke into it."

Judge and I are both glowering at her when he speaks up.

"What the hell were you thinking?"

"I had to see for myself," she bites out. "It could have been nothing. But it wasn't."

"What was in the storage unit?" I ask.

She dips her head down and shrugs. "A bunch of file boxes. Papers. They all belonged to Chambers."

Judge and I glance at each other as an idea begins to take shape in my mind.

"That wasn't it," Mercedes continues on. "There was something else."

"What?" Judge asks.

"In the back of the unit, beneath a tarp, there was a rolled-up blanket. It was bloody, and when I picked it up to look at it, a wallet fell out. It belonged to Chambers."

My blood runs cold as the weight of her words settle over me, casting an accusation that can't be refuted.

"He's dangerous, Santi." She looks at me. "And I overheard him say something on the phone. Something I can't stop thinking about."

"What was it?" I rasp.

"He said he would sooner rot than let you impregnate Ivy. And if you did, he would cut the baby out of her himself."

35

IVY

I'm still shivering hours after Santiago left. I feel so cold. Did he only marry me to gain physical custody of me? To have me within his home, within his power to do with me as he pleased?

Why am I asking the question? I know the answer.

"Your body will be a healthy host for my child."

My mind is still reeling. I'm pregnant with his baby.

His.

I didn't miss the fact that not once did he say it was our baby. I am a host. A body. A thing to breed.

The nurse pokes her head inside and warily searches the room. She smiles and pushes the door all the way open when she sees I'm alone.

"How are you feeling, love? I'm glad to see you ate all your breakfast."

"Am I really pregnant?" I ask her.

She smiles warmly. "Yes, just a few weeks, but you have a strong baby in there." Her expression changes, pity creeping into it. "You know we have psychologists on staff. They're approved by The Society so your husband can rest assured—"

"I'm in a Society hospital?"

She looks confused.

I shake my head. "Never mind." Of course, I am. I am where Santiago can and will control everything. "Can we take this off?" I gesture to the IV.

"That's why I'm here. Now that you're up and feeling better, you'll be sure to eat and drink to feed that little baby of yours."

I nod, and she gets to work.

"The doctor will release you as soon as he's here in a few hours. Mr. De La Rosa is anxious to have you home." She glances at me momentarily when she says that part and finishes taking the needle out of my arm.

I look around the room. "Can I call my sister?" I ask her. "I don't have my cell phone…" I trail off, and it's not really a lie. I don't have my cell phone. Or any cell phone.

"Oh." She looks around too. "They must have taken the phone out when cleaning. I'll tell you what," she says, reaching into her pocket. "Use mine. It'll be easier than tracking down the one that belongs in here. It's not one of the fancy ones, but it works just fine." She hands it to me and cleans up the last of the bandages. "I'll be back in a few minutes. Let me get these things sorted and pick up your lunch."

"Thank you," I say, trying not to sound too anxious as I flip her phone open. It's one of the ones my dad used to have when I was little.

As soon as she's gone, I dial Abel's cell phone, hoping he'll pick up even though he won't recognize the number. When I hear the click as he does, I breathe a sigh of relief.

"Yes?" he answers short and sharp.

"Abel. It's me. Ivy."

"Ivy? What number is this?"

"It doesn't matter. It's not mine. I...I'm in the hospital."

"What?" There's an urgency in his tone I don't expect. "What did he do to you?"

I don't want to tell him about the aspirin. I feel too ashamed. And I can't stand the thought that he'll call me weak. I am. I know it already.

"Ivy?"

"I'm pregnant, Abel." I hold back a sob when the words spill out, my throat tight. Pregnant. I know if I go back to that house, I will be Santiago's prisoner forever. And my forever may not be that long. Is that the silver lining?

I hear something crash on Abel's end of the phone.

"Abel? Can you hear me?"

"Yes."

"I really need your help now. Okay?" I can't help the tears that flow, and I know he hears them, but I go on before he can say anything. "I can't go back there. I'm a prisoner. I'll die. I know I will."

"I'm assuming you're at The Society hospital?"

"Yes."

"Do you know your room number?"

I shake my head. "No. Let me go see." I push the blanket aside and swing my legs off the bed. I move slowly, not trusting my limbs, feeling so weak. My legs are bare beneath the gown, and the floor is cold under my feet. I pad across the room to open the door, and the first thing I see is a man leaning against the opposite wall talking to a nurse. The moment he sees me, he straightens, his expression changing, darkening.

Santiago has a guard watching me.

I slip back inside and lean my forehead against the door.

"Ivy? What the fuck is going on?"

I force myself to breathe. Try to calm my heart rate. "I'm on the fifth floor," I say, having seen the number of the room across from mine. "I don't know the number, but it's across from 566. Abel, there's a guard outside."

"Okay. I need to think."

I walk back toward the bed and sit down, my toes

barely grazing the floor. I feel like a child. Like a scared little girl and I think about how Hazel left. How she managed to stay gone.

"Please, I can't go back. I would rather die." I wipe the back of my hand across my eyes.

"Just give me a little time. Can I call you back at this number?"

"I don't think so. The nurse—"

"It's fine. I'll figure something out."

"How?"

He snorts. "Your husband isn't the only one with connections. Sit tight, little sister." With that, he disconnects, and I'm left holding the phone, wondering about the last part. *Little sister*. It sounded almost affectionate, and I have to remind myself that this is Abel. He hates me.

But he hates Santiago more.

I'VE ALMOST GIVEN up on Abel when, two hours later, there's a knock on my door, and I sit up to see Evangeline's face peer inside.

"Eva!"

"Knock, knock," she says, slipping in and coming to me. I hug her so tight I don't ever want to let her go. It's been so long. Months.

"Eva, where's Abel?" I ask when she pulls the chair Santiago had sat in up to the bed and glances to the door.

"He sent me. He thought they wouldn't let him in to see you, but I'm just a kid." She shrugs her shoulder with a wide grin. She reaches into her small backpack, pulls out a couple of Snickers bars, and sets them on the nightstand. "Hospital food sucks, right? And you got skinny."

Her expression falters. I see worry. And I find I can't speak without crying.

She glances back at the door. "The guard is at the door, but he's flirting with some of the nurses. Your car's outside," she whispers. "At the back of the lot."

"My car?"

She nods, slips her hand in her pocket, and pulls out a familiar keychain.

I smile.

She puts it back in the pocket. "Can I use the bathroom real quick?"

I nod. "Over there."

"BRB," she says almost cheerily. She goes into the bathroom. I wonder what's going on when a few minutes later, she returns and when she does, I notice instead of the bulky sweater and jeans she had on when she walked in here, she's wearing a pair of black leggings and a Henley.

"I didn't figure you'd want to leave in a hospital gown," she says.

"You thought of everything."

"It was Abel mostly. Shocking."

"Is he outside?"

She shakes her head. "He dropped me off down the street just in case. You probably want to get going. Abel left an address to a safe house in the glove compartment. And there's a cell phone in the car. Maybe you can call me when you get out of here?"

"A safe house?"

She nods. "I don't know what's going on, but you don't look good, Ivy."

"I'll be okay," I tell her. "The guard?"

"Go get changed. When you're ready, I'll cause some commotion. Pull a fire alarm maybe. I've always wanted to do that. When you get out, make a left out of the room. The stairs at the end of the hall are unlocked." She studies me. "Do you think you can get there on your own?"

"I don't look that bad, do I?"

"No, of course not," she says, her voice a little too high. It's a lie. I must look like hell. "But we should hurry probably."

I get up, and while my sister stands guard, I enter the bathroom and change into the clothes she brought, thinking there's no way this will work. And even if it does, Santiago will find me. Even if I get out of the hospital or manage to get to the safe house, he won't just let me walk away. Especially not now. But maybe I have to trust my brother. Maybe he'll come through, and finally, do the right thing for us. His family.

I think about Dad. Wonder where he is. How he is.

"Ivy?" My sister knocks.

"I'm ready," I say, slipping my feet into the ballet slippers she brought.

"You look better already," she says and hurries to the nightstand. "Don't forget the Snickers." I have to laugh when she shoves them into my pockets, then pulls me in for a hug. "Please call me as soon as you're at the safe house, okay? Please don't forget."

"I won't. I promise."

"Give me a two-minute head start."

"Okay."

With that, she hurries out of my room and, on cue, not two minutes later, the fire alarm rings, and I hear the confusion in the hallway. I give it another minute before opening the door, and when I see the guard who was standing outside earlier with his back turned, I step out of my room. It takes all I have to walk, not run toward the exit sign marking the stairwell, and slip through the door and out of sight.

36

IVY

I don't breathe a sigh of relief until I'm sitting in the driver's seat of my car, the door locked, my shaking hands over my pounding heart.

I'm out. I made it.

And now I need to move. If they haven't already noticed that I'm gone, they will soon enough, and Santiago will send an army after me. But before I reach over to open the glove box, I take a moment to look down at my stomach. It's still flat, and I put my hands over it, not really believing that I'm pregnant just yet. Not quite processing the fact.

Which makes it so much more important that I hurry now.

It takes a little wiggling of the handle to open the glove compartment. It always did get stuck. And when I do, and the contents spill out onto the floor of the passenger side, I'm momentarily stunned.

Because there along with a sheet of paper upon which I see Abel's hurried scrawl, the three hundred-dollar bills, and the phone is a small, black pistol.

I look at it. I've never seen one in person before, only on TV. I've never touched one.

Reaching down now, I pick it up and feel the weight of it, the cool steel hard and deadly in my hands. Does he think I would use this? Would I?

No.

Even if Santiago found me, I wouldn't. It makes no sense for Abel to have given it to me.

I quickly shove it back into the glove box and close it, then bend to pick up the rest of the things. I fold the bills and set them in the cup holder with the phone on top. I then read the address Abel wrote out. I'm surprised because I know the town. It's about twenty minutes from my apartment at school.

Strange.

But I set the piece of paper aside and put the key into the ignition, remembering the hiccup the car always makes before the engine turns over. The familiarity makes me smile. Takes me at least momentarily to a different time, a different place. A different life.

God. Has it only been months since the night Abel came to bring me back? Only a few months since my life changed so irrevocably?

I put the car in gear and glance behind me to see

people gathering outside as they evacuate the building, and the fire engines with their screeching sirens turn perilously into the parking lot. I try to see if I can find my sister, but there are too many people, and as I glimpse the first of the police cars heading toward the lot, I put my foot on the gas pedal and ease out, trying not to make this appear like a getaway.

And when I'm on the road, and I watch the police cars turn into the lot, their lights and sirens fading as I get farther away, I breathe a sigh of relief.

I did it. I got away.

At least for now.

The weather changes as I drive the long stretch of highway to Lafayette. I consider driving by my old school, the apartment building, but I find I don't want to. It's like that life's not mine. Was it ever?

By the time I get to the small, quiet neighborhood, the sky has darkened with storm clouds. I have to drive up and down a few of the streets until I find Raymond Road. The houses are small but quaint in this middle-income neighborhood of Louisiana. They're each painted a different vibrant color, reminiscent of The Garden District although so obviously not. I find number 13, which is yellow, and as I pull up into the driveway, I wonder at that number. Thirteen. It's always been unlucky for me.

But maybe that's changing.

My stomach growls as I put the car into park and

pull up the emergency brake. It'll roll down the driveway if I don't. I then grab the money and the phone along with the car keys and the sheet of paper that contains the address and head up to the yellow house with the dark windows.

Although it's quiet, I can hear the road from here. It makes me think of how still Santiago's house is. How deadly silent.

It feels so far away now.

Once I get up to the porch, I see the electronic keypad, which is strange. It's too high-end to fit here. It would be more appropriate for The Manor. I shake off the thought and punch in the code Abel had written under the address, grateful when I hear the sound of the door unlocking and a green light blinks.

I push the door open and step into the dark house. I feel for the light switch and turn it on before I close the door behind me. As soon as I do, I hear the lock re-engage.

Setting the car keys on the table beside the door, I shove the paper with the entry code into my pocket and enter the foreign space. It's obvious from the stale air and sparse mismatch of furnishings—a couch, a coffee table littered with newspapers and junk, and one chair—no one lives here. No table in the small dining room. The kitchen is the size of my bathroom at Santiago's house. I open the refrigerator to find a couple of takeout containers of spoiled food. I leave them but grab a bottle of water of which there are plenty stacked, taking up two of the shelves.

I open it and drink half, then remember the candy bars Eva shoved into my pocket and take one out. I rip the wrapper and take a bite as I open the freezer, curious to see if there's anything inside. I'm surprised to find stacks of frozen dinners and a half-full bottle of vodka.

No one lives here, but someone does use this place. This safe house. I am curious who.

I finish the candy bar and take out one of the dinners, a lasagna dish. Before heating it, I grab the phone out of my pocket and dial Abel. He answers on the first ring.

"Yes?"

"I'm here."

He exhales. "Good. Okay. Stay put while I figure out what to do with you."

"Did Evangeline make it out?"

"Of course, she did." He sounds almost proud.

"Can I talk to her?"

"No, you need to hang up. I'm sure your husband has a search party out by now."

"I promised I'd call her."

"I'll let her know you made it."

"Whose house is this?" I ask.

He goes quiet for a moment, then snorts. "Dad's. Don't touch anything."

"Dad's? What?"

"Don't touch anything, understand? You just go up to bed. Wait for me to call you."

"But I don't understand. What do you mean it's Dad's?"

I hear the doorbell ring on his end. "I have to go," Abel says.

"Is it him? Santiago?"

"I can't see through closed doors, can I? Don't call me, I'll call you. You just stay put. Do not go anywhere."

"I won't."

He disconnects the call, and I busy myself opening the frozen dinner. I pop it into the microwave and look out the window onto the big, empty lot of the fenced-in backyard with its brown grass while it cooks. The clouds have darkened, the first drops of rain falling, and my gaze shifts from the garden to my own reflection.

My sister was right. I look bad.

I touch a hand to my stomach, turn sideways even though I know it'll still be flat. I'm having a baby. Santiago's baby.

And some part of me knows no matter what he won't just let me walk away. He will hunt me down. He would do it even if I wasn't pregnant.

So why is Abel helping me? Why risk it? Why when he must know Santiago will win. He always does.

I blink away from my reflection as the microwave dings. I'm not hungry anymore but I take the lasagna out and force myself to eat it, burning my tongue on the too-hot sauce.

I just need some time to think. To figure this out. Make a plan.

Because I have no doubt Santiago will come for me and I have to be ready for him when he does.

37
IVY

I think about what Abel said, that it's Dad's house. Dad doesn't have a house apart from the one we lived in.

Although I remember the picture in his wallet from when I was little. The beautiful woman. The one I didn't know.

Was my dad having an affair and keeping this house for that affair?

In addition to the living and dining rooms and the kitchen on the first floor is a small office. There's no light in there, though, and the windows are boarded up, so I leave it alone.

Upstairs are three small, sparse bedrooms. Only one has a proper bed in it. I guess it'd be the master. There's one bathroom with a tiny shower. On the shelf is a worn-down bar of soap, and under the sink is a package of men's razors and shaving cream.

The two bedrooms are empty except for two twin-size mattresses laid on the floor of each. But if they've been used, it's very gently. In the small linen closet in the hallway, I find folded sheets in pinks and yellows and a couple of towels. Nothing fancy. More leftover things picked up here and there, but everything smells clean at least.

I carry the sheets into the master to make the bed, but I keep thinking about Dad. I sit down on the edge of it and look across to the chest of drawers. Leaving the sheets on the bed, I get up and go to it, opening the first drawer. I find it empty, as I expect. Same with the second.

The third one is jammed, and when I manage to tug it out, I almost fall backward from the force and hear something clatter to the back of the drawer. I'm more careful when I pull it farther, and for a moment, I'm not sure if what I'm seeing is right.

My heart races as a chill covers my skin with goose bumps.

I reach in and take out the bracelet. It's a small gold chain with a name written in cursive across a narrow gold bar. I know this bracelet. I have one just like it. It's at home. Eva has one too. I don't know if she wears hers, though. I don't wear mine. I stopped the day Hazel left.

I brush my thumb over the name inscribed on the bar.

Hazel.

And beside it the symbol that I hate. *IVI*.

A gift for the daughters of The Society. Like we're all some big, creepy family. They give them to the parents with each female birth. My parents kept extending the chain as we grew, proud that we were Society's daughters.

This is Hazel's. She never took hers off. Never.

Was she here?

I slip the bracelet around my wrist and close the clasp.

Was Hazel here? And did Dad know?

Suddenly no longer tired, I go downstairs. There was a flashlight in one of the drawers in the kitchen. I get it and switch it on. It's a good one. Strong. I walk to the small study and open the door. I shine the light over the interior, see the messy desk that's too big for this tiny house, too grand. I see the worn Chesterfield against the far wall. The empty bottle of whiskey in the trashcan, the one that's only a third full on the desk beside a tumbler with whiskey residue inside it.

I roll the chair back behind the desk and sit down, shining the light over the top of the desk, opening folders and peering at the papers inside. But they don't mean anything to me, and honestly, I'm not sure what I'm looking for. Well, I guess I am. I want to see if there's more evidence of Hazel having been here. I want to know if this is truly Dad's house.

But I don't find anything in here useful. Nothing

in the drawers but more folders containing names I don't know.

The sound of a police siren demands my attention, and I gasp, my heart racing as I fumble to switch off the flashlight. I sit in the pitch-black, trying to remember if I'd left any lights on. The kitchen.

Shit.

But then the sound fades, and I realize how paranoid I'm being. Santiago can't find me here. Not yet. I have some time. And I'm dead on my feet.

I'll have a look around in the morning when I'm fresh. So I switch off the kitchen light, double-check that the doors are locked, and make my way to the bedroom where I make the bed and lie down, wondering if Hazel had slept on this very bed years ago. If this was a safe house for her, too. And if that was Dad's doing. If he'd helped her run away.

38

SANTIAGO

"Boss, I need a word with you." Marco pokes his head into Ivy's room, and I grunt a response.

"Give me a hand with these, will you?" I shift the window cover, setting one piece aside.

Marco doesn't move. "I think you should come down here so we can talk."

I glance at him over my shoulder and frown at the strained expression on his face. My fucking nerves are already shot, and this isn't helping. The moment I left Judge's house, I sent ten of my best guards to the hospital to collect my wife early while I came home to prepare for her arrival. That was an hour ago. They should have given me a status update by now.

My gut sours, and I know Marco came to deliver bad news. What else could it be?

I turn back to the window, tugging at the piece

that won't seem to budge. Much like me, it's stubborn. Unyielding.

"Fucking piece of shit." I growl, slamming against it in frustration. "I need your help, Marco."

"Boss, I really think you should come down here." He's quieter now. Uncertain how to handle me like this. I can't say I blame him.

I don't want to hear whatever it is he came to say. Maybe that's why I'm still prying at the window cover as if I can alter it. Avoid it.

"I have to get this out," I snarl. "Her room has to be ready when she gets home."

Silence. He doesn't bother to respond this time, and a cold chill moves over me when I release the cover and finally turn to him. I look down at him from the sill, a lead weight settling over my chest.

Marco shifts from one foot to the other. He clears his throat then stuffs his hands into his pockets. And finally, he delivers the news he doesn't want to tell me.

"Sir, your wife slipped the guard and escaped the hospital. I've had my men out scouring the city for her from the moment I became aware, but she hasn't turned up anywhere. I waited to tell you because I had hoped we might find her."

My hands fall open at my sides. My breathing slows. And I stare at him, blank.

Several minutes pass. Maybe more. Marco stares

back, his face growing more uncomfortable the longer I stand there, silent.

I turn back to the window cover and yank again, grunting out in frustration when it refuses to budge. Marco doesn't say anything else as I continue to grapple with the piece. Or if he does, I don't hear it.

"I need to get this out," I bark at him. "She'll be home soon. Her room should be ready. It should have been ready..."

My voice falters, and a hand settles onto my arm, gently guiding me away from the window. Marco helps me down from the sill, meeting my gaze with sorrowful eyes.

"She's gone, sir. I'm so sorry."

A tremor moves through me. I can't accept it. She wouldn't leave me. Ivy hates me, but she wouldn't leave me.

"You're wrong." I brush past him, determined to prove it myself.

Marco follows me all the way down the stairs and to the car still parked in the driveway. When I try and fail to open the door, he unlocks it with the keys in his hand and gently guides me around to the passenger seat.

"I'll drive you, sir."

The ride is quiet. I can't accept that this is anything other than a mistake. Ivy wouldn't do this. She wouldn't take away my light.

Marco pulls up to the curb of The Society

hospital and follows me inside. We take the elevator up to the fifth floor, passing the army of guards that has now multiplied under Marco's command. They are scouring the halls, some checking each room and peeking into laundry carts while others interview hospital staff.

I can't focus on any of it. I can only focus on each step. Each breath.

When I enter her room, I come to a halt just past the doorway. Her bed is empty, and a glance inside the bathroom confirms that is too. And for a minute, I don't know what else to do.

Marco lingers beside me, waiting patiently for my sanity to return. But it never does.

I move robotically, a phantom in search of the beating heart that's been ripped from his chest. There's nothing left inside that gaping space. Nothing but agony.

"I was going to make things right," I murmur as my hand settles onto the pillow where she lay this morning. "She would have seen it. The windows. Her new clothes. The lock removed from her bedroom door. I removed the rosary and the mask... I was going to make things right."

Marco has grace enough not to interrupt my fragmented thoughts as I bring the pillow to my face and inhale her scent. I breathe it in, and then it slips from my hands, falling to the floor as my gaze drifts out the window. At the vast city beyond.

She is out there somewhere. My wife and our child.

I turn to Marco, a familiar anger steeling me against these unrecognizable weaknesses stirring up inside me.

"Where is Abel?"

"We haven't been able to locate him, sir," he answers apologetically. "But the nurse mentioned that Ivy's youngest sister came by to visit. We haven't spoken with her yet."

"Take me to her."

He nods, and thirty minutes later, I'm standing on the doorstep of the pathetic structure the Moreno's call home. I've been to this house many times. Sat in the office with Eli and said hello to his family in passing. I remember it vividly. Back then, it looked very much like a family home. Now, it looks like it should be burned to the ground.

The door opens, and Mrs. Moreno squeaks when she sees the grim reaper standing on the threshold to greet her. She never could look directly at me. Not even when my face wasn't a skull.

"Where is Evangeline?" I demand.

"Eva?" she repeats, her voice too high.

"Bring her to me. Now."

She steps back, nodding fast as her hands begin to tremble. "Of course, Mr. De La Rosa. I'll bring her to you."

She leads us into the sitting room, offering us a

drink, to which I don't reply. After a moment, she scurries away in search of her daughter.

"Search the house," I tell Marco.

He nods and disappears while I stand in the middle of the sitting room, scanning the space for any signs of my wife. After a few more moments, the smallest Moreno girl enters the room, eyes cast down, cheeks red.

"Mr. De La Rosa," she grits out. "My mother said you'd like to speak to me."

The mother she speaks of sent her into the room alone, courageous as she is. She's too afraid to face me herself but does not hesitate to send her young child to speak with me. That tells me everything I need to know about the coward of a woman.

"Evangeline." I glance down at her, the little girl much like a younger version of Ivy. This miniature human reminds me of that girl, the one who stumbled into her father's office in tears so many years ago. The one who gifted me a pen and didn't hesitate to look me directly in the eye, unlike most of the people in my life.

Evangeline tips her chin up, squaring her shoulders. "What do you want?"

My lip tilts at the corner, despite the gravity of the situation. She is very much like Ivy, indeed.

"Where is your brother?"

"I don't know." She shrugs. "He hasn't been home since I got here."

"Tell me about the hospital. You went to visit your sister. What happened when you were there?"

She swallows and shakes her head. "Nothing. It was just a visit."

She's lying, and I know she's lying. It only makes sense that Abel sent her. Nobody would think twice about the young, innocent girl coming to see her sister. The hospital staff already knew Abel was not allowed visitation rights. This was his way in. And I am a fool for not considering that he would use anyone, even a child, even at the risk of her own severe punishment. He fed her to the wolves, completely disregarding the consequences for her. It does not inspire confidence that he will have any mercy for my wife.

I study Evangeline for a long moment, considering how to handle this. I don't often deal with children. I know almost nothing about them, except for what I learned from looking after Mercedes. But that was different.

I lower myself to one knee, meeting Evangeline's gaze directly. She sucks in a sharp breath, her eyes moving rapidly over the ink on my face. She does not seem scared but fascinated, and it surprises me.

"I need you to tell me where your sister is. It's for her own safety."

"She isn't safe with you." She glares at me. "I saw her. She was a wreck."

Shame washes over me as I dip my head in acknowledgment. "I know. And I regret that."

Evangeline watches me curiously, her brows pinching together.

"But she isn't safe with Abel either. I know he's your brother, but he has plans for Ivy that you aren't aware of. He will harm her if you don't tell me where she is."

"He wouldn't." Her lip wavers as she denies it, but I can see the questions in her eyes.

"He would. And I think you already know he's capable of it."

She's quiet for a pause, and when she blinks again, tears splash against her cheeks. "I couldn't tell you even if I wanted to. I don't know where she is."

Marco returns, capturing my attention from the landing. Mrs. Moreno is beside him, watching him with annoyance after he rifled through her belongings.

"I didn't find anything, boss."

I stand and direct my sharp gaze at Mrs. Moreno. "Anything else you'd like to tell me?"

"I don't know where Abel is," she huffs. "Or Ivy for that matter. Whatever plan they concocted is between them. I am terribly ashamed of them right now, truth be told. If this gets out to The Society, it will ruin us. They think of nobody but themselves."

"Very well." I turn to Marco, gesturing to the little

girl. "Take her for collateral. We'll bring her back if my wife is returned alive."

Evangeline looks at her mother, eyes pleading. Mrs. Moreno does not utter so much as a protest.

DUSK SLIPS to darkness as we drive around the city, searching every place Abel has ever been known to frequent. Using the power of IVI's connections, we have also traced his phone, only to learn that it's been turned off. With no other leads, we resort to dispersing my men to every hotel, alleyway, and street corner with Ivy's photo, asking for witnesses and offering a reward.

Still, the results yield nothing.

As the light of morning settles over us, my frustrations grow. She isn't safe, and I can't get to her. I can't protect her.

My wife.

My sweet, infuriating, intoxicating wife.

Doesn't she understand what she's doing to me? I can't be without her. Not now. Not after everything. It's something that's only become painfully clear in her absence. Even when she was just down the hall, stowed away in her room, out of my sight, I knew she was always there. And now that she isn't, the blood in my veins has slowed to a crawl. The thumping beat of my heart is dimming, fading.

I need her.

"Antonia says the girl is awake," Marco glances at his phone briefly to read the information from his texts. "She's still not talking."

I stare out the passenger window, watching the buildings as we pass. The gloomy fog around us is as heavy as my mood. Where the fuck could she be?

I've tried not to think about the haunting words Mercedes left me with. Abel's intentions for the baby inside Ivy. But the images come back, again and again, violent and excruciating. *Is it too late?* Has he destroyed the only good thing we have left?

Coldness seeps into my chest, icing over the warring emotions I don't know how to deal with. There is one option left. The one option I didn't want to consider. It would make me a truly weak man to walk into Eli Moreno's room and beg him for his help.

But what choice do I have?

I close my eyes briefly, prioritizing my thoughts. Revenge has always been of the foremost importance in my life. Six months ago, I wanted every Moreno to suffer. I wanted Eli and Abel and even Ivy dead. But Judge was right. Somewhere along the line, things have changed.

I'll never let her go, even if she condemns me to her hatred for an eternity. I understand that now. Because the loss of her for even these few hours has strained me beyond comprehension. I can't think. I can't eat. I can't even breathe without the pain reminding me of one simple truth.

She should be here beside me.

"Take me back to the hospital."

Marco glances at me. "The hospital?"

"Yes," I grit out. "I'm going to see Eli."

39

SANTIAGO

Eli glances up at me from his wheelchair, his eyes widening in surprise and then narrowing slightly. He looks different than I remember. More like a frail old man and less like the capable figure who mentored me. The man I spent countless hours with. He offered me guidance, praise, things I was not accustomed to. He told me he was in awe of my mind, and I allowed myself to believe him. Now, I can hardly stand to look at him.

"Santiago," he rasps.

The nurse holds up a cup of water for him, giving him a drink from the straw. I watch him struggle with the basic task, and it makes me uncomfortable in a way I did not expect. They told me he was recovering, regaining his strength every day. But if this is progress, I can't imagine how far he still has to go.

It would be so easy to kill him now. It would require little effort at all to wrap my hands around his throat and squeeze while I demand the answers I seek. It would undoubtedly do the job, but it would bring me no pleasure. Not right now.

"Leave us," I tell the nurse.

She nods and leaves the room, shutting the door and sealing Eli into the room with his worst enemy.

"They tell me you control everything regarding my care." He sputters the words out through broken gasps. "That is why my family has not been to see me."

"Your family doesn't care," I answer him coldly.

He stares at me, blank. His face that of someone who is on their death bed, and I suppose in many ways, he still is.

"It hurts me to see you this way, son," he says. "Your heart has become so dark."

"I am not your son," I snarl. "I am a De La Rosa, and you aren't even worth the oxygen in this room."

A pained expression flashes in his eyes, or at least, that's what he'd like me to believe. I can't deny that Eli knows my weaknesses because he exploited them at every turn, pretending to be a friend. A father figure. But I won't be fooled again.

"The nurses tell me you married my daughter," he says quietly. "Is she... safe?"

I choke down the response I've waited years to give him. The plans I had made to destroy him. I had intended to tell him in detail of Ivy's suffering. Now I can't even consider it.

"She's the reason I'm here." I pace along the wall, trying to keep my calm. "I need to know where Abel would take her to hide her."

Eli doesn't reply, and when I glance at him, he appears confused. "If he took her into hiding, I'm sure he had his reasons."

"I'm not here to entertain your noble father act," I bite out. "It's too late for that now. You have failed your own family miserably. That much is obvious. But you have a chance to protect your daughter now. Tell me what I want to know so I can retrieve her before any real harm comes to her."

His eyes shine with emotion as he shakes his head. "I don't know where Abel would take her."

"I could choke the life out of you right now, and nobody would stop me." I stare through him. "Is that what you want?"

"Would that bring you peace?" he asks, catching me off guard.

My eyes move over his hunched frame as I shake my head in disgust.

"Tell. Me. Where. She. Is."

"I don't know, Santiago." His voice breaks. "I honestly don't know. Take me with you. We can find her together."

I slam my fist into the wall in frustration, howling like a madman. And then slowly, I pull myself together, turning back to face the man I despise more than anything.

"I'll drag Hazel out of hiding. I'll bring her before The Tribunal to pay for her desertion. What have you to say now?"

"You won't." His eyes are soft and too calm when they meet mine. "I know you won't, Santiago. Because you are better than that."

"You know nothing about me. You never did."

"I know what I can see before me," he replies. "A broken man whose anger has controlled his life for far too long. You have so much anger inside you, it's poisoning you."

"That anger was a gift," I remind him. "From you to me. And someday soon, I will repay the favor."

He frowns, and I turn for the door, his voice following me out and down the hall.

"I know who you really are, Santiago. You won't hurt my daughters."

THE SMALL, gray house in Oakdale blends in amongst all the others. It is not the first time I have visited, but it will be the first time I have stood on the doorstep.

I know every detail of her schedule. When she leaves each day. Where she goes. What groceries she buys, how often she fuels her car. There isn't a single thing I don't know. And as I count the time passing on my watch, I know in fifteen seconds, she will open the door, rushing out to her car to take her son to school.

I stand and wait. Moments later, there is a commotion on the other side of the door. Something clatters to the floor, and she curses. She yells for her son, telling him they have to go. The knob turns, and when the door opens, she spills out in a rush, nearly colliding with me.

A small gasp flies from her lips, and horror washes over her face as she scrambles back inside, trying to shut the door to seal the monster out. My palm slams against it, and a dark smile bleeds across my face.

"Hello, Hazel. It's been a while."

40

IVY

I wake up to sunshine. Glorious sunshine. I smile, open my eyes, and take in the soft yellow light filtered by old-fashioned lace curtains.

And I remember where I am.

Sitting up with renewed anxiety, I fumble for the phone on the bed beside me. I check the time, surprised when I see it's ten o'clock. I didn't wake up once in this foreign bed, this foreign house knowing my husband is hunting me.

I'm tempted to call Abel but remember what he said and slip the phone into my pocket. I push the blankets off, slide my feet into my shoes, and go to the window. The lace is torn in places, and the windowsill has a layer of dust. I push the curtain open just a little. Outside all is quiet. My car is still where I left it. The army I'd expected Santiago to come with not there.

I make my way into the bathroom, where I splash water on my face and rinse my mouth before heading downstairs to the kitchen. In one of the cupboards, I find a tin of coffee and filters for the machine, but then I remember the baby. Caffeine isn't good for a baby, right? I don't really know much about pregnancy. I put the coffee back into the cabinet and look for tea but don't find any, so instead, I pour water from one of the bottles into a mug and set it into the microwave. At least it'll be warm.

While sipping that, I look through the frozen meals and find a breakfast burrito. I pop it into the microwave, and it makes my mouth water when I take it out. I carry it into the living room to eat, glancing out the window through the curtains, which are heavier downstairs, before taking a seat on the couch. I bite into the burrito, the eggs and cheese tasting great. I sit back and just eat for a few minutes. I'm so hungry, and I can't remember the last time I ate something like this. Santiago would lose his mind, I'm sure. The food at home... no, I catch myself. The food *at his house* is healthy. Delicious even but never anything like this, so I savor the fat of the sausage, licking it away when it drips down my chin.

I wonder what Santiago is thinking now. He must be furious with me. Probably hurling curses at me for having stolen his baby. His. Not ours. It makes me angry to remember it. How dare he? This is my body, and it's our baby. He can't just use me as some host to grow a human being then take the child away from me. I don't know what world he thinks we live in, but even The Society cannot have that kind of power.

I put the dish down and wipe my hands on a napkin I find on the coffee table. It's clean. There's a stack of them and beside them packets of ketchup from a fast-food place. I pick up my mug of now warm water and finish it, then look at the newspapers around me. I read the date on the first one, and it surprises me, so I look at another. It's a different paper but the same date. The day after the gala. There are several gossip magazines underneath the pile of papers, about a week's worth. Again, the week following the gala.

It's nothing, I tell myself as I stand to carry my dish and mug back to the kitchen. Just a coincidence. In the kitchen, I wash my things and set them on the drying rack before returning to the living room.

Was Abel here that week? Why? He called this a safe house. What would he have needed to be safe from?

But no, Abel doesn't read gossip magazines. He does devour the papers, though. I check my phone to make sure I haven't missed his call. I haven't, but he'd better call me soon. The battery is running low, and I don't have a charger. Although I could charge it in the car if I need to. The one I keep plugged into the power outlet would fit.

I make my way into the study. It's still not as bright as the rest of the house, but with the light coming in from the open door and my flashlight, it'll do. I sit back down in the big chair, switch on the flashlight and start to go through the folders one by one, seeing if I recognize any names. Abel's voice telling me not to touch anything echoes in my mind, but I ignore it.

When I'm about halfway through the files, I finally come across one I recognize. One that makes me shudder.

Judge.

It's in italics beside what I guess to be his real name. Lawson Montgomery. I flip through the pages of the file and, like the others, see a date of birth, parents' names—some seem to have a whole family tree, but this one doesn't. He does have a brother, but according to this, they're estranged. I see his address and wonder if that's where the cellar is. It would match up to the length of time it took us to drive to IVI.

I close the file and set it aside. I don't want to read about him. I don't want to think about that time.

I don't recognize the next set of names, but then I come to another one I do. Van Der Smit. Jackson's last name. The file is about another man, though. Marcus Van Der Smit. From the date of Marcus's birth, I'd say he's maybe an uncle? Are these all members of IVI? And why does my brother have detailed files on all of them? Is it my brother or my father, though, who's kept these?

Opening another one of the drawers, I find more of the same stacks. I don't have the energy to go through them, though, and there's nothing about my father or Hazel in here, so I get up and go back to the kitchen to try the back door. I can at least walk around in the backyard to get some exercise and fresh air.

The door has the same keypad on it as at the front, and I dig out the sheet of paper from my pocket to unlock it, not sure how it works to get out once I'm in, but when I punch in the code, I hear the same sounds and see the green light. Just in case, though, I drag a chair over to keep the door open. The day is cool, and I don't have a jacket, but it's nice to be outside, so I hug my arms around myself and walk around the yard. I can hear cars drive by. A baby cries somewhere not too far away. And I think about my own baby and then about Santiago. How it could have been different for us. How I'd felt like it was getting there, at least a little.

I still remember his face the night I burned the bloody sheet. I'd never seen him look like that before, and I'd thought I'd seen Santiago at his worst. But I understand, too. The fire must have triggered an old memory. I wonder about his memories of the night of the explosion. He never talks about it. Does he remember? And did seeing that fire, seeing the photos of his father and brother just beyond the flames, did I stir something up in him that made him so angry? Did it remind him of the night they died?

God. Did he watch them die?

I shake my head. There are moments I think how ridiculous this is. How if he'd just let me talk, if he'd listen, he'd know I don't mean him harm. But as long as he doesn't tell me his secrets, doesn't tell me what it is that happened that made him hate my family and me so much, it won't matter anyway.

My phone rings then, startling me even though I've been expecting Abel's call. I fumble to drag it out of my pocket and answer.

"Abel?"

"Yes," he says, sounding on edge. "You're still at the house?"

"Yeah. My phone's almost dead. I think it hooks up to the cord I have in the car, though. If we get disconnected, I'll—"

"No, it's fine. I'll just be a minute. You won't need it. Stay inside the house, Ivy. Don't fuck this up."

"Okay. It's not a big deal."

"Good. I've got some friends coming to get you later tonight."

"Friends? Why don't you come?"

"I can't. Your husband has eyes on me."

"Oh. Have you seen him?" I ask, hearing that little upward turn of my words, wondering how he'll read it.

"You want an update on the man who put you in the hospital?"

"He didn't...No. I just...never mind."

"Good. You'll need to be ready to go when they get there between eleven and midnight."

"Where are they going to take me?"

"I'm working that out now."

"Who are they? Do I know them?"

"They're just some people I work with. Listen, they're doing me a favor. You just be ready and don't give them any trouble, understand?"

"I wouldn't give them trouble."

"Good. I have to go."

"Can I talk to Eva? I called her, but she isn't picking up."

"She forgot her phone, and she's not here. I'll let her know you called."

"Why isn't she there? Is she okay?"

"She's at school, Ivy. It's a school day, and believe it or not, life goes on. Has been even without you in it. Now, I really have to go."

I don't know why his words hurt me. "Abel?"

"Yes?" he asks, tone frustrated.

"Do you use this house?"

"I told you, it's Dad's."

"I just saw papers from the week of the gala, and since Dad's been in the hospital, I just wondered if it was you."

"Are you playing detective?"

"No, I just...I didn't know."

"Well, remember, don't touch anything."

"Is something going on? I mean, why do you need a safe house?"

"Jesus Christ, Ivy. I'm saving your ass at a great risk to my own, I might add, and you're giving me the third degree?"

"No, it's not like that. I just was curious."

"Curiosity killed the cat."

"What?"

"Nothing. Be ready to go when they come."

"Can I know their names at least?" I hurry to ask before he disconnects.

"Just be ready." He hangs up.

41

IVY

I sit in the living room, flashlight in hand, waiting for the men Abel is sending to get here. I feel on edge since our conversation, but I keep telling myself it's just how Abel is. He's under pressure too. I'm sure Santiago has men watching him. I wonder if he's interrogated him already.

My phone is long out of charge, but I keep it beside me anyway. I pick up another one of the magazines to pass the time and flip through some pages before setting it aside. I get up and pace the room, anxious to leave now, to get to the next phase of this, but it's barely nine o'clock.

I have decided one thing. I need to talk to Santiago. It wasn't ever really an option to just disappear out of his life—even if he somehow didn't catch up with me. I can't leave Evangeline or the rest of my family behind. I can't take a chance that he'll hurt them. I just need a few more days to think before I make contact.

To pass the time, I start to fold up the newspapers and stack them. I wipe off the coffee table, then enter the study to pick up the whiskey glass sitting on the desk and carry it into the kitchen to wash. I set it on the drying rack, then empty the moldy food containers from the fridge. The trash can hadn't been emptied since before I came, so I pull the bag out of the bin and carry it into the study. There, I take out the empty bottle of whiskey and set it aside, then pick up the bin and turn it over into the bag but only manage to get half the contents in. The other half spills out onto the carpet.

"Crap." I tie the bag off and set it down, then get on the floor to pick up the things that fell out, pieces of crumpled paper, a paper cup of what was once coffee. I reach my arm under the desk to grab whatever it is that rolled there. When my fingers close around it, I pull my arm out, and I'm surprised to find lipstick.

I look at it. It's a smooth matte-black tube, simple, like any hundreds of this particular brand that I recognize. And I can't help but pull the lid off and twist it so I can see the lipstick itself.

Leaving everything, I get up and go into the living room where I have a little more light to study it. To double-check.

It's just a red lipstick. But I turn it over and read the name of this particular shade. Russian Red.

It's the shade I wore at the gala.

I find my hands are trembling as I feel for the phone in my pocket, but when I take it out, I remember it's out of charge. And I remember Abel's warning to stay inside the house.

But I make my way to the door anyway and punch in the code. Pulling it open, I grab my car keys from the table beside the door before going outside. I fumble with the lock, my hands are shaking, but I get the door open and slip into the driver's seat. I put the lipstick down and start the car, my door still open as I let it run and feel for the charger cable that's disappeared somewhere under the passenger seat. It's still plugged into the power outlet, so I find it and tug it out, then plug the phone in and wait. And while I wait, I look at that lipstick again. It's used but hardly. And my mind is running with an idea, but it makes no sense. None.

A few minutes later, the phone switches on, and I dial Abel's number. It rings and rings, then goes to voicemail, so I disconnect and try again. I catch my reflection in the rearview mirror. The light is on since the door is still open. I should probably close it, but Abel answers then.

"I told you not to call me again."

"Whose lipstick is in the house?"

"What?"

"The lipstick. Whose is it?"

"What the fuck are you talking about?" he asks but only after a pause I might have missed if I wasn't paying attention.

"Abel, the lipstick. It's the same brand and shade I wore to the gala. The same shade the woman who pretended to be me wore when she tried to kill my husband." God. To say the words is still unreal. Someone tried to murder Santiago. And what I'm holding in my hand...no. No. It can't be.

"Ivy. Where are you?"

"Was it you?" I ask, my voice small.

"Where. Are. You?"

"Tell me, Abel. Tell me you didn't do this to him. To me. Please."

There's silence then, just before I hear the sound of a car. A glance in the rearview mirror tells me it's two cars, actually. One parking along the street, one directly at the end of the driveway. My brain is slow to process what's happening until I see the men climb out, two from each vehicle. One flips his cigarette onto the lawn.

These are the friends Abel sent. They're not Santiago's men. He wouldn't send these particular men. I know it.

They're early.

I drop the phone, the lipstick slipping from my hand when I try to grab the door handle, almost managing to pull it closed as I put the car in reverse and slam my foot on the gas, instinct taking over now. Adrenaline as one of the men jumps out of the way while another yanks my door open, and I ram my car into the one parked at the end of the drive, my forehead slamming into the steering wheel with the impact.

One of them yanks me out roughly. I open my mouth to scream, but someone slaps his hand over it, and I just see one of them slip into the driver's seat of my car as I'm lifted off the ground, my kicking, my struggles meaning nothing. I'm carried into one of the waiting vehicles, the stench of cigarette smoke overpowering as my hands are dragged behind my back and bound just as I manage to bite the hand still closed over my mouth and scream the instant I can. But almost in that same instant, I'm struck so hard, my head whirls to the side, the impact of the man's knuckles against my temple making my brain rattle and my ears ring.

The driver is in the car a moment later, and we're moving as the man beside me slaps tape across my mouth, and I turn my head just enough to see the two cars behind ours, mine and the other sedan, the one with the huge dent I put in the side. But it's the last thing I see before the man beside me slides a sack over my head and forces me down onto my knees, holding me there with a foot at the back of my neck, my forehead pressed to the floor vibrating beneath me as we speed off into the night and I think about that lipstick. About Abel's silence.

I think about Santiago almost dying. Santiago out there looking for me. And I know I've made a terrible mistake.

One that won't cost only me but possibly the baby inside me.

THANK YOU

*Thank you for reading **Reparation of Sin**. We hope you enjoyed this continuation of Santiago and Ivy's story.*

*Their story concludes in **Resurrection of the Heart**.*
One-click Resurrection of the Heart.

ALSO BY A. ZAVARELLI

Boston Underworld Series

CROW: Boston Underworld #1

REAPER: Boston Underworld #2

GHOST: Boston Underworld #3

SAINT: Boston Underworld #4

THIEF: Boston Underworld #5

CONOR: Boston Underworld #6

Sin City Salvation Series

Confess

Convict

Bleeding Hearts Series

Echo: A Bleeding Hearts Novel Volume One

Stutter: A Bleeding Hearts Novel Volume Two

Twisted Ever After Series

BEAST: Twisted Ever After #1

Standalones

Tap Left

Hate Crush

For a complete list of books and audios, visit http://www.azavarelli.com/books

ALSO BY NATASHA KNIGHT

To Have and To Hold Duet
With This Ring
I Thee Take

The Society Trilogy
Requiem of the Soul
Reparation of Sin
Resurrection of the Heart

Dark Legacy Trilogy
Taken (Dark Legacy, Book 1)
Torn (Dark Legacy, Book 2)
Twisted (Dark Legacy, Book 3)

Unholy Union Duet

Unholy Union
Unholy Intent

Collateral Damage Duet

Collateral: an Arranged Marriage Mafia Romance
Damage: an Arranged Marriage Mafia Romance

Ties that Bind Duet

Mine

His

MacLeod Brothers

Devil's Bargain

Benedetti Mafia World

Salvatore: a Dark Mafia Romance

Dominic: a Dark Mafia Romance

Sergio: a Dark Mafia Romance

The Benedetti Brothers Box Set (Contains Salvatore, Dominic and Sergio)

Killian: a Dark Mafia Romance

Giovanni: a Dark Mafia Romance

The Amado Brothers

Dishonorable

Disgraced

Unhinged

Standalone Dark Romance

Descent

Deviant

Beautiful Liar

Retribution

Theirs To Take

Captive, Mine

Alpha

Given to the Savage

Taken by the Beast

Claimed by the Beast

Captive's Desire

Protective Custody

Amy's Strict Doctor

Taming Emma

Taming Megan

Taming Naia

Reclaiming Sophie

The Firefighter's Girl

Dangerous Defiance

Her Rogue Knight

Taught To Kneel

Tamed: the Roark Brothers Trilogy

ABOUT A. ZAVARELLI

A. Zavarelli is a USA Today and Amazon bestselling author of dark and contemporary romance.

When she's not putting her characters through hell, she can usually be found watching bizarre and twisted documentaries in the name of research.

She currently lives in the Northwest with her lumberjack and an entire brood of fur babies.

Want to stay up to date on Ashleigh and Natasha's releases? Sign up for our newsletters here: https://landing.mailerlite.com/webforms/landing/x3s0k6

ABOUT NATASHA KNIGHT

Natasha Knight is the *USA Today* Bestselling author of Romantic Suspense and Dark Romance Novels. She has sold over half a million books and is translated into six languages. She currently lives in The Netherlands with her husband and two daughters and when she's not writing, she's walking in the woods listening to a book, sitting in a corner reading or off exploring the world as often as she can get away.

Write Natasha here: natasha@natasha-knight.com

Click here to sign up for my newsletter to receive new release news and updates!

www.natasha-knight.com
natasha-knight@outlook.com

Printed in Great Britain
by Amazon